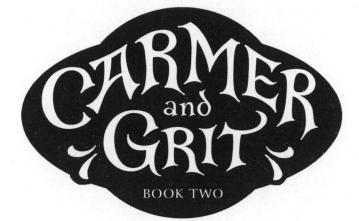

BOOK TWO

The Crooked Castle

ALSO BY SARAH JEAN HORWITZ

Carmer and Grit, Book One: *The Wingsnatchers*

SARAH JEAN HORWITZ

BOOK TWO

The Crooked Castle

ALGONQUIN YOUNG READERS 2018

Published by
Algonquin Young Readers
an imprint of Algonquin Books of Chapel Hill
Post Office Box 2225
Chapel Hill, North Carolina 27515-2225

a division of
Workman Publishing
225 Varick Street
New York, New York 10014

LIBRARY OF CONGRESS CATALOGING-IN-PUBLICATION DATA
Names: Horwitz, Sarah Jean, author. I Horwitz, Sarah Jean. Carmer and Grit ; bk. 2.
Title: The crooked castle / Sarah Jean Horwitz.
Description: First edition. I Chapel Hill, North Carolina : Algonquin Young
Readers, 2018. I Series: Carmer and Grit ; book two I Summary: When
magician's apprentice Felix Carmer III and his faerie companion Grit come
across a magical flying circus, it becomes clear that there is something not normal
about it or its inventor, and that it may be related to regional airship disasters.
Identifiers: LCCN 2017032158 I ISBN 9781616206642 (hardcover : alk. paper)
Subjects: I CYAC: Magicians—Fiction. I Fairies—Fiction. I Circus—Fiction.
I Airships—Fiction. I Aircraft accidents—Fiction. I LCGFT: Fantasy fiction.
Classification: LCC PZ7.1.H665 Cr 2018 I DDC [Fic]—dc23
LC record available at https://lccn.loc.gov/2017032158

10 9 8 7 6 5 4 3 2 1
First Edition

For Brooke, obviously.
This one doesn't have any cats at all.

BOOK TWO

The Crooked Castle

THE *JASCONIUS*

THE DAY THE *JASCONIUS* CRASHED, THE CABIN BOY
was late for his shift. He was *never* late.

He was never late because he loved his job. He loved
his ship and every moment he spent on it, soaring over
the ocean from one continent to the other. The *Jasconius*
was one of only three transatlantic airships in the world,
making the journey from London to Driftside City, Virginia,
every few weeks like clockwork. How many young men
could say they flew across the ocean not once in their life,
not even twice, but a dozen times a year? How many could
say they lived in an impossible thing, a machine great and
powerful enough to defy gravity itself, with nothing but
open skies ahead and the wind at their backs?

The cabin boy knew he was lucky. But his luck was about to turn.

That day, he was late *because* he loved the ship. He'd been coming off a shift with strict orders to report straight to the crew quarters and *get some sleep, young man*. But he knew the ship would be docking in the early morning, and he didn't want to miss the first sight of land for anything in the world. He wanted to be the first one to see it, to feel that little jolt that came with every landing after a few days over open water—the miraculous reminder that they'd made it, that there was a world beyond the endless blue below. So he nodded to his superior officer, quickly changed into his civilian clothes, and tucked himself into his favorite secluded nook on the observation deck to watch the sunrise. It was a tight fit these days—he was still getting taller every year—but he managed.

He hadn't meant to fall asleep.

When he woke up, they were already preparing to land. He'd missed his first glimpse of his favorite city in the world. And something felt wrong.

But there were no shouts of alarm, no explosions, no panicked passengers clinging to the railings as the ship reeled. In fact, all was quiet.

The cabin boy stretched and crept out of his nook, surprising a few early-bird passengers nibbling at their breakfasts on the observation deck. He mumbled his apologies and distractedly brushed past them, determined to both find the source of his unease and sneak back to his quarters without being seen. He'd overslept in his hiding spot, and he'd be in for a dressing-down if he showed up for duty late *and* out of uniform.

He took a shortcut along the keel catwalk, waving to a few other crew members as he hurried past. But a moment later he was alone, with only the hum of the engines to keep him company. The corridor was deserted, and it should not have been so. Not when they were preparing to land.

"Hello?" called the cabin boy. He shivered. The air was chilly, but the steam pumping through the pipes in the ship's envelope should have been keeping them all warm. He slowed down, though he couldn't say why, and made his way toward the hatch that led to the engine car. The crew would be hard at work coordinating the landing.

The cabin boy slipped and fell, too quickly to even reach out and catch himself. He lay there on the cold metal floor of the catwalk, a wetness seeping into his back. He sat up, groaning at the bruises already blossoming on his elbows, and rubbed the back of his head. He put a hand to the ground, and his fingers couldn't quite believe what they were feeling.

He'd slipped on a patch of ice.

This was impossible, of course. He looked around for any source of water—a leaky pipe, a spilled bucket abandoned by someone who had been cleaning, but there was nothing. He slowly got up. A trail of the stuff led all the way to the hatch.

The cabin boy knew he should turn around and get help straightaway, because something was clearly not right. But his feet seemed to move forward of their own accord, carefully dodging the slippery patches. His breath fogged in the air.

When the young woman darted in front of him, he nearly fell again.

"Miss, excuse me!" he said, trying to remember his professional courtesies. "Passengers aren't allowed back here!"

But then she was gone, only the ghost of a laugh in her wake, and he couldn't be sure there'd been anyone standing there at all. He shook his head, like he was trying to clear cobwebs out of his brain, when suddenly his face was trapped in the grip of cold, pale hands.

"Oh, don't worry," said the young woman. She looked like a girl, really—except for her eyes. There was something older in their gray depths. Something darker. "I'm not a passenger."

The boy staggered back, but her icy hands had already clawed up into his hair, fingers snagging in his short, tight curls.

"You should probably run," she said, staring straight into his eyes. "Run, little boy, and don't look back."

The cabin boy ran. He didn't remember much after that.

1.

WHERE THERE'S A WILL, THERE'S A WISP

FELIX CASSIUS TIBERIUS CARMER III SPENT HIS DAYS learning about all the things that wanted to kill him.

There were not as many of these things as there used to be, for which he was thankful, but there were still enough to be getting on with. He learned about redcaps, who kept their namesake hats soaked with the blood of their victims. He learned about sirens, who lured sailors to their doom among jagged rocks with nothing but a song. He learned about kelpies and banshees and ghouls: where to find them (and how to escape when you did), what they looked like (or how they disguised themselves), even what they ate for breakfast (which was usually never anything good). These creatures all had one thing in common, besides their murderous impulses: they were part of the Unseelie fae. And that made them part of Carmer's world, whether he liked it or not.

When one's new best friend was a faerie princess—and a *Seelie* one at that—it was important to stay on top of one's magical education.

It was for the sake of Carmer's magical education, or so Grit claimed, that he was now ankle deep in stagnant, freezing water in near-total darkness, trying to distinguish the difference between half a dozen floating balls of light.

"I think a leech just bit me," Carmer complained. He shook his leg, sending ripples sloshing through the pond. He could have sworn one of the glowing orbs tittered in amusement.

"Pay attention to the lights," Grit scolded from somewhere up ahead. He could tell her golden faerie light apart from the others' easily, though he couldn't say why. It was as unique to her as a fingerprint was to humans, though it should have been indistinguishable from the others from this far away.

"I thought I wasn't supposed to!" Carmer protested. "Or else they'll . . . 'enthrall' me, or whatever it is you called it."

"You've got to look at them *sideways*, like I told you," explained Grit. "Catch a glimpse out of the corner of your eye. That's all you need. Then *focus*." Her light bobbed up and down.

Carmer tried to do as he was told, but like so many things in the faerie world, "looking sideways" was hardly an exact science—a fact that frustrated him to no end. He closed his eyes and took a deep breath, shivering in the December air. He opened them again, slowly this time, and looked at the reflections in the water below instead of directly out across the pond. Trying to keep his mind blank, he peered through dark lashes and the bits of hair that fell in front of his eyes. And he *saw*.

He saw that most of the balls of light had small figures at their centers—faeries, he knew. Only one or two were truly nothing more than swirling orbs of glowing gas and malicious intent—will-o'-the-wisps and jack-o'-lanterns who (in a less controlled scenario) wanted nothing more than to lure him into the depths of the dark water. Carmer smiled to himself; maybe he really *was* getting better at this sort of thing. He flicked his gaze upward, more confident now that he'd chosen the right ones, and stared into the center of one of the lights. Was there really nothing inside it at all?

He didn't think so. He took a few steps closer, just to make sure. His knees bumped against the thin sheets of ice floating on the pond's surface, but his legs were already so numb from the cold, he barely felt it. The orb glowed brighter, illuminating more of the pond. Carmer could even see a house on the other side of it. Was that the glow of a fire he spotted through the windows? A fire sounded lovely on a night like this. One more step, just for a closer look . . .

"CARMER."

A streak of gold sparks shot across his field of vision, disrupting his view of both the orbs and the house. Carmer stumbled backward and nearly fell, but the muddy bottom of the pond sucked at his boots, reluctant to let such a willing prisoner go.

"That's enough, you lot!" Grit darted in and out of the other lights. "Show's over! Thank you for your time!"

The lights dispersed with shrugs of tiny shoulders, more than a few curious backward glances, and one or two teasing giggles. Grit stuck her tongue out at the retreating backs of the gigglers while Carmer staggered onto solid ground. The will-o'-the-wisps sank back into the pond, winking out of sight with little gurgles as they submerged themselves in the inky water. Grit kept an eye on them as she flew to Carmer's side.

"Congratulations," she said, hovering at his knee as he sat down. "You've just been enthralled."

Carmer shook his head vigorously and ran his hands through his hair. His head felt fuzzy, much like the last time he'd fallen under the influence of faerie magic, but he was already starting to feel the true bite of the cold night air.

"I-I thought I had them," he said, a round of shivers clacking his teeth together.

"You did," agreed Grit. "Until they had you."

Carmer shivered harder. "The house wasn't real," he guessed.

Grit shook her head; tufts of frizzy red and gold curls escaped from her messy bun. "And you should have known that."

"Well," said Carmer with a shrug. He tried to wring out the ends of his sodden pants, but his fingers were numb with cold. "You know what they say. P-practice m-makes p-p-perfect."

Grit flew right in front of his face. "Hands," she ordered.

"I—I'm fine," Carmer stuttered through white lips.

"And I'm a giantess," she said. "Hands. Now."

Carmer blew on his fingers a few times before cupping his hands and extending them out to Grit, who promptly stepped inside them. Almost instantly, warmth began to radiate into his frozen fingers. Having a fire faerie for a best friend did have *some* benefits, after all. Carmer sighed with relief.

"That's the best I can do for now," Grit said, sitting cross-legged in his palms. "Let's call it a night, shall we?"

Carmer couldn't have agreed more.

THE NEXT MORNING dawned bright and clear and cold, though not nearly as chilly as the night before. As Carmer had said would happen, their days were growing warmer as they traveled south for the winter, away from Grit's home city of Skemantis and the rest of New England.

Grit stood on her favorite perch at the very topmost turret of the Moto-Manse, Carmer's three-story motorized house on wheels, and stretched from the points of her tiny toes all the way to the tips of her fingers, yawning. As usual, she was up much earlier than Carmer—faeries didn't need to sleep at all, strictly speaking, but with her only traveling companion in dreamland for most of the night, there wasn't much else to keep her occupied. (Carmer, of course, couldn't understand why she didn't use the extra time to study his lessons on the *human* world, but that was because he was *boring*, and she was not.)

Grit lowered her arms, watching the pale sunrise, and rolled her shoulders experimentally. The muscles around her left wing had gotten stiff and sore in the night, and the cold wasn't helping. She held on to the tip of the turret for support—the wind was quite strong that day—and slowly opened and closed both wings. The brass outline of the metal one glinted in the corner of her eye. Grit wondered if she would ever get used to that.

The Seelie faerie princess hadn't always had two wings. She'd been born with only one, and it wasn't until the engineering prowess of Felix Cassius Tiberius Carmer III, combined with the perfect dose of faerie magic, that she flew for the first time. Her new wing—had it really been only a few short weeks since she'd gotten it?—was a mechanical *and* a magical marvel. But it didn't come without its own fair share of problems—like a tendency to literally freeze up in the cold. Grit was learning to use her magic to account for such drawbacks, but it was a process that involved a *lot* of trial and error (and occasionally setting things on fire).

Grit squinted into the sunrise, where a floating black spot had suddenly appeared over the horizon. It dipped dangerously close to the tree line in the distance before bobbing unsteadily back up again.

Grit scurried halfway down the Moto-Manse's roof before she remembered to fly—that was another thing to get used to—the rest of the way to Carmer's window. He was still asleep, his black hair tousled every which way, snoring soundly. She was loath to wake him, as she knew he didn't always sleep as well as he could; the nightmares that plagued him from their last major encounter with Unseelie faeries made sure of that. But a skyward glance showed the black spot getting bigger—and therefore closer. It was teardrop-shaped, and not actually black at all, but striped in bright colors.

She decided to investigate. She pushed off Carmer's windowsill with only the slightest twinge of guilt—she would turn *right back* if anything were amiss, she promised herself—and the moment the wind caught under her wings, she couldn't help but break into a smile. *This* was the way good days started—with clear skies and the possibility of adventure sailing straight at you—not by burying your nose in books and beakers and belching engines the way Carmer did.

Truthfully, the possibility of adventure in question seemed to be having a tough time sailing straight in any direction. As she flew closer, Grit recognized the shape as a balloon. These weren't as big as the hulking airships the humans sometimes traveled in, and they usually carried only one or two people in a hanging wicker basket.

In addition to being in obvious distress, this one also seemed to be missing a key element: the basket. A lone figure hung directly from the balloon itself, suspended in the air by nothing but a few ropes and straps.

Grit hung back, hesitating as she glided closer. She landed in a copse of trees a short way from the road and flitted from treetop to treetop, following the balloon's progress. Surely, someone else would come driving along and see the balloonist. And there was a town just over the next rise—perhaps they could see the mysterious shape floating on the horizon. *They* could call for help.

But a needling voice told her it was still very early, and as untraveled as the country roads they were taking were, the likelihood of anyone else calling for help was slim. Contrary to what Carmer thought, she really *did* try to pay attention to the human world. Or at least, the practical bits that were *worth* paying attention to.

The balloon passed directly overhead, and Grit got her first look at the unfortunate passenger. He was tall, with long legs currently occupied in thrashing about in a panic; gloved hands fiddled helplessly with his harness. He looked down at the ground, which was growing nearer by the second, and then at the countryside around him—and *laughed.* A small, bemused laugh, to be sure, but a laugh all the same.

Only a fellow adventurer could find himself in a predicament like that and *laugh.* And Grit was always game to meet a fellow adventurer. She sprang up from the trees before she could second-guess the impulse and launched herself past the clueless balloonist and straight under the balloon itself.

I'm a fire faerie, Grit thought. Surely, she'd heard these things called *hot* air balloons for a reason.

CARMER DREAMED OF trains.

He dreamed of trains spewing smoke into claustrophobic underground tunnels, brakes and whistles and *other things* shrieking into a dark void. Black vines crept along cold concrete walls. Black iron rails twisted with magic. The very mud beneath his feet became grasping hands, ready to drag him down forever. A three-eyed man with a dripping red conductor's cap beckoned him forward with a pointy-toothed smile.

He dreamed of running until his lungs and his legs were on fire and feeling, *knowing*, that he could never run fast or far enough. The train was coming for him. The Wild Hunt was coming for him, just as it had come for Gideon Sharpe.

Carmer's eyes snapped open, the image of a blond boy being thrown into that very train still burning across his vision. He shook his head, forced himself to take deep breaths, and focused on the sound that had woken him.

It was the sound of something very large crashing into his roof.

"Grit?!" Carmer called. She had a habit of watching the sunrise from the turret in the mornings, and at five inches tall, she wasn't exactly squish-proof.

"Urmngmf" was all he could make out of the reply.

He jumped out of his bunk and scrambled down the stairs and out the door. The sight that greeted him outside the Moto-Manse was not one he expected.

There was a balloon on his roof.

Perhaps more alarmingly, there was a *man* on his roof. He was fairly certain it was a man, at least, from the look of the khaki-clad limbs sprawled every which way.

"Um," said Carmer.

"I said I'm here!" said Grit, a little more clearly this time, though he could barely hear her. A glowing light switched on somewhere *under* the fabric of the balloon, which had caught itself quite dramatically on the topmost turret of the Moto-Manse.

Carmer scrambled forward, unsure of what to do. The man groaned and pushed himself up onto his elbows, and then, probably realizing he wasn't actually on the ground yet, plastered himself even more firmly to the

14

roof. One of his boots found the peaked trim of one of the windows.

"I wouldn't put your weight on—"

That, Carmer thought, just as the decorative molding gave way. The man's legs swung wildly, and Carmer saw that he was attached to the balloon. The hole where the turret had pierced the fabric was getting bigger, tearing as the balloonist's weight pulled it. A glowing light—*Grit's* glowing light—tumbled a few feet down, still trapped underneath the balloon.

"Grit!" called Carmer.

"I'm fine!" came the breathless reply.

He pictured her clinging to the shingles of the roof for dear life, even as the iron in them burned her hands. Iron repelled all things fae. He hoped she'd been wearing her gloves this morning when she decided to go chasing balloons.

"Me too," said the man hanging from Carmer's house. "Thanks for asking!"

"Wait a minute," said Carmer, frowning. "I'll climb up to the attic and pull you inside."

But Carmer's plan never came to fruition. With a great ripping sound, the balloon tore almost all the way, dropping the balloonist down the side of the Moto-Manse until he was only a few feet off the ground. Somewhere underneath the canvas, Grit shrieked, and her light went out.

The balloonist swung around to face Carmer. He was

young—perhaps only a few years older than Carmer—with smooth ebony skin and closely cropped black hair. He smiled, a blinding smile that lit up his face all the way to his eyes, hidden as they were behind thick aviator goggles (now hanging crookedly, of course). He removed the goggles with a flourish and looked down at Carmer.

"Bell Daisimer," said the balloonist. "Professional aeronaut, at your service."

And then the balloon tore from the roof completely, dropping him into a tangled heap at Carmer's front door.

2.

BELL THE BALLOONIST

"I'M FINE," PROTESTED GRIT, CRINGING AWAY FROM Carmer's touch. Her wings were folded protectively against her back, but Carmer could see that the mechanical one lay at an odd angle. Carmer, Grit, and their uninvited houseguest sat in the Moto-Manse's kitchen, the latter two taking stock of their various bumps and bruises. Carmer had put on a pot of tea; that's what Kitty Delphine, a girl he'd spent most of his childhood traveling with, seemed to do in the face of difficult or awkward situations. He assured himself it was just one of those things people did.

"And I'm king of the—"

Faeries, he was about to joke, when the full ramifications of the balloonist named Bell Daisimer sitting in his kitchen hit him like a brick wall. Carmer stared at Grit, then at Bell, who was twisting his ankle experimentally with a grimace, and back at Grit.

"Spirits and zits," Carmer exclaimed. The figure of speech was another one of Kitty Delphine's influences he would probably never shake. "What do we do about *him*?" he whispered. As a Friend of the Fae, Carmer had sworn an oath to guard the secrets of faerie magic with his life. It hadn't been six weeks since he'd sworn that oath, and now he was making tea for his very obviously faerie best friend and a clueless errant balloonist.

"Why don't you make sure the lunatic hasn't broken his ankle, for a start?" suggested Grit.

"I think we can confidently say this lunatic has *not*," said Bell cheerfully. He placed his foot on the ground and prodded at a blossoming bruise over his temple. "And my lunacy is debatable."

You attached yourself to a balloon and lit a fire under it until it blasted you off into the air with no means of controlling it, thought Carmer. The teakettle whistled.

Carmer's skepticism must have shown on his face, because Bell said, "Aw, come on there, Mr. . . ."

"Um, Carmer."

"Mr. Carmer. Don't tell me you've never seen a barnstorming act before?"

Carmer could have pointed out that most barnstormers were called such because the balloons and airships they performed with *actually* took up enough space to fill entire barns. He shrugged and busied himself with the teacups.

"Barn . . . *storming?*" piped up Grit, frowning. "I didn't even see any barns around here . . ."

Bell laughed. "It's just a few aerial tricks for the local yokels," he explained to her. "Nothing so fancy as the real flying circuses. But a man's gotta eat, right?" At that, he looked around the kitchen rather hopefully.

Carmer sighed and handed him the cookie tin with his tea.

"Thanks!" said Bell. "But I gotta say, I must've hit my head harder than I thought on the way down, because was I or was I not just crash-landed by a *faerie?*" He took a sizable chomp out of his cookie and looked at Carmer and Grit expectantly.

Carmer nearly dropped the rest of the cups.

Grit, on the other hand, hopped to her feet. "*Crash-landed?!*" she demanded, wincing as pain lanced through her shoulder. "You'd have had a very pointy encounter with some evergreens if it weren't for my help, mister."

"I had the situation perfectly under control," protested Bell. "Just got a little off course, is all. It's not every day an airman gets multiple foreign objects stuck under his canvas at the same time—"

"I am not a *foreign object,*" Grit fumed.

Carmer busied himself with the tea while they bickered; it was useless to try to get any information out of

Grit when she was in a temper, and Bell didn't seem particularly inclined to explain himself properly, either. He picked up his cup and ventured outside to look at the state of his house.

The remnants of the balloon flapped in the breeze from the Moto-Manse's turret like a sad banner on a miniature castle. Most of it wouldn't be salvageable—Bell had been so tangled in his straps they'd had to cut him out—and the balloon was in pieces. Carmer examined it, but it didn't take much deduction to see how Bell made his living. It was a cheap trick, the sole province of twopenny entertainers with a balloon and not much else. Most modern balloons were gas balloons; they were lifted by hydrogen and equipped with ballast for ascending and a vent in the envelope for descending. But in the absence of a proper lifting gas, anyone could light a coal fire under a balloon, wait until it got hot enough, and *bam*! Liftoff. The practice was foolhardy at best. The balloons often caught fire, endangering the unfortunate barnstormers attached to them, and they had no means of control up in the air.

The other reason coal gas wasn't often used was that it wasn't nearly as powerful. The balloonists were usually aloft for only a short while before they came drifting back down, but the strong winds that morning must've had their own ideas for Bell.

Carmer shook his head. Winds didn't have *ideas*. Clearly, he'd been spending more time in the company of mythical beings than was strictly good for the scientific mind.

That's when he noticed the balloon was *moving*—and it was most definitely not because of the wind. Something was caught under the shredded mass of canvas, trapped between the wreck of the balloon and Carmer's roof, and it was . . . *buzzing*? About the size of Carmer's hand, it rattled with a soft metallic clang against the roof as it struggled to free itself from under the weight of the balloon.

Multiple foreign objects, Bell had said. Grit hadn't been the only thing to get caught in Bell the Balloonist's operation this morning.

"Um, hello?" Carmer called out, a little hesitantly. He knew he was supposed to be getting better at recognizing magic, but whatever this was didn't sound much like a faerie. It sounded like . . . a machine.

Carmer picked up a long piece of broken window frame, squared his shoulders, and gave the canvas a good shove.

A small, white, and birdlike metallic object skittered out from under the balloon and across the roof tiles, bumping along like a poorly thrown skipping stone. It made a strained ticking noise as it fell off the roof and sailed straight over Carmer's head—he ducked just in time—and shakily flew a dozen or so feet before plummeting to the ground.

Carmer stayed in his crouch, his heart pounding as he watched the object twitch across the packed earth of the dirt road. The last time he had seen mechanical birds, they'd been the tools of Gideon Sharpe, apprentice to the evil, faerie-enslaving mastermind Titus Archer, also known as the Mechanist—and Carmer had barely escaped their pointy beaks with both eyes still inside his head. Was this Gideon, somehow out of fae captivity, coming for his retribution already?

There was only one way to find out. Carmer forced himself to stand up and edged closer to the twitching device—and saw, with no small amount of relief, that this object had very little in common with Gideon's ornate, realistic automata. "Birdlike" was a generous description; it was, in fact, a miniature glider. Once gleaming white, it was scuffed and dented from its rough journey. A bit of gold foil peeked out of a small chamber on its underside, winking in the morning sun as the glider bounced around.

So this was what had gotten caught in Bell's balloon while Grit had been trying to help him. Unfortunately, it had probably gotten caught *because* she'd been there. Mechanical devices had a tendency to go on the fritz around too much faerie magic, and if this glider had been flying in the area at just the right (or in this case, the wrong) time, well . . . their collision suddenly made a lot more sense. But whose was it, and how had it even flown high enough to get caught there in the first place?

The glider wouldn't be flying anywhere anytime soon—not with those bent wings and the noises coming from its insides. In a different life, Carmer would have scooped it up and run upstairs to his laboratory to gleefully take it apart piece by piece. He still planned on doing that, of course, but now, he also took the extra precaution of hefting his handy piece of window frame and whacking the glider as hard as he could.

The grinding and ticking noises ceased, and Carmer shook off the sad, guilty feeling that came over him, as if he'd killed something small and defenseless. It was just a machine, after all. He picked it up and gently placed it in his coat pocket.

"Carmer!" Bell Daisimer's panicked voice came from inside the Moto-Manse. "Hey, that's your name, right?" Bell ran out the door, still limping a bit on his right leg. "I think something's wrong with Grit."

Carmer dashed past him and into the house, where Grit was lying on the kitchen table, pale and panting.

"She, well, she got kind of mad at me," admitted Bell, "but when she jumped up to fly, she just fell."

Carmer pulled out his portable magnifying glass from his pocket and sat at the table. "Let's take a look."

"Something bent when I got caught under the balloon," admitted Grit, breathing shallowly.

"Can you sit up?" Carmer asked.

Grit nodded and eased herself into a sitting position. "It only hurts when I try to extend it."

"What were you *doing*, Grit?" Carmer asked, examining her wing as gently as he could.

Grit explained how she'd seen Bell bobbing around the skyline that morning. "I couldn't just let him plow into the trees," she said. "I've seen the fire in other kinds of balloons before. I thought I could give him a boost without him even seeing me. But then something else flew underneath us, too, and . . ." A red flush of embarrassment crept up her neck.

"It wasn't a bad idea, little miss," said Bell fairly.

He seemed to be taking the revelation that faeries were real in stride.

Then again, Carmer thought, *anyone who willingly launches themselves hundreds of feet in the air for spectator sport can't be too easily rattled.*

Carmer sat back. "The frame is fractured," he told Grit grimly. "On the apex of the forewing."

Grit stared at him.

"It's small," he assured her. "I could probably weld it back together, but I worry about burning you." Thanks to a dose of magic from Grit's mother, Seelie Queen Ombrienne, Grit's wing was part machine and part real faerie wing; the glass panes between the tiny gears and wires had been replaced with actual membranes, and the device was permanently fused to Grit's back. But that same magic, while making the wing more functional, also made repairs tricky.

"I'm a *fire* faerie," Grit reminded him. "You could probably drop me headfirst in a volcano."

"Have you ever *seen* a volcano?" asked Bell.

"Have you?" countered Grit.

Carmer interrupted before they could get going again. "I'll do my best." He sighed. "I wish I could've made it more durable. I'm sorry, Grit."

Grit blushed again. "I probably should've made more of an effort not to get myself squished."

"And I sincerely apologize for any role I may have played in said squishing," added Bell, placing a hand on his heart. "Now, I don't mean to be indelicate, but as it seems *we* will all live to see another day . . . can I ask if the same is true for my balloon?"

Carmer grimaced. At this rate, they were all going to need a *lot* more tea.

"WHAT DO YOU think?" asked Grit, lying under one of the lamps in the Moto-Manse's attic laboratory. She was trying to distract herself from the fact that her best friend was about to melt part of her body.

"Think about what?" asked Carmer, intent on the diagram of Grit's wing in front of him.

"About Bell, silly. About what we're going to . . . well, *do* with him," said Grit. She almost shrugged, then remembered she wasn't supposed to move. "You've been awfully quiet since the . . . um, accident."

Carmer looked down. "I don't know," he said, and sighed. Bell Daisimer had become an unexpected guest at the Moto-Manse for the past day and a half, as his primary form of transportation had been reduced to scrap fabric.

"I'm just . . . I'm not like you, Grit. I don't make friends with every person I meet. And it's odd for me, having someone else in the Moto-Manse, after all those years with just Kitty and the Amazifier." Until recently, Carmer had been apprenticed to traveling magician Antoine the Amazifier, but the old man had retired.

"Bell and I are hardly friends," said Grit. "Or at least, we won't be until he admits I saved his backside."

Carmer smiled as he checked over his tools.

"And I thought since his balloon was wrecked, and that was a little bit my fault . . ." She trailed off.

"I'm nearly ready," said Carmer, tugging on the ends of his safety gloves. "You may want to, er . . . do the magic thing."

"Do the magic thing?" Grit laughed nervously. "I'm so glad I've spent the last month teaching you about faerie lore." She closed her eyes and breathed deeply, focusing on channeling her magic to make herself as hot as the metal poking at her wing. She was glad of the cement surface of the lab table.

"Speaking of faerie lore, it's just . . ." Carmer said. "Is it okay that Bell's in the loop? Your mother was furious when you revealed yourself to me."

The muscles in Grit's back tensed. "Well, my mother's not here, is she?" she asked testily. Carmer paused in his work until she sighed. "I . . . I'm sorry. I know I messed up. But he seems to be taking it well, right?"

"Remarkably so," admitted Carmer. "But he could also be blabbing to every soul he meets about the faerie princess in the moto-mansion parked just outside town." Bell had gone into the nearest town earlier that morning to see if they had any supplies that might fix his balloon.

"I don't think so," said Grit. "And even *I* haven't mentioned the princess part, thank you very much." And she hadn't done so on purpose—this far south, few fae would recognize her for what she was, and she wanted to make the most of it. No one had to know she was a sheltered Northern princess who'd barely left her own kingdom.

"But if he does talk," continued Grit, "I . . . I'll take care of it."

Carmer paused, so briefly that Grit barely noticed, before he finished fusing the two broken pieces of her wing together. He didn't ask *how* Grit planned to take care of it, but he had an idea, and he didn't like it one bit.

Carmer watched in fascination as Grit's wing glowed a bright gold, the membrane stretching to accommodate the new repair. Just when he'd thought magic couldn't amaze him any more.

"That should do for now," Carmer said. "But take it easy for a bit, all right? I promise, I really *will* do my best to see if I can improve the design."

Grit scurried up Carmer's shoulder, as she used to do before her wing. But this time, she did something she'd never done before, and jumped up to peck him quickly on the cheek. He blushed.

"I think it'll be good to have Bell around," Grit said as Carmer made his way back down to the cab of the Moto-Manse. He'd promised to pick up Bell at the town's main square soon. "At least until we can drop him off somewhere that he can get a new balloon. He's passionate about learning how things work, just like you."

Carmer thought Bell was more passionate about seeing how high he could get in the air before he came crashing down, regardless of the vehicle, but he kept his thoughts to himself.

"You need someone you've got something in common with to talk to," Grit chattered while Carmer finished starting the engine. "And what are the odds you'll run into another Friend of the Fae who's like that? I mean, someone besides—"

She broke off, but Carmer knew what she'd been about to say.

Someone besides Gideon Sharpe.

Gideon Sharpe was—had been?—around Carmer's age. Maybe a year or two older. He'd been a magician's apprentice, like Carmer. He'd been a Friend of the Fae, like Carmer. But he'd also been a kidnapper, a faerie murderer, and a magic stealer—a past that caught up with him right around the time Carmer met him. And when he was finally free from the man he claimed made him do those things—the

Mechanist—Gideon had come to Carmer and Grit asking for forgiveness. Asking for help. Gideon Sharpe had been a thorn in Carmer's side, but he was also just a boy—a fascinating one at that. Grit's mother had said he was an Unseelie changeling—a healthy human baby swapped with a sickly faerie child and raised by the fae instead.

Gideon Sharpe was what happened when one caught the interest of a very different kind of faerie than Grit, and Carmer couldn't help feeling a strange kinship with him.

Carmer and Grit had tried to help him, but it wasn't enough. Gideon was taken prisoner by the Wild Hunt, a horde of trapped human and faerie souls led by the Unseelie fae creature known as Mister Moon, as punishment for his crimes against the fae. Carmer didn't know if he would ever be freed.

"It's all right," Carmer said to Grit. "You're right." But he couldn't stop his memories of the Wild Hunt from roaring back. The ghostly train screeching down the abandoned underground tracks, the howls of the warrior-prisoners trapped inside, the clash of their weapons against the glass windows. And then, unbidden, the sound of faerie music, eerie and enchanting all at once . . . Carmer gripped the Moto-Manse's steering wheel so hard his knuckles went white.

"Carmer," Grit said. "Do you hear that?"

The music wasn't in his memories. It was all around him.

3.

DON'T YOU WANT
TO KNOW?

WITHOUT A SECOND THOUGHT, CARMER NEARLY
put his foot through the accelerator. The Moto-Manse
bucked under his rough treatment, her engine not yet
warm enough, and Grit was forced to jump off Carmer's
shoulder and onto the dashboard.

"Carmer, wait!" she said, but even the hint of faerie
music had brought a manic gleam to her friend's eyes.
It was coming from the town to the east, the town Bell
was visiting for supplies—the town whose skyline was
now littered with half a dozen balloons. The lilting song
floated toward them. Carmer and Grit heard every word
as if there were faeries inside the Moto-Manse at that very
moment.

Come fly so high
You'll touch the sky,
However the wind may blow.

Browning fields and ramshackle cottages whizzed by as Carmer drove faster, giving way to clusters of statelier brick buildings that made up the small town's main street. People stopped and gaped, first up at the sky, and then at the three-story house on wheels tearing past them.

"Carmer, stop!" said Grit. "Look!"

Small white balloons covered in delicate gold and silver filigree were winding their way between the buildings. The balloons were shaped like airships, and a beautiful girl in a fancy, glittering costume was suspended from almost every one. They held megaphones to their mouths as they sang.

We see that you're curious,
So won't you come join us
At the Roving Wonder Show?

Carmer was finally forced to slow as more and more locals crowded the streets, pointing with delight up at the pretty girls. The women were obviously human—at least, they looked that way to Carmer—and now that he'd had a moment to calm down, he realized the music wasn't really faerie music at all. At least, not entirely. It had a tinny quality from being distorted by the megaphones that was decidedly unfaerie-like. Some of the balloons had no girls attached at all, but bunches of colorfully painted gramophones that looked like flowers in a bouquet. They all broadcast the same song. Carmer couldn't see anyone steering them, but he had a sneaking suspicion that tiny winged creatures were involved somewhere in the equation.

They were criers, Carmer realized—the circus members responsible for getting into town a few days ahead of the show to spread the word and sell tickets. But the criers Carmer had grown up watching were usually men in dusty top hats nailing a single flyer to a town notice board while they shouted from a stool in the main square. *Flying* criers were something he'd never seen in his life.

We don't have beasts
And we don't have freaks,
So boy don't you want to know
What makes us so special,
What's teeming with magic
At the Roving Wonder Show?

The girls reached into the sandbag pouches at their waists—Carmer doubted they had any true function as ballast—and withdrew handfuls of white, black, and gold objects that he couldn't quite make out from this distance.

They stopped singing, but echoes of the melody still hung in the air, as if someone were humming it faintly in Carmer's ear.

"Atteeeeeention!" said the girls in unison, their balloons stopped in midair. "Put your hands together and glue your eyes to the skies for the amazing, the death-defying, the aeronautic feast for the eyes that is RINKA TINKA'S ROVING WONDER SHOW!"

The girls tossed the objects from their hands, and Carmer saw that they were miniature paper gliders—simple toy versions of the downed glider currently stashed in his desk. People leapt off their bicycles and leaned out of the windows of buildings to try to catch them.

"What *is* this?" Grit asked, and Carmer heard the undercurrent of unease in her voice. The last time Grit had sensed faerie magic combined with human technology, they'd discovered a plot to enslave all the faeries of her city—and eventually the world—to force them into generating power for humans.

"It's a flying circus," said Carmer. "They've been around for a few years. I've heard of them, but I've never actually seen it." The man known as Rinka Tinka, the owner of the Wonder Show, was supposedly a genius aeronautical engineer. He was notorious for being both selective about his crew and secretive about his technology.

"Arriving in Driftside City for one week only TOMORROW NIGHT!" chorused the girls. "Come one, come all . . ."

The gold and white balloons started drifting again, edging across the rest of town and beyond. The locals were already over their surprise at the criers' dramatic appearance and were now chatting excitedly about how they would find the time to make the trek into the city, and which cousin they would stay with, and did they think Old Joe would let them borrow his steam carriage? Carmer watched as the last of the paper gliders flew this way and that on the wind. A group of schoolchildren rushed out of a white-painted church and tussled over one of the golden ones—a shade of gold that looked strikingly familiar.

We don't have beasts
And we don't have freaks,
So boy don't you want to know
What makes us so special,
What's teeming with magic
At the Roving Wonder Show?

"Well, *I* certainly do," said Grit flatly.

Carmer loosened his grip on the steering wheel and cracked his knuckles. "There's something I think you should see."

GRIT LOOKED AT the white metallic device on the lab table for approximately five seconds before striding up to the hatch in its center and blasting enough sparks from her fingertips to send the whole thing careening off the end·of the lab table and crashing to the floor. The compartment fell open with a soft *pop*.

"What?" Grit said at Carmer's warning look. Bell, for his part, had skidded back into a shelf of the Amazifier's old pickled specimens and nearly sent the whole thing toppling over. "You said you couldn't get it open!"

Carmer rolled his eyes and bent to pick up the (slightly singed) glider and place it on the lab table. Bell righted the jars behind him with a casual salute to one of the floating salamanders and stepped forward to join them.

"*And* you said this thing isn't at all like Gideon's evil mechanical birds," Grit reminded Carmer. ". . . Right?"

"I said it didn't *look* like one of Gideon's evil mechanical birds," corrected Carmer with a sigh. At least, this one didn't seem designed explicitly for inflicting terror. The metal plates he had been able to unscrew before revealed a complicated network of grooves inside the device— it was a map, he'd realized, designed to steer the glider toward its intended recipient. Only this glider had been intercepted by a certain balloonist—and now its message was in their hands.

Or rather, in Bell Daisimer's hands. Bell had already unfurled the tightly rolled golden paper that Carmer had seen peeking out of the glider's center hatch. He stared at it with a worshipful expression. A second, plainer piece of paper fell to the tabletop.

"What is it?" Grit asked. "Is that one of those papers the crowd was fighting over in town?"

"A golden glider," Bell breathed, carefully unfolding each corner of the paper to reveal the flowing calligraphy inside:

The holder of this golden glider

Is entitled to TWO first class boarding passes

For

RINKA TINKA'S ROVING WONDER SHOW

On the mythical

WHALE OF TALES

Please present your ticket at the dock at the Topside Hotel.

Boarding begins promptly at 2:00pm.

"It's a ticket, see? The criers always pass out a few of these to the crowd, to get people excited," explained Bell. "But the golden ones aren't just any ticket—they're *the* VIP experience. You get to fly with the show itself! I never thought I'd even *see* a real golden glider, never mind get one!" He danced around the attic with the ticket in hand, too-long limbs nearly cracking Carmer over the head in the small space.

"Watch the glassware, please," Carmer said, cringing. "And it's not exactly ours, is it?"

"It *did* crash into *my* balloon," Bell pointed out. "I'd say I've earned it."

"And I'd say it's our best chance to get inside this 'Wonder Show,'" said Grit, her mouth set in a firm line. "There's faerie magic at work there, and I want to know why." She bent down to unroll the plain note that had also accompanied the golden ticket. "Now, Bell, why don't you tell me everything you know about this flying circus?"

"It's not *just* a flying circus," said Bell, as if this were the most obvious thing in the world. "They've got balloon rides and ornithopters and aerial acrobatics, sure, but there's stuff that's just as amazing on the ground! And that's saying a lot, coming from me . . ."

He stopped, leaning over Carmer's shoulder to read the note, which had probably come from within the Wonder Show itself. In small, shaky handwriting, it read simply:

With my compliments.
I hope you enjoy the show.

Carmer gulped. It probably wasn't a good time to mention that he was a *little* afraid of heights.

"WELCOME," BELL DAISIMER said, "to Driff City!"

Bell hung out the door of the Moto-Manse, long arm swinging out to greet the approaching city skyline. He'd spent much of their approach to Driftside City nervously pacing around the few feet that constituted their living quarters and sneaking glances out the windows, but he couldn't seem to help himself from bursting outside eventually. The young man was incapable of sitting still; he climbed all over the Moto-Manse like he'd take off into the sky at any moment if he had the chance. Carmer told him to get inside before oncoming traffic finished the job his balloon accident had started.

Driftside City—or "Driff City," as Bell said the locals called it—didn't loom up overhead the way other cities did, so much as slowly *surround* you. It was more flat than anything else, built on swampy marshland surrounded by rivers and spitting distance from the coast. The milder Virginia climate meant the weather conditions that spelled disaster for most airships—snow and ice—weren't as big a threat. All these factors combined made it a hub for transatlantic travel—first by boat, in the shelter of the Chesapeake Bay, and years later by airship. Now it was a manufacturing capital for everything that flew—a bonus for both Bell and his ballooning needs *and* Carmer's hopes to improve Grit's wing. If Carmer wanted to learn more about aerodynamics, there was no better place.

There was also no *bigger* place, it seemed. The city was huge; the necessity for large, open spaces for airship takeoffs, landings, construction, and storage meant the city had expanded out, not up. There were no clusters of skyscrapers here. And from his view in the cab of the Moto-Manse, the first words that sprang to mind to describe Driff City, cliché as they might have been, were *lighter than air*.

Airships of every shape and size imaginable, from transatlantic luxury liners to local taxis, and even a smattering of balloons, dotted the sky. Almost every building had a mooring mast attached to its top. The buildings *themselves* gave off the impression that they, too, could be neatly folded into compact packages, ready to be loaded onto a ship at any moment.

Though some sort of vehicle seemed necessary for traveling around Driff City, the Moto-Manse immediately stuck out like a sore thumb. Other than a few cargo trucks, the three-story house on wheels was the heaviest, slowest, bulkiest vehicle on the road. In a city where even the paper delivery boy knew something about the complex weight calculations that went into getting an airship off the ground, lightness was a prized quality. There were distinct lanes on the major roads—one for wide-load vehicles and airships being towed at ground level, and another for the much lighter (and much faster) bicycles and velocycles. Even most of the steam cars had been stripped of all but their essential components, leaving the drivers open to the elements except for small canvases stretched across thin frames over their heads.

Carmer glanced overhead to see the sky choked with low-flying airships. Brave air-traffic directors perched in crow's nests attached to buildings or were suspended all by themselves at various "intersections" that seemed invisible to Carmer but no doubt made perfect sense to the fliers above. Advertisements and notices were placed at every height interval imaginable, displaying everything from announcements (*Monsieur Giland's Flying Monkeys!—One Night Only!*) to news headlines (Jasconius *Crash Mystifies Authorities—$500 REWARD for Information!*).

Carmer frowned at the *Jasconius* sign. It didn't help his slight case of nerves at the thought of flying on Rinka Tinka's Roving Wonder Show that the biggest airship disaster of the decade had occurred just two weeks prior. The great transatlantic passenger ship had crash-landed into a Driftside airfield and literally gone up in flames, killing five crew, three passengers, and a firefighter trying to combat the blaze. It was a miracle that more people hadn't been killed, and no one knew what had caused the disaster, though engine failure was suspected.

Yet Driftside City appeared to be taking the disaster in stride. The skies were still full of ships and the streets still full of people, as if they had all collectively shrugged their shoulders and said, "Well, that's what happens sometimes when you fill a flying passenger vehicle with tons of highly flammable gas, right?"

Carmer, frankly, was interested in machines that had a bit less of a chance of erupting into giant fireballs.

Something whizzed by the Moto-Manse, snapping Carmer's attention back to the road; he had to swerve to make sure Bell retained all his limbs. Up in the attic window, Grit shouted down a few choice words about his driving.

"Sorry!" Carmer called.

The balloonist galloped into the cab and clapped Carmer on the shoulder. "Velocycles!" Bell said, pointing ahead. "They're made extra light and fast here, for travel between the ships. Pretty fabulous, right?"

The motorized bicycles dodged and weaved around the Moto-Manse, forcing Carmer to coax his mobile house into more subtle maneuvering than it was accustomed to. There was a whole pack of them—all ridden by young men whose appearances ranged from handsomely rakish to outright disreputable—and they laughed and pointed at the bulky Moto-Manse as they darted around it.

"Yeah," Carmer said, finally relaxing when the last hollering hooligan had sped away. "Fabulous." He pulled over into the "wide loads" lane.

"The velocycle clubs don't have the best reputations," conceded Bell. "You'll want to steer clear of gangs like that, traveling on your own."

Gangs?! Carmer thought, but he didn't want to seem like a *total* country bumpkin, so he said, "You're not staying in the city, then? After the show?"

Bell seemed to deflate a little, as if *he* were the balloon that had just been popped.

"Just until I can get a new balloon," said Bell, "and

point you and the little miss in the right direction for getting her wing spruced up. To tell you the truth . . . Driff City wasn't exactly on my itinerary, either. I'll be out of your hair in no time."

Carmer flushed. He hadn't realized his discomfort with Bell as a traveling companion had been that obvious. And perhaps, as a balloonist with a rather small operation, Bell avoided Driftside City for the same reasons Carmer and the Amazifier did with their magic show: city crowds (and markets saturated with entertainers) were tough customers.

"I'm sorry about your balloon. I have . . ." Carmer hesitated. *Finances*—both Carmer's and Bell's—were just another thing that Grit hadn't been thinking about when she took on another houseguest by effectively destroying Bell's livelihood. "I have a little bit of money saved up, from a magic competition Grit and I just won. We could, um, help you out a bit with the new one, if you like."

"You're a stand-up fellow, Carmer," Bell said. "I'm not gonna lie, I could use the help. I barely had enough cash to— Well. You know how it is. And don't worry, I'll be more careful with the next one. And if all goes well, I won't be Bell the Balloonist forever."

Carmer drove for a few moments in silence before he realized that he was probably supposed to express curiosity over what Bell's future plans actually were.

"I hope not" was what eventually came out of Carmer's

mouth. "Because the odds of setting yourself on fire the way you perform now are pretty high."

Fortunately, Bell didn't seem to hear him, but instead stared out through the Moto-Manse's front window at the city before them with such intense longing that it almost felt rude to watch.

"I'm going to be a pilot someday, Carmer," said Bell after a moment. "You can bet on it."

"You mean a captain?" Carmer suggested. He didn't know much about airships, but he was fairly certain they shared similar terminology with sailing.

"Nope," said Bell, his dark eyes twinkling. "I mean a pilot. Airships won't be the only machines in the sky forever, Carmer. You can bet on *that*, too."

4.

THE ROVING
WONDER SHOW

CARMER, GRIT, AND BELL FOUND THEMSELVES staring down the belly of a whale.

They were actually staring *up*, and the whale in question was not an *actual* whale, but Carmer found he suddenly empathized much more with the heroes in the stories Grit insisted he read, who were so often being swallowed by some giant creature or another.

"Welcome," said a deep voice from somewhere within the bowels of the airship in front of them, "to the *Whale of Tales*. Your journey is about to begin . . ."

Carmer and Bell had been the first to approach the ship, painted in such detail to look like a giant blue whale that some of the other passengers had actually screamed when it came into view. It even had full-scale fins attached to either side that bobbed gently in the cold afternoon breeze.

The criers' song drifted out from the *Whale of Tales*' "mouth"—the hatchway where the lucky golden ticket–holders were being urged to board. The pearly gangplank under Carmer's feet felt like standing on a set of monstrous teeth, ready to gobble him up at any second—which, he supposed, was the intended effect. The Amazifier would have liked it.

As Carmer moved farther into the whale's mouth, he noticed the song's words were different from before.

> *One who seeks*
> *A hint of mystique*
> *Must also be willing to pay*
> *The sum of a story*
> *The tax of a tall tale*
> *If they wish to be on their way.*

"What the devil does that mean?" asked a mustached man in line behind Carmer. "Haven't we already paid a fortune to get on this thing?"

The gentleman standing in front of the complainer, a giant of a man with a thick black beard, rolled his eyes and smiled at Carmer conspiratorially.

The truth was, they probably *had* paid a fortune. Carmer and Bell stood out like mismatched sore thumbs on the roof of the Topside Hotel—Carmer in his magician's top hat and patchwork coat, and Bell in his dusty khakis and old, crusty leather jacket. The Topside Hotel was the grandest in the city, so imposing that the entire wealthy neighborhood where it was located was called "Topside" by association. A single meal there, Carmer was sure, cost more than he made in half a year.

The "upper lobby," as it was called, was really the semi-enclosed roof of the hotel, where luxury passenger airships docked temporarily to drop off the rich and famous directly at the hotel—presumably so they didn't have to mingle with the unwashed masses of the city below. Unlike Carmer and Bell, the finely dressed hotel guests' tickets obviously hadn't been free.

"Shall I give one of them a good poke with my sword?" whispered Grit. She was perched on the small balcony built on the *inside* of Carmer's top hat, with a small peephole to look out of. "Come on, just a little one." She brandished her hatpin sword so forcefully it almost got caught in Carmer's hair.

"Only if you never want to find out what's going on with the Wonder Show," Carmer warned under his breath. This was their best shot at getting close to the flying circus; they couldn't afford to get kicked off the ship now. A ticket on the *Whale of Tales* meant they got to fly *with* the fleet as it paraded into town and landed in the airfield. Most spectators watched from the fairgrounds, or made do with the roofs of the tallest buildings they could find.

A woman in a long black evening gown and a thin lace shawl sniffed her nose at Carmer and turned away to complain to her neighbor about the cold. It was late December, but most of the hotel guests were curiously inappropriately dressed for spending hours hundreds of feet in the air on a winter afternoon.

"They think I'm talking to myself now, too," said Carmer glumly.

"No, you're not," said Bell, linking his arm with Carmer's. "You're talking to me!"

Carmer felt his cheeks grow warm and ducked out from under Bell's grip.

"Let's get on with it, shall we?" muttered Carmer, and took the first step into the belly of the whale.

There wasn't much to see. A shimmering curtain, made of glittering white-and-silver thread, blocked the way up a set of stairs ahead. As soon as Bell stepped next to Carmer, a silver door promptly slid shut behind them. Bell scooted backward, his heels bumping into the door, but Carmer stood frozen on the spot. His breath quickened. They'd been trapped.

"Hey, what's the big idea?" complained Grit, racing to her peephole in Carmer's hat.

Vaguely, Carmer could hear the concerned noises of the rest of the crowd outside. Again, the song sounded:

One who seeks
A hint of mystique
Must also be willing to pay
The sum of a story
The tax of a tall tale
If they wish to be on their way.

"The Whale of Tales," Grit whispered excitedly. "Of course! It feeds on stories!"

"Feeds?" asked Carmer.

"You know what I mean." Grit nudged him with her toe. "You've got to tell it a story to get in."

Though Carmer hadn't paid for his ticket, he was starting to understand the point of the man behind him who'd complained.

"Oh, I've got loads!" said Bell cheerfully. "But which terrifying tale of adventure to regale this great beast with—"

"Once upon a time, I made a friend and we saved an entire population from destruction by an evil mastermind, and now he's dead and we're not," said Carmer tersely. "The end."

"That works, too," said Bell with a shrug, but he looked at Carmer appraisingly.

The silver curtains at the top of the stairs parted, revealing the corridor beyond, and the door behind them began to slide open to admit the next guest.

He wondered what kind of story they would tell, and who was listening.

CARMER HAD NEVER been on an airship before, but he guessed that the *Whale*'s design was fairly standard once one got past the giant mouth. Instead of the red, squirming insides he half expected to find, the hallway was just a hallway, albeit a beautiful one. The theme of the Wonder Show's performance was "Myths from Around the Globe," and the hall leading to the observation deck was painted with sweeping murals so vivid that the gods and goddesses, nymphs, monsters, and ghosts they depicted looked ready to pop out of the walls.

On second glance, Carmer saw that they *were* popping out of the walls. Many of the figures were made of a thin layer of painted wood sculpted on top of the wall itself, and as Carmer walked down the hall, they ever so subtly moved. The naiad Daphne, her arms already transforming into the branches of a laurel tree, leapt just a bit farther, Apollo in hot pursuit. Zigzags of lightning escaped from a brightly colored thunderbird's eyes while its wings flapped up and down. A handsome prince waved a blade at a menacing nine-tailed fox.

Carmer would have liked to stay in that hall of stories longer, but Bell dragged him along impatiently; others had already passed them by on the way to the observation deck ahead, and Bell wanted to snag the perfect spot to view the rest of the show.

The deck was simple but elegant, with floor-to-ceiling windows on all sides. Carmer didn't get too close, though Bell ran right up to the edge, nearly jumping onto the guardrail that kept the passengers from pressing up against the glass itself. Those rails were probably made expressly for the Bell Daisimers of the world.

"I wonder if we'll meet Mr. Tinka himself," said Bell. "He's a genius! Done more for aeronautics in the last five years than anyone else has managed in forty. We'd *all* still be drifting around in balloons if it weren't for him."

That wasn't strictly true, but Carmer didn't want to dampen Bell's obvious excitement. He remembered how it felt to want to meet the role model you idolized; he just hoped Bell's hero didn't end up being a faerie-enslaving villain, too.

"I bet *he* doesn't think airplanes are a bunch of hooey," continued Bell. He was convinced that so-called airplanes—heavier-than-air aircraft—were the future of flight. Carmer had heard of a few successful attempts, but no one really thought it would catch on. Airships, filled with hydrogen or helium that made them lighter than air, were the tried-and-true method of aerial transportation.

Then again, most people didn't think magic was real, either. Carmer reserved his judgment for the moment.

More people began to file onto the observation deck,

oohing and *aahing* over the view of the city below and the other ships passing by. The show probably opened the windows in warmer weather. As it was, Carmer felt curiously warm for being up so high in the middle of winter, and the wealthy spectators' lack of winter wear was starting to make sense: the ship was *heated*.

"Do you see that?" Carmer asked Bell excitedly, inching toward the windows. Carmer tried his best to remain focused on the heating and ventilation, as opposed to the several-hundred-foot drop onto concrete below. He pointed to some of the pipes running along the frame in the ceiling. "They use the steam from the boiler for heating *and* running the engines. You can pump in hot air that way. A perk for the passengers *and* a way to keep ice from freezing on the envelope. No *wonder* they still tour in the winter, when everyone else has closed down for the season!"

Bell was looking at Carmer like he had two heads.

"First of all," said Bell. He lowered his voice, but the other passengers were so busy mingling and pointing out the sights that no one noticed. "I think that's the first time I've ever heard you say more than two sentences at a time to anyone but that faerie of yours."

"I am not *his*," Grit corrected him from inside Carmer's hat. "But don't feel bad. He just likes me more than you."

Carmer wanted to look down at his feet, but since that was dangerously close to looking down at the ground so far below them, he shrugged instead.

"Second," Bell continued, "we're hundreds of feet up in the air, with a first-class ticket on a first-class airship, about to see the best flying circus in the *world*, and you're excited about the *heating system*."

"It's really very sophisticated," muttered Carmer.

A handful of stewards entered, carrying drink trays among the guests.

"You think this is great," said Bell, grabbing a fizzy-looking drink from a passing tray, "just wait until we get to the fairgrounds! Of course, the greatest part about being on the *Whale* is getting to be *in* the parade—did you know they had to close down air *and* street traffic on Main Street just for the show?—but—"

"Look!" Grit whispered to Carmer, her eyes keener than the humans', even through her peephole. "What is *that?*"

A glowing shape was coming into focus in the distance—a very *large* glowing shape. A few of the other passengers took notice, including the big bearded man from the line.

"Is that . . . a *giant?*" Carmer asked.

So many of the guests rushed to the guardrail that Carmer was surprised the ship didn't tilt.

He peeked between the heads in front of him to see several human-shaped figures, taller than most of the buildings on either side of them, walking down the street. They were faceless, glowing gold from head to toe, but for all of their size, they made no sound as they trod on the earth below.

"They're floating lanterns," said Bell. He reached out a hand toward the glass as if to touch them.

He was right. Each giant was made of hundreds—if not thousands—of clusters of paper lanterns controlled by Wonder Show workers from tethered points below.

One of the giants came so close to the *Whale of Tales* that everyone backed away from the windows when it waved a mighty hand—and then burst apart from the inside, scattering hundreds of lanterns to ride on the wind. Carmer risked a brief look down to see the onlookers outside reach out to catch them or to tap them upward and onward to continue their journey down the parade route.

The menagerie came next. The *Whale of Tales* suddenly fit right in as balloons and airships modeled after creatures of every shape and size floated through the air. There were snail shells with perfectly proportioned spirals. There were sea horses and honeybees; gliders that Carmer had only ever read about, designed to look like delicate dragonflies but actually bigger than he was; a turtle that retracted its head in and out of its shell; even a fierce dragon airship that roared as it approached.

The *Whale of Tales* joined in the procession, and the crowd inside shifted, either to wave to the spectators outside or to watch the rear of the parade, where the human element of the Wonder Show had finally been introduced. Half a dozen brightly painted gliders, along with three ornithopter pilots expertly flapping their immense artificial wings, followed just behind them. Trapeze artists swung suspended from the criers' black, white, and gold balloons, completing death-defying somersaults with apparent ease.

Before Carmer knew it, they had reached the end of the parade. The *Whale of Tales* was tethered in a circle with the rest of the floating animals, leaving the broad expanse of the fairgrounds open for the rest of the air show. In the middle of the field, a white spiral staircase reached so high it seemed to touch the clouds, ready and waiting for the first act to begin. The show's theme song began playing through the megaphones mounted in the corners of the *Whale*'s ceiling.

Come fly so high
You'll touch the sky . . .

Carmer swayed on his feet, the memory of faerie song bringing him crashing back down to reality.

"You all right there, Carmer?" asked Bell, looking concerned.

Carmer waved him off. "I'm fine."

"And I'm a water horse," Grit muttered. "Let's find out what makes this show so wonderful, shall we?"

WHILE BELL AND Carmer watched the swooping airships, daring barnstormers, and jumping gymnasts of the Roving Wonder Show, Grit watched the ceiling. Specifically, she watched the heating vents that Carmer had pointed out, waiting for another glimpse of the movement she'd spotted there shortly after they boarded. She occasionally snuck a glance at the spectacle outside—a red-haired girl was currently walking a wire suspended between two balloons—but she knew her best chance at investigating the show would come from the inside, not out.

She was just about to give up, her eyes watering, when she saw it—a flash of tiny running feet across the vent, so fast a human would never have seen them. She concentrated on keeping herself invisible and slowly, ever so slowly, opened the secret door that led out onto the brim of Carmer's top hat. She needn't have worried about the humans—all *their* eyes were glued to the show outside—but she couldn't be sure what sorts of faeries were watching.

She had a mind to find out.

Grit knew Carmer wouldn't think much of her going exploring on her own, but really, what was the use in being the faerie in the operation if you couldn't use your size to your advantage?

I'll be back before he notices I'm gone, thought Grit, and launched herself toward the ceiling.

5.

THE WORLD'S SMALLEST COWBOY

GRIT FOLLOWED THE FAERIE THROUGH THE BOWELS of the ship, away from the other passengers. She ran along the metal framework as quietly as she could. It really did feel like running inside the skeleton of a very large beast—one that was still alive and ready to devour her at any minute.

There were so many crisscrossing bars and other obstacles that it was actually easier to run than fly. Having spent most of her life relying on her legs instead of her wings, Grit was a swift runner, but the other faerie—faeries?—knew the territory. Grit would catch just a glimpse of running feet turning a corner or the shadow of a small silhouette, or would hear the ghost of a teasing chuckle before the air turned utterly still again.

Grit paused to get her bearings. She was high above a small corridor. A skinny girl with a mane of messy dark hair hurried along below, her footfalls so quiet even Grit barely heard her—one of the acrobats, perhaps. Grit waited for her to pass before calling out.

"I know you're here," she said, trying her best to keep her tone light and friendly. "And you know I'm here. So we might as well introduce ourselves, don't you think?"

A soft titter was barely audible above the roar of the engines—they were much louder in this part of the ship—and a pair of bright wings fluttered into view farther down the walkway before darting out of sight again. They were either playfully shy or toying with her. Grit was certain now there was more than one other faerie on board.

The question was *why*. What were a bunch of faeries doing on a human airship, blatantly (at least to the right audience) using their magic, *and* hiding from one of their own?

She walked toward the direction she'd seen the wings, more casually this time.

"This is an impressive ship," she said. "You probably know loads about it. How the engines work . . ."

She jumped lightly from her perch by the wall toward the center of the ceiling.

"The propellers . . ." Another jump, to another level of the framework. "They're called propellers, right?"

The air was very, very still. Only soft echoes of the show's musical score drifted into this part of the ship.

"But the thing is," Grit said, with one last hop into the skeleton ceiling, "I just spent the last few days listening to someone natter on and on about airships, so I know a little bit about how they work, too."

More silence. These faeries clearly had no plans to reveal themselves or their business on this ship to her. But with over a dozen people on board, she wasn't in the mood to take any chances.

Grit looked at the gasbag now directly above her.

"These big bags," she said, trying to keep her voice from wavering, "are filled with a gas the humans call 'hydrogen.' It's lighter than air, which is what makes the *Whale of Tales* fly. But I hear it's also *highly flammable*."

Grit took one last, long look around, and raised her hand in the air. She had no intention of using her powers here, but if they weren't going to talk willingly . . .

"So I would suggest you tell me what you're doing on a human flying circus," she said. "Because with a snap of my fingers, I could send this whole ship up in flames."

There was a heavy pause, and then—out of nowhere—a thin rope shot out, curled around Grit's wrist, and yanked it down by her side.

A faerie strolled out of the shadows, dressed in human-style shirt and trousers, with the world's tiniest cowboy hat pulled low over his eyes. Those clothes could mean only one thing: the faerie was a member of the Free Folk— faeries who had forsworn both the Seelie and Unseelie courts—and therefore had no love for Seelie faeries like Grit.

"That was the wrong thing to say, miss," he said, a pleasant twang in his voice. Quick as lightning, he spun another length of rope around his head a few times and cast it out. Brown, curling vines sprouted from his wrists and intertwined with the rope, elongating it until it reached up and snatched Grit around the waist, pulling her away from the gasbag before she could even cry out.

And then she was falling.

But all she could think about was the faerie—and the first thing she'd noticed when he stepped into the light.

He didn't have any wings.

THE WONDER SHOW was ending, and Icarus was falling.

The man piloting the ornithopter somersaulted in dizzying loops as he descended, expertly maneuvering the wings as if he were a real bird in flight. The "feathers" of his wings somehow changed color from tawny brown to fiery reds and oranges, mimicking the fatal rays of the sun that melted the wax holding them together in the Greek myth. Icarus had been warned by his father not to fly too close to the sun with his artificial wings. But too thrilled by the freedom of flight, he'd failed to listen—and had met his doom in the sea below.

This fall was far from uncontrolled, though it might have looked that way to the audience. Carmer had never seen an ornithopter capable of such finely tuned movements. But Faerie aid could go only so far when machines were involved. Not only did mechanical devices tend to behave erratically around the presence of too much concentrated magic, most faeries wouldn't even get *near* machines, if they had a say in the matter. Whoever had designed these devices—including the messenger glider—was clearly a genius.

As soon as Icarus descended from view, the other ships quickly swooped back into place for the finale. The music pumping through the gramophones changed from the somber, dramatic violins accompanying Icarus's fall to a cheerful orchestral romp that felt rather jarring to Carmer. Though he knew it was all part of the show, he couldn't get the image of the falling ornithopter pilot out of his head. He'd been much too far away to see the man's face, but he imagined the look of terror there—the moment when Icarus realized his wings were gone and all he could do was flap his arms until he fell to his death.

By the time Carmer snapped back to attention, the Wonder Show ships were already dispersing, and Bell was shaking him by the shoulders and practically hopping up and down with excitement.

"Did you *see* that airman?!" Bell exclaimed. "It was so beautiful, I thought I might cry." He fanned himself with his hand like one of the fashionable ladies around them.

It *was* beautiful, but it also wasn't helpful. Other than

the undercurrents of faerie song in the music, Carmer hadn't detected a hint of actual magic. He was still learning, but he was willing to bet Grit felt the same.

"What do you think?" Carmer asked, staring out at the city as the ship began to circle back to the hotel.

Bell was about to open his mouth to answer when he realized Carmer was talking to Grit.

But Grit didn't answer, and Carmer's hat felt *curiously* light.

"YOU GUYS REALLY, really can't take a joke," Grit said weakly. She was tied up in the cargo hold of the *Whale of Tales*, facing a handful of decidedly unhappy Free Folk, and she had definitely *not* made a good first impression. "I wasn't *really* going to set your ship on fire!"

The faerie with the pearly white wings she'd glimpsed in the hall tightened Grit's bindings with a harrumph. They squeezed her newly healed wing painfully.

"Oh, that's all fine and dandy, then," said the wingless cowboy faerie, who seemed to be the leader of the bunch. (He was unlikely to have wrangled many actual cattle in his life, being about five and a half inches tall, but she couldn't think of any other word that suited him better.) He leaned against a box labeled *ORANGES* with his arms crossed. "Nothin' but a misunderstandin', right?"

"I would *never* do something like that," Grit assured him. "Not with all—"

The humans on board, she had almost said, but stopped herself just in time. She had no idea what these faeries' relationship to the humans on the Roving Wonder Show was. Despite living in the human world, most Free Folk had no great love for the big folk themselves.

"Not with everyone here," she finished lamely, blushing. "I've no quarrel with Free Folk."

One or two of them seemed slightly mollified at her use of their preferred name. Most of the Fair Folk, as faeries in the courts called themselves, referred to the others as "street fae."

"Good to hear it, miss," said the cowboy. He stepped into the light, revealing a weathered face with a strong jaw. Brown curls snuck out from under his hat, touched by gray; this was unusual for a faerie of his apparent age. "But you threatened to burn down our ship. And that means we might have a quarrel with *you*."

"*Your* ship?" Grit asked, looking him square in the eye.

The faerie raised an eyebrow. "'Scuse me?"

"I was just curious." She shrugged, trying not to wince at the ropes squeezing her wings. "You called it 'our' ship. Maybe I'm out of line for saying this, but it seems like there's a bit too many humans crawling about for it to be *entirely* your ship." Grit looked up at him as innocently as she could. Something about this tiny cowboy didn't sit right with her, kidnapping notwithstanding. And she was going to find out what it was.

He tugged at the bandana around his neck—his human-style clothes, Grit thought, suited him about as well as a wolf wearing a dog sweater—and cracked a smile.

"We have a . . . special arrangement with the Wonder Show here," admitted the cowboy. "It looks like that might be an arrangement you're familiar with." He nodded to her mechanical wing.

"I am," said Grit. She considered avoiding mentioning Carmer—there was no sense in getting him in trouble if she could help it—but she had no idea what the Wonder Show faeries had seen and what they hadn't. For all she knew, they had Carmer socked away in another corner of the ship somewhere. "I'm traveling with a Friend of the Fae. We came here because we were . . . curious."

And wondering if you were in need of rescuing, Grit thought wryly. *Which, clearly, you were not.* It was altogether more probable that someone was going to need to rescue *her*.

"You've got questions," said the cowboy. "Just so happens I might have some for you, too. Whatcha say, darlin'? An answer for an answer."

Grit set her teeth. Either these fae were going to let her go, or they were going to toss her trussed-up rump over the edge of the ship, and it hardly seemed like anything she had to say would change their minds one way or the other. But she could at least stall for time.

"Sure thing," Grit said gamely. "Me first."

"PARDON ME, GENTLEMEN, but passengers aren't allowed in that part of the ship."

Carmer and Bell halted, barely two steps onto the keel catwalk of the *Whale of Tales*, and turned around to see a young redheaded woman hanging upside down from the ceiling.

"I, um . . ." said Carmer. "I was just looking for my friend."

She's about five inches tall, with a penchant for setting things on fire with her bare hands.

The girl smiled knowingly and gracefully swung down to stand before them. She was wearing a polka dot dress loud enough to wake the dead and carrying a pink parasol and a large basket. All in all, she looked more prepared for picnicking than manning an airship. Carmer thought he recognized her as one of the tightrope walkers.

"Seems to me like you've already got one," said the girl, nodding to Bell. "Plus, all the other passengers have already disembarked. I'm going to have to ask you to do the same."

Bell clapped Carmer on the back. Carmer was starting to hate it when he did that.

"Don't mind my friend here, miss," said Bell. "Nan Tucket, right? I saw your act. Walking the high wire across those ships with *baskets* on your feet? That's crazy!"

The girl's mouth quirked, and a small blush crept into her pale cheeks. She was clearly, like Bell, a person who accepted "crazy" as a compliment.

"It's an *homage*, really," Nan explained, twirling her parasol. "To Maria Spelterini."

"First woman to cross Niagara Falls on the high wire." Bell mimed a tip of the hat. "With . . . was it peach baskets, I believe?"

Nan looked grudgingly impressed.

"Truth is, we're aerial enthusiasts ourselves," continued Bell. "Bell Daisimer, current balloonist and future pilot." He reached out and shook the girl's hand. "And this is . . ." Bell drifted off, just for a moment, and Carmer realized he'd never even told Bell his full name.

"Felix Cassius Tiberius Carmer III," muttered Carmer, looking down at his feet.

Bell and the girl called Nan Tucket turned toward him in unison.

"This is Carmer," said Bell, suppressing a laugh. "One of the brightest engineering minds from Skemantis."

Carmer's eyes widened, but he held his tongue. He'd spent barely a week in Skemantis, and had in fact been instrumental in *dismantling* one of the city's crowning engineering achievements. (Granted, it had been corrupt technology running on stolen faerie magic, but still.)

"We were *hoping* to see a bit more of the ship," said Bell. "Carmer here would just about wet himself if he got a glimpse of the latest Lilienthal engine we hear you're using. Any chance we could get a bit of a private tour?" Bell flashed his most dazzling smile, but it appeared Nan was unimpressed.

"Sorry," she said with a shrug. "Captain's orders. I'd sneak you in my basket, but I don't think you'd fit." She winked, but gestured outside all the same. "Though you'd have a better shot at it than the other gent who tried sneaking backstage just now. Nearly as big as the ship, that one! Now come along, please. Unless you *also* plan on trying to convince me you've got a 'personal invitation' from Mr. Tinka?" Nan let out an unladylike snort—fortunately missing the guilty look exchanged by her two wayward passengers—and steered Bell out by the elbow, apparently confident that Carmer would follow.

"Honestly, what is it with you rubes tonight?" she muttered.

Before long, they were out in the cold night air, being shooed away from the Topside Hotel by a bellhop who looked relieved to see the backs of them.

"What are we going to do now?" Carmer asked Bell when they were out on the street.

"We're going back to get a better look around the Wonder Show, of course," said Bell, as if this were the most obvious answer in the world. He held up a small slip of paper.

"This is where the *Whale* is docking," said Bell. The paper was of the same fine material as the glider invitations, but this one contained only a hastily scrawled note that read, *ELYSIAN FIELD, WEST HANGAR*. Bell frowned at it, despite being obviously pleased with his success.

"Where did you get *that?*" demanded Carmer.

"Oh, Felix Cassius Tiberius Carmer III," said Bell, resuming his casual stroll along the sidewalk, "you underestimate the power of my charms."

A SUBTLE CHANGE in the rhythm of the engine was the only indication that the ship had changed direction, but Grit felt it all the same. They'd stashed her in a windowless cargo hold, and there was no way to tell where in the world the ship was going.

"Okay," she said. "First question: Who are you, and what are so many Free Folk doing here on the Wonder Show?"

"You don't mess around, do you, miss?" asked the cowboy faerie with a barking laugh. "The name's Yarlo, and I do believe that was two questions in one."

Grit pressed her lips together.

"What do they call *you?*" Yarlo asked, absentmindedly twirling one of his vines around his gloved wrist.

"They call me Grit," she said, trying to look as confident as she could while tied to a pole and surrounded by fruit crates. She wasn't strictly *lying*. She just left out the part about *also* being called Grettifrida Lonewing, princess of the Seelie faerie kingdom of Skemantis. (Carmer did not have the premium on silly names in their relationship, a fact that delighted him to no end. *Grettifrida*, thought Grit. *Honestly.*)

"Pleased to make your acquaintance, Grit," said Yarlo.

"Clearly," Grit said. "Now. This ship. I've met my fair share of Free Folk"—*well, a handful from the local faerie pub*—"and while they like to share a strong potion and a good revel every now and again, they're hardly known for sticking together through thick and thin, if you don't mind me saying so. But you lot seem to be traveling together."

"I'm a relative newcomer to the Wonder Show, myself," admitted Yarlo.

Grit was surprised; he was clearly in charge here.

"But it's true, we stick together around here. I think you'll agree that tough times make unlikely alliances." He glanced knowingly again at her mechanical wing.

"Unlikely alliances," Grit repeated. "You use your magic to help the Wonder Show in exchange for a place to stay?"

"The Wonder Show doesn't *need* our magic to fly," piped up the faerie with the white wings who had tied up Grit. She had light green hair, so pale it was almost white, too; it swirled up on the top of her head like a pearl onion. Her cheeks glowed with fluorescent light in place of the usual blush. "Its creator made it without any help from anyone."

Yarlo's eyes tensed, just a touch. "Grit," he said, "meet Beamsprout."

Beamsprout stepped forward. "And we don't *need* to stay here. Free Folk may go wherever they wish, unbound by the confines of kingdoms and the rules of noble faeries."

The two other faeries in the room nodded their approval, glowering.

Grit gulped, glad she'd kept her own noble status quiet.

Yarlo put up a hand to speak. "We have a healthy respect for the great mind behind the Wonder Show," he allowed. "And Beamsprout is right. We *choose* to be here. And you'll find we've never garnered any unwanted attention with the small amount of magic we do lend them."

"Until now," said Beamsprout, crossing her arms.

"Beamsprout, darlin'," said Yarlo, "why don't you check on the cables for docking? We must be nearly back to the camp. Thundrumble, Canippy, you go on, too. Tell the folks on the other ships we'll meet at the . . . usual place."

The other two faeries shrugged and flew off, but Beamsprout lingered with a final, narrow look at Grit before Yarlo shooed her away.

"I'll take it from here with our visitor," Yarlo said with a smirk. He stepped forward and whipped his vines to the floor with a crack, striking a hairsbreadth from Grit's toes. She gasped.

As angry as the other Free Folk had been about her storming their home, there was something . . . different about Yarlo. He was *toying* with her—all friendly and smooth "y'all"s and "ma'am"s one minute, and stone cold the next—and he was enjoying it.

Grit had no idea how he would react to what she said next, but it couldn't hurt to try.

"Well, before you decide whether to strangle me with those vines of yours or not, there's one thing you should know," she said. "I think . . . I think I know who stole your wings."

6.

A NAUTILUS, ACTUALLY

"HOW DO WE KNOW WE'RE GOING TO THE RIGHT place?"

The icy wind whipped against Carmer's face as he and Bell pedaled furiously on the bicycles they'd rented for their stay in Driff City. It was nearly dark already; Elysian Field was miles farther from downtown than the fairgrounds had been. If Nan Tucket was just toying with them—a couple of "rubes," as she'd said—they would lose precious time. *Grit* would lose precious time, wherever she was on the *Whale of Tales*. If she was still on the *Whale of Tales*.

"We don't!" said Bell over his shoulder.

Well, that was comforting.

"The Wonder Show docks its ships all over the cities it visits—keeps them looking extra impressive when the whole fleet takes off at once. Plus, it's easier for them to keep out nosy folks like us if no one knows *exactly* where the sausage gets made." Bell pedaled harder, shooting ahead.

Carmer, whose legs were much shorter, struggled to keep up.

"But the *Whale* will be here, at least," added Bell, "and that's a good place to start!" Of course, they both knew that Grit might not even be on the *Whale of Tales* anymore, which meant that unless Bell Daisimer had a *lot* of charm stored up to bribe the crew, they might bike all night and never find the other ships.

They veered off the main road. Boxy, utilitarian buildings in shades of gray and brown surrounded the airfield before dissolving into marshy wetlands and outlying farmland. Carmer had only heard of Elysian Field, one of the largest airfields in the country, for the same reason that most people had heard of it: this was where the *Jasconius* had crashed just a few weeks before. Carmer looked for any telltale signs of an accident—scorched earth, ruts in the ground, even bits of wreckage—but the Driftsiders had cleaned up well. There was little indication that the field had just played host to a disaster.

And though the Wonder Show might have taken pains to hide its ships, it was a lot harder to hide its people. The lights and sounds of merriment from the circus camp in the southern end of the field cut sharply through the industrial gloom surrounding it. Carmer and Bell gave the caravan a wide berth.

Nan Tucket met them at one of the outer storage sheds near the western hangar, as promised. Her freckled face was washed free of her heavy stage makeup, and she wore a clean-cut—if rather plain—navy dress and coat.

"We nearly didn't recognize you there," said Bell, gesturing to her layman's clothes.

"What did you expect?" she asked, a bit of a challenge in her voice. "More silk and garters?"

"I wasn't expecting anything, miss," said Bell, "I'm just delighted by the pleasant surprise of your company."

"And you brought your friend," said Nan, scrunching up her nose. But she waved hello to Carmer all the same, and said, "You could learn a thing or two from him."

She hiked up her dress a few scandalous inches to reveal a polka dot petticoat and grinned at them both. "What, did you think I left *all* the fun behind when we hit the ground?" She turned on her heel, evidently expecting them to follow.

"I think I like this tour already," said Bell, taking off after her.

Carmer hurried to follow them.

"Keep quiet," Nan warned, "and don't get caught, or I'll be stuck on dish duty for weeks, and you . . ."

She looked Bell up and down.

"You'll be in *very* big trouble."

As they scurried toward the hulking outline of the tethered *Whale*, Bell didn't look like he minded being in trouble with Nan Tucket very much at all.

THE WORLD'S SMALLEST cowboy did not look very impressed at Grit's declaration.

"That's amazing, you know," Grit tried again, nodding to the coils around his wrists. "What you can do with those ropes, and your vines. You're an earth faerie, right?"

Yarlo nodded slowly.

"I was born without a wing," said Grit. "And maybe I'm wrong, but . . . I don't think you were."

Yarlo merely leaned back against the crate behind him. "That seems like a statement, to me."

"Sorry?"

"I thought we was askin' questions," he pointed out, his drawl thickening.

"The man who did that to you," Grit went on, ignoring his attempt to be disarming. "I think I know who it was. His name was the Mechanist. Well, it was really Titus Archer, but his magician's persona was named the Mechanist, and he had a whole *cloak* of faerie wings—"

Yarlo flinched.

"I'm sorry," Grit said breathlessly. "I'm so sorry. But he did. And some pretty nasty mechanical cats to do his dirty work."

Yarlo's face darkened, and Grit knew she was on the right track.

"And eventually, he figured out how to use faerie magic in a machine to make electricity for humans. You know, to turn their lights on and things. But my friend Car—a Friend of the Fae and I stopped him. I destroyed his machine myself, and we freed all the faeries inside."

Grit stood up a little taller.

Yarlo let out a low whistle, leaning more heavily against the orange crate. "I've got an actual question for ya, then." His knees shook, ever so slightly. "What happened to him? What happened to the son of a harpy who took my wings?"

"The Unseelies . . ." Grit said. "Well, the Wild Hunt came, and their leader was representing the Unseelie king."

Grit took a deep breath.

"They killed him. They killed him right in front of us."

CARMER HAD EXPECTED Nan Tucket to take them straight to the *Whale of Tales*, but she veered off before they reached it, darting around all the giant aircraft in the dark with practiced skill. On the other side of the field was the hangar, an enormous barn-shaped building designed for holding airships.

"With any luck, they'll have left the side door unlatched," Nan whispered. "Come on, now. You said you wanted to see engines . . ."

She led them away from the main horizontal doors that would slide open to admit the aircraft to a much smaller side door. Carmer could barely hear the revelry from the Wonder Show's camp from here.

Nan tossed her fiery hair over her shoulder, her eyes sparkling in the moonlight, and opened the door.

Inside the hangar were half a dozen airplanes.

Not airships, but air*planes*—the buzzing, smoking contraptions that Bell was determined to fly one day. Carmer had only seen them in the scientific journals the Amazifier subscribed to, but he recognized them right away—the smooth wings jutting out on either side, the slender fuselage. These planes were small; they would hold only a man or two. Some of them were incomplete, innards exposed or wings not fully attached.

"Spirits and zits," breathed Carmer.

"Whatever he said," said Bell.

Nan shut the door behind them. "I knew you'd like it."

"Like it?!" Bell walked into the hangar as uncertainly as a new father might walk into a nursery, afraid of waking the sleeping infants all around him. "I've never seen planes like these!"

Moonlight spilled in from ten-foot windows on both sides, bathing the hangar in an eerie glow.

"That's because they don't exist yet," said Nan. "But Mr. Tinka's on the verge of a breakthrough, we all know it. Something about using 'internal combustion engines,' I heard him say."

"Internal combustion engines?" asked Carmer, hurrying to one of the planes to take a closer look.

"See, I knew you'd be glad you came," said Bell fondly.

"That's what I heard," said Nan, shrugging. "Don't know what it means, but I don't really have to, do I? I'll worry about these buzzards the day I have to jump from them."

She gave the plane a friendly pat on the wing; it echoed too loudly in the space, and she cringed.

"Who's there?" demanded a man's voice from somewhere in the dark.

They froze.

"Oh, dishes," whispered Nan ruefully.

"GOOD," SAID YARLO, his voice harsh. "He got what was comin' to him, then."

"It's faerie justice," Grit allowed. She wasn't quite prepared to dance on the Mechanist's grave, whether or not she felt he deserved it.

"And what about this . . . cloak of his?" Yarlo asked.

Grit sighed. "I'm not sure." Her best guess was that it was moldering down in the abandoned subway tunnels of Skemantis with the rest of the Mechanist. "It all happened so fast. And Yarlo, I'm sorry, but . . . even if we could get the cloak back, I don't think . . ."

"You don't think I could reattach my wings, do ya?"

Grit shook her head.

Yarlo sat down across from her, a faraway look in his eyes. "I wonder if I'd even recognize them," he mused. "Could I pick them out, out of a whole cloak of—"

"Yarlo," said Grit. "Don't. I'm sorry if I only made this harder for you. But I thought you had a right to know."

Yarlo shook his head, like a dog shaking off water, and managed a wink in Grit's direction. "And," he said, "you thought it might get you off my ship."

"I thought it couldn't hurt," Grit said.

Yarlo barked out a laugh and stood up, brushing his knees. "You're a young one yet, Grit," he said. "I'll allow that you don't seem the likeliest candidate for sending a ship full of Free Folk up in flames." He looked again at her wing; she kept expecting him to ask her about it. She had to admit he was probably more polite about it than she would've been.

"But you'll learn soon enough. A faerie can't be too careful in this world. In these times." He moved forward, and Grit tensed. But all he did was cut her bindings with a small knife she'd never even seen him draw. Grit fell to her knees—she couldn't help it—and rubbed the feeling back into her shoulders where the ropes had squeezed her wings together.

"I know *that*," she muttered. Did this cowboy think she was some little sprout with only a handful of summers under her belt? (Granted, twelve summers was not that much longer than five on the scale of the typical faerie life span, but still.)

Yarlo helped her to her feet. "Do you?"

Grit looked into his honey-colored eyes. The street fae she'd met before were a little rough, that was true, but this bunch had outnumbered her four (and probably more) to one, and still they'd practically demanded her head. But underneath the tough cowboy act, Yarlo—and the rest of them—seemed almost . . . *scared.*

"Yarlo," Grit said slowly, "is something wrong with the Wonder Show?"

He took half a step back. "Now what makes you ask that, darlin'?"

"My excellent people skills," said Grit. "My Friend's kind of a lost cause on that front, so I'm developing enough for two."

Yarlo chuckled. "Why don't I see you out, Grit?"

"But—"

"As you said, nothing but a misunderstandin'."

Yarlo turned without waiting for her to answer, and she followed him out into another one of the *Whale*'s internal passageways. Yarlo turned on his light, his body illuminating from the inside with a soft golden glow.

They passed under a gasbag. Grit blushed in the dark, embarrassed by her earlier behavior.

A white blur fluttered to a standstill in front of them, stopping Grit in her tracks. Beamsprout looked displeased to see Grit walking without restraints. Or maybe just walking at all.

"A pair of silly human boys have snuck into the hangar," she said to Yarlo. "Tinka's about to flay them alive." Beamsprout didn't seem too upset about it. She looked at Grit. "Friends of yours?"

"Probably yes, actually," said Grit, relief flooding through her. "And one of them's a Friend of the Fae, period."

Beamsprout's smug smile quickly turned into a frown.

"So," said Grit brightly, "is it too early to ask for a quick favor?"

CARMER LOOKED AROUND the hangar for the source of the voice, but the planes blocked much of his view, and it was impossible to see every dark corner of the huge space. He, Bell, and Nan crouched behind one of the aircraft.

"Sorry, Charlies," whispered Nan. "But you're on your own." She dashed away from them and off into the shadows.

Carmer heard the side door slam. *Great.*

"Hey, wait!" hissed Bell, running after her.

Carmer tried to grab him—he was sure Nan Tucket would never be caught unless she wanted to be—but Bell was too fast.

Bell did, however, lack the silence and grace of a

trained acrobat, and his loud footfalls across the hangar floor might as well have been a target on his back. Somewhere, a switch flipped, and rows of huge arc lights buzzed and snapped to life overhead, blindingly bright. Bell was caught out in the open. He skidded to a halt at the door.

"Who are you and what are you doing here?" asked the voice. It was smooth and deep and sounded slightly familiar.

Bell slowly turned around. Carmer, still crouched near the plane, started to stand up, but Bell subtly shook his head, and Carmer got the message. *Stay where you are.*

From underneath the plane, he watched a set of legs walk by—legs, he was somewhat amused to note, wearing decidedly adventurous pinstripe pants.

"The name's Bell, sir," said Bell, but his usual charming smile wavered. "Bell Daisimer."

The footsteps stopped a safe distance from Bell; Carmer still couldn't see the pinstripe pants' owner.

Bell held up his hands. "And would you believe it if I said I was looking for a job?"

"It's my experience that most people," said the other man, "approach their prospective employers at an interview. In the light of day."

"Even us loons who want to join a flying circus?"

A small laugh escaped the man. "Even you loons, Mr. Daisimer."

"Mr. Tinka," said Bell, and Carmer stifled a sharp intake of breath—of *course* it would be none other than the most important person in the Wonder Show who caught them. "I'm really sorry to meet you like this. I'm a huge admirer of your work, and an aspiring pilot as well, and I heard about your planes—"

"Which is quite astonishing," Tinka interrupted, "because these planes have nothing to do with the Roving Wonder Show."

"They . . . they don't?" asked Bell, his voice cracking.

"I'm afraid not," said Tinka. "Elysian Field includes three landing strips and several hangars. My ships are docked all over Driftside City. So we're hardly the only 'tenants,' if you will, at any one base here."

"But I heard—"

"You seem to hear an awful lot, Mr. Daisimer," said Tinka. "But I would be careful where you get your information. There are many rival airship manufacturers here in Driff City. *I've* heard they sometimes plant misinformation on purpose, to throw off their competitors."

"Do they?" asked Bell, tugging at the collar of his shirt.

"Sometimes they even *spy*."

Carmer could feel the man's pointed look, even if he couldn't see it.

"Oh, sir, I'm not a spy!" insisted Bell. "Honestly, I just wanted a closer look. Because, um . . . ." Bell trailed off.

The pinstripe pants took a step closer.

"Because . . . ?" asked Tinka impatiently. Another step.

Carmer racked his brains for a more plausible excuse—*any* excuse.

And then he remembered where they were, and the news marquee he'd seen when he entered the city: Jasconius *Crash Mystifies Authorities—$500 REWARD for Information!*

"Pardon me, sir," said Carmer loudly, standing up. "But it's because we were looking for clues." Carmer slowly walked around the plane he was hiding behind, hands in the air.

"Clues?" asked Tinka. He was a tan-skinned, angular-faced man, somewhere in his late forties, with a thick handlebar mustache, wire-rimmed glasses, and a bald head that glinted faintly under the lights. He looked surprised at Carmer's declaration—*but not*, Carmer thought, *as surprised as he should.*

"About the *Jasconius*, sir," clarified Carmer. "We saw there was a reward. For anyone with information about the crash. This seemed like a good place to start."

Bell looked at Carmer with wide eyes.

"We were just . . . poking around, sir," finished Carmer. "We didn't mean any harm by it."

But Tinka looked far from mollified by Carmer's answer. In fact, he'd gone pale. "How did you know of my connection to the *Jasconius*?"

Carmer had not, in fact, known of any such connection. He took half a step back. "I . . . well, that is . . ."

Tinka looked like he was about to realize he'd spoken too soon.

"We made it our business to know, Mr. Tinka," said Bell. "My friend Carmer here just happens to be top-notch at solving local mysteries."

Between Carmer being one of the greatest minds of Skemantis and now, apparently, a detective, Bell hadn't left him much room for being a traveling magician.

"Is he," said Tinka. He was of average height, but the stripes in his suit made him look almost as tall as one of his looming lantern giants. He looked from Bell to Carmer, obviously sizing up their knowledge.

"I'm mostly just a magician," Carmer admitted. Bell gave him a pointed look. "We saw the advertisement, and I needed the money, and so I did some digging. We're sorry to have trespassed, sir. We won't trouble you again."

Carmer was backing away, hoping that Tinka would even *let* them leave, when Tinka spoke.

"Actually," he said, holding up a hand, "Carmer the magician-slash-detective, you might be just what I need."

"He is?" asked Bell.

"I need someone to investigate the *Jasconius*," Tinka admitted. "*Quietly.* And since you seem to have gotten farther than anyone else, you just might be the gentlemen for the job."

Carmer's mind raced. Grit was still missing. Tinka's

show used faerie magic in some way. For all Carmer knew, he could be walking straight into a trap.

"I'll pay the reward myself," continued Tinka. "In fact, if you figure out what happened to my ship, I'll double it."

The implication was clear: *I'll pay double for you not to tell the police.* If there *was* faerie magic powering Tinka's show, he certainly wouldn't want the authorities to look too closely at his affairs.

Yet it seemed unlikely that an evildoing Tinka would allow someone he barely knew to investigate what was apparently his *own* ship. And the truth was, Carmer's share of the Symposium of Magickal Arts' winnings wouldn't last forever.

"All right," Carmer finally said. "I'll do it."

He didn't want to speak for Bell, who seemed keen to leave the city.

"Very well," said Tinka, bouncing on his heels. "Come back in the morning, then, and report to my tent. Nan can show you the way." Tinka rolled his eyes.

"We're thankful for the gig, sir," said Bell, his gaze turning to the window at the other end of the hangar. "And since we're all friends now, I feel obligated to ask . . . isn't that giant snail-shaped balloon *yours?*"

"It's a *nautilus*, actually," said Tinka rather testily, as if he'd corrected this misnomer many times. "But . . . oh, crickets!"

Carmer glanced out the window himself. Sure enough, a giant snail—*nautilus*—was slowly meandering off into Driff City, apparently unsupervised.

"I can help you with that, if you like, sir," offered Bell. "I'm an excellent balloonist."

Tinka turned on his heel, muttering, "Better you were a pilot, too, if you were serious about that job. All he had to do was watch a few balloons . . . Come back tomorrow, boys!"

"Wait," Bell cried excitedly after Tinka's retreating figure, "but I *am* a pilot!"

"Tomorrow!"

As Tinka ran off to wrangle his runaway snail, Carmer smiled with relief. He had a feeling Grit was just fine.

CARMER AND BELL were nearly to the edge of the airfield when Carmer felt a familiar collision with his hat. He sighed with relief, but quickened his pace; Wonder Show workers were coming out of the woodwork to track down the snail balloon.

"Nice to see you, too," Grit groused, peeking down over the edge of Carmer's hat. "And 'Thanks for coordinating that diversion, Grit. Whatever would I do without you?'"

"I'm thrilled to see you," said Carmer. "I'll be even more thrilled when we're not trespassing on private property."

"We're not trespassing!" said Bell, loping along. "Well, not anymore. Carmer's got himself a job!"

"A *what?*" asked Grit.

"Tinka caught us," said Carmer, and filled Grit in on the details.

"It does seem odd that he'd ask you to investigate his own ship, if he were up to anything bad. But we were right, there's *definitely* something magical going on in that show of his . . ."

While he and Bell biked back to the Moto-Manse, Grit told Carmer about her capture by Yarlo and the Free Folk of the Wonder Show. They rode slowly, so as not to dislodge Grit from Carmer's hat. She wasn't up for a long-distance flight; her wing was still smarting from Yarlo's ropes.

The streets of Driff City were eerily empty at night. There didn't seem to be any theater scene or night markets, and the low-flying airships needed the light of day to fly. It was very different from the nonstop hustle and bustle of Skemantis.

When Grit was finished with her story—and Carmer had silently congratulated himself on not flinging his hat away in reaction to her sheer recklessness—he considered the other faeries.

"I don't understand," Carmer said. "You seem worried. But I would've thought you'd like them—Free Folk banding together like that. And Tinka may not seem likely, but let's not forget, the queen made *me* a Friend of the Fae. And I wasn't exactly anybody's first pick."

"But that's just it," said Grit. "I don't think they *have* made him a Friend. Only a king or queen can bestow Friendship, and most of these faeries haven't belonged to a court in ages. I'm not sure Tinka knows about the faeries at all."

"So they're just giving away their magic for free?" asked Carmer, frowning.

"In my experience," said Grit, her mouth twisting, "not a lot that comes from the fae is free. Especially for humans."

Carmer and Bell dismounted as they approached the lot where the Moto-Manse was parked.

"Not to interrupt this meeting of the minds," said Bell as he locked his bike to the horse trailer hitch at the back of the house, "but it sounds to me like the two of you should tag-team this operation. Carmer can take the *Jasconius*, and Grit, you can keep an eye on the faeries. Cover all your bases." He scrunched up his face. "I think there's a mixed metaphor somewhere in there, but you get it."

"What about you?" Grit asked. "Have you found someone to fix your balloon?"

"Actually . . ." said Bell, rubbing the back of his neck, "I was thinking of staying around a little longer . . . if that's all right with you, little miss." He grinned at Grit, but she couldn't shake the feeling that he wouldn't be too sad if she told him to get lost anyway.

Grit flitted down from Carmer's hat and poked Bell's shoulder reassuringly. "It's all right with me, if it's all right with Carmer."

There was an excruciating pause. Grit was *really* going to have to help him with those people skills.

"Lucky for you," Carmer finally said, "it sounds like Tinka could use a detective *and* a pilot."

Bell flashed Carmer his bright smile.

Grit chuckled and followed them into the house. Carmer's cheeks were flushed, and she was pretty sure it wasn't just from the cold.

7.

ICARUS

THE YOUNG WOMAN WITH THE PURPLE HAIR SAID,
"I saw your wings."

Mikhail Hunt ran a hand over his face, displeased to
notice that his fingers were shaking. He blinked vigorously,
trying to keep his focus on the beautiful young woman in
front of him. The beautiful young woman with black hair,
he told himself. A hard look confirmed it. He must've really
had a lot to drink. Normal broads didn't have purple hair.

"Did you?" He was normally a lot smoother in front of
the ladies, but it was awfully late, and those fellows at the
bar by the docks had been awfully generous to a visiting
airman. He was a bit proud of forming words at this point,
actually. And it was just his luck he'd run into the best

gal—the gal he *really* wanted to impress, out of all the others he'd met that evening, and all the other girls on the Wonder Show—when he'd been out having too good of a time.

"I did," said the woman. "You are a very convincing Icarus."

Mikhail was the lead ornithopter pilot in Rinka Tinka's Roving Wonder Show. It was his best gig in a long time—heck, probably his best gig ever. If only his boss weren't such a . . . well, *boss*—always on his case for being late or ruffling the feathers on his costume—it'd be perfect. It also *really* didn't hurt his chances with the ladies.

Some women liked men in uniform, and some women liked men with feathers. Mikhail was eternally grateful for the latter.

There was something strange about this girl, though. Something strange about sitting on the edge of the docks with her—wow, they really *were* pretty far out—with their legs dangling over the black water. Her face was as pale as her hair was dark. Almost *too* pale, with blue around her lips . . . like someone who'd been out in the cold too long.

"How do you ever manage to flap those wings so fast?" she asked. "With those puny human arms of yours?"

Some part of Mikhail's brain remembered to be slightly offended that the well-cultivated specimens that were his arm muscles had just been called "puny" by a waif, but mostly, he hardly noticed the slight.

"Well, uh." He tried to explain how he piloted the orni-thopter with his legs, as well as his arms, but it was a complicated system, really, and he was not in the mood for complicated. The girl was *so pale*. Like someone . . .

Like someone who's drowned, his brain prompted. A pale hand clamped around his wrist, surprisingly strong. He could almost see her veins popping out against her skin.

"Can I tell you a secret, Icarus?" asked the woman. She tossed her hair, and the cloak she wore around her shoulders caught the moonlight, scattering it around them like tiny shards of sparkling glass.

"I've got wings, too."

8.

THE HAND
IN THE WINDOW

"TELL ME, YOUNG MAN, HOW WELL CAN YOU FLY an ornithopter?" Tinka asked Bell as they walked through the Wonder Show camp the next morning.

Carmer followed along behind, shaking dew off his trousers and blinking in the early light. He'd nearly had to restrain Bell from setting out as soon as the sun had risen.

"Well, I mostly learned, uh, unofficially, you know, from off-duty airmen from the base," Bell explained. The military kept a naval base north of the city with a small airfield; the air traffic (and the soldiers) often spilled over into Driff City. "I grew up working on a passenger liner, and whenever we'd dock in Driff City—"

"If you're worried about whether I care if you've got an academy education, Mr. Daisimer, I can assure you that I don't," said Tinka, stopping short. "I didn't ask you where you learned to fly. I asked if you can do it *well.*"

Bell smiled and tipped his hat. "Frankly, Mr. Tinka, some've said I was born to be in the air. Goodness knows, it's where I'd rather be at any minute."

Carmer thought this was rather dodging the question, but Tinka seemed charmed.

"Another minute," Tinka said, "and we'll see how true that is. And please, call me Mr. Tinkerton—Julius Tinkerton. The stage name's just for putting on the handbills." He bounced on his heels and set off.

They climbed to the top of a hill, where a small wooden tower had been erected—the catapult to launch Tinkerton's ornithopter. The ornithopter perched at the top, ready and waiting, wings as long as three men head to foot, and looking very much like a large bird of prey. A few men milled about, checking the wings and levers, the handholds and footholds, and the rubber cord that would launch the device.

Tinkerton gestured toward the tower. "Icarus," he said, "your wings await."

"Icarus?" asked Bell. "But you've already got one."

"Not for long, if he keeps gadding about and showing up late to performances," said Tinkerton. "Consider this an audition to be his understudy."

"Oh, Mr. Tinkerton, thank you!" The urge to jump in the air was clearly requiring all of Bell's restraint. "I won't let you down, sir." And he vaulted onto the tower and began climbing up the side as easily as climbing a set of stairs.

Carmer smiled, but his amusement was short-lived; something white and gleaming whipped past his ear. He jumped backward, nearly sending his hat flying off his head, and yelped.

"There's no need for alarm, Mr. Carmer!" said Tinkerton, laughing. He bent to pick up the object, which had fallen into the grass, and Carmer saw that it was not a bird at all, but a miniature glider exactly like the one that had flown into Bell Daisimer's balloon.

"Self-propelled gliders," Tinkerton explained while Carmer did his best to look suitably surprised. "They're no more than windup toys, really, but for sending casual messages around the camps, they're more than suitable."

Tinkerton extracted a slip of rolled-up paper from the small chamber in the center of the device, read the message inside, and tucked it into his breast pocket. He fiddled with the insides of the glider and turned a small crank in a practiced, swift motion.

"Just the camps, sir?" asked Carmer.

Tinkerton noticed Carmer staring and handed him the glider to examine.

"I could've sworn I'd, um, seen a glider like this before." Carmer focused on examining the complicated array of grooves inlaid into the glider. He didn't feel that he and Tinkerton were at the point in their relationship where it would be wise to confess he'd *sort of* stolen a prized golden ticket to the show.

"No doubt you have," said Tinkerton, "but none as accurate as mine." He grinned as Carmer handed the glider back to him. "Each 'messenger bird' is carefully calibrated for a specific route in each place we make camp. Time-consuming to make, but useful to communicate over short distances. It doesn't hurt our image that they're charming, too." A final twist, and he sent the glider sailing back to the main camp.

By this time, Bell was fully strapped into the ornithop-ter and grinning like he was about to walk down the aisle to marry it.

"Whenever you're ready, Mr. Daisimer!" cried Tinkerton toward the top of the tower.

Bell gave a thumbs-up, as well as some other signals to the crew that Carmer didn't know. The catapult was released, and the ornithopter was launched into the air.

There was a terrifying moment when Bell just hung there, suspended in midair, giant wings extended—and then, with a powerful flap of the ornithopter's wings that made a breeze stiff enough to nearly knock off Carmer's hat, Bell was in the air. He ascended, wings rising and fall-ing, steadier with every beat. Bell whooped, and Carmer let out a deep breath.

"Never seen an ornithopter launch before?" asked Tinkerton with a knowing smile.

"No, sir."

They watched Bell angle the wings to make a turn around the field.

"That's not a Frost model, is it, sir?" Carmer asked. He'd studied some of the latest developments in aeronautics on their way to Driff City, mostly to see if he could find any improvements to Grit's wing, but also to give Bell someone to talk at. Edward Frost's ornithopter looked the closest in design to this one, but it wasn't an exact match.

"A what model?" Tinkerton asked, his attention turned to Bell's flight.

"A Frost model, sir," Carmer repeated. "Edward Frost?"

"Ah, yes!" Tinkerton nodded and bent to clean his glasses with his handkerchief. "You have a keen eye, Mr. Carmer." He leaned back on his heels. "But that machine is one of my own. As you and your friend have guessed, the Wonder Show isn't my only aerial endeavor. And as much as I love it, it's also not my most profitable."

Carmer was surprised, but then again, he supposed it *was* rather hard to charge admission for a show that people could at least partially see from miles away for free.

"What makes all of this possible," Tinkerton said, gesturing to Bell, "is the sale of my patents. I design gliders, ornithopters, steam engines for airships—anything that goes up in the sky that you can legally claim as your own idea, I have. And I'm not the only one. The competition between manufacturers, inventors—even the military—is fierce. Everyone wants their invention to be the next great flying machine."

Tinkerton looked up at Bell, circling the field in a graceful glide. He cleared his throat. "This I tell you in the strictest confidence for the purposes of this investigation, Mr. Carmer. It is to remain between you, Mr. Daisimer, and myself. Do I have your word?"

Carmer nodded. "Yes, sir."

"There have been a series of . . . accidents, lately," said Tinkerton, as if it pained him to admit it. "All in the vicinity of Driff City. They started small, at first. Things that could be attributed to human error, or even just bad luck. But then they got bigger. Disabled low-water trips. Jammed pumps. Severe buildup in the boilers that couldn't be explained."

Carmer gasped as Bell performed a particularly daring loop-de-loop. Tinkerton applauded.

"I had recently put out a new model of condenser," continued Tinkerton. "I advertised it—quietly, of course— as the lightest and most efficient on the market. In addition to a few aerial enthusiasts—I believed it would be particularly valuable to the growing airplane industry—I had one very large, very important client: the Brendan Company, owner of the transcontinental cruiser the *Jasconius*."

Bell dove from impossibly high above, wings wrapped in tightly as he fell headfirst. All Carmer could think of was the pictures he'd seen of the *Jasconius* crashing nose-first into Elysian Field and going up in flames.

Bell pulled up at the last possible second, and Carmer could practically hear the sound of the ornithopter's straining mechanisms from across the field, but he made it. Thankfully, the demonstration seemed to be enough for Tinkerton. He waved for Bell to come down.

"The one thing all of these accidents had in common," said Tinkerton, "was my patents."

Carmer couldn't help but come to the obvious conclusion, but Tinkerton shook his head.

"I know what you're thinking, Mr. Carmer," said Tinkerton as Bell flew toward them, beginning his descent. "But my designs were not to blame. I have looked over every schematic. I have tested and retested every model. I have traced every purchase order down the supply line, down to the man who forged the steel, and I could find no evidence to suggest that my inventions were to blame. If I had, would I continue to let them fly?"

Carmer said nothing at that, but Tinkerton only let out a short, dark laugh.

"No. The only possible conclusion I can draw is this," said Tinkerton as Bell touched down, the ornithopter's wheels carving ruts in the wet grass as it slowed to a stop. Bell removed a gloved hand from the handholds and waved at them enthusiastically.

"I have a saboteur on my hands."

And with that, Tinkerton turned on his heel and stalked back toward the *Whale of Tales*, his expression stormy enough to take down a fleet of ornithopters.

WHILE CARMER CONTEMPLATED sabotage, Grit rode her first bicycle.

"This," Grit called to Yarlo over her shoulder, "is the most amazing thing I've ever done!"

Her voice was sucked up by rushing air. She was in no danger of being heard over the whizzing of the rushing bicycles and the motorized velocycles that passed them on either side. She and Yarlo clutched the frame of the bike they rode—unbeknownst to its actual human rider—as they sped along one of Driff City's many bike paths. Bicycles were all the rage these days, but in a close, crowded city like Skemantis (which also had an elevated railway), it was just as easy for most people to walk. Grit hadn't known it was possible to move this fast.

Yarlo was even more daring, using his ropes and the vines that sprang from his wrists to swing from spoke to spoke of the bicycle's wheels as they turned. Grit wasn't one for fussing over others—a lifetime of being on the receiving end of that sort of talk ensured *that*—yet she couldn't help but worry that if Yarlo fell, or one of his ropes missed their mark, he'd have a one-way ticket to the ground underneath the bike's wheels. It was dizzying to watch.

The gray buildings on either side gave way to a stretch of greenery that took Grit's breath away even more than the rushing wind. Massive oak trees with sprawling tentacle limbs formed a shaded arch over the entire trail for at least a mile. Most surprisingly, the trees were still *green*, though it was nearly the end of December. A cheery, sunbleached sign she barely had time to read welcomed her to the Driftside Trailway.

"This is us," Yarlo yelled, now perched on the top tube of the bike's frame above her.

"What is?" Grit yelled back.

"This is where we get off!" he said. "Watch out for oncomin' traffic!"

"Get off?" asked Grit. She hadn't thought that far in advance. "But how do I—"

"Yee-haw!" cried Yarlo, shooting out a vine to wrap around a thin branch of the nearest tree on the path. He was yanked from the bicycle and gone from Grit's view in less than a second.

"Spirits and zits," she gasped, glancing at the human above her, a dapper young man in a straw hat. He continued pedaling as if nothing had changed.

Grit climbed up as high as she could on the bicycle's frame without getting too close to the cyclist and looked to the left, then the right, then left again, waiting for a break in the line—and launched herself toward the greenway with all her might.

She twisted in the air, falling back toward oncoming traffic, and it was only with a panicked and painful flapping of her wings that she was able to gain any upward momentum at all. She tumbled into the landing—narrowly dodging the deadly grind of another bicycle wheel—and ended up a tangled pile of limbs in a bed of cobwebby dead leaves.

"Urgh," Grit said, gingerly getting to her knees and shaking as much sandy dirt out of her wings as she could. Her left side throbbed—so much for following Carmer's advice to "take it easy"—and she felt like the world would never stop spinning.

"Yarlo?" Grit called. She removed a dead beetle from her hair and kicked away the last of the leaves tickling her legs. The few seconds between their departures from the bike could have put a considerable distance between Grit and the cowboy faerie, as fast as they'd been riding. She tried to tune out the whizzing of the bicycles and rumbling velocycle engines to listen for any sign of him—or whatever else might be living in the shadow of these miraculously green trees.

The faint sound of wind chimes carried from just up ahead. Grit squinted into the maze of intertwining branches around her, and her eyes quickly found a flash of white—Beamsprout, perhaps? But no, the object fluttering in the wind wasn't a faerie, or even magical at all; it looked like a strip of some sort of fabric, or the silly ribbons the human girls sometimes wore in their hair. Grit took a few steps forward and saw more ribbons tied from the trees in shades of blue and green, gold, and purple. Perhaps she'd stumbled upon some sort of wishing tree? Grit had heard of such things before; they were often tributes to the fae. Her Arboretum back home had its own landmark—an old, crumbling wall where humans would whisper their secrets in exchange for the hope of a magical favor.

She walked on. But soon the softness of the wind chimes and fluttering ribbons was overpowered by a strange buzzing sound. Grit whipped around and looked overhead just in time to see a miniature windup glider, exactly like the kind that had crashed into Bell's balloon, fly over the trees—and straight toward the decorated branches.

Grit picked up her pace and followed. Carmer would say it was probably just a coincidence, but Carmer was not a faerie, and definitely not a faerie princess. Something on this Driftside Trailway was calling to her, just as the insides of the glider guided it to its destination. She ducked under low, snaking branches and dodged the pointed edges of ferns dusted with frost—and then stopped.

There, under another archway of oak branches, fitting so perfectly it might have been made with the trees in mind, was a small, docked airship—and a very peculiar one at that. It took Grit a moment to realize she was looking at a tower . . . on its side. The nose of the ship was a pointed turret, like the top of the Moto-Manse, but much bigger. The envelope was painted to look like stonework, with thorny roses and vines growing along the sides. Grit tilted her head to see the full effect: standing up, it would have been fit for a storybook princess.

The mechanical glider soared toward an open window, and—so quickly Grit almost thought she imagined it—a small brown hand reached out to pluck it from the air. Grit blinked, and the hand was gone. She flew toward the Crooked Castle—she could think of no other name for it—only to be cut off by a scowling and *literally* prickly faerie.

Grit recognized her as one of her captors on the *Whale of Tales*.

"If you're looking for your friend," said the round-faced faerie with hair like a porcupine, hovering in front of Grit and blocking her view of the ship, "he's back in Tinka's office, in the *Whale*."

"'In the whale'? Oh, right!" That name was going to take some getting used to. Grit pointed to the docked ship. "Hey, is that one of the Wonder Show's?" It seemed unlikely this faerie—Grit thought her name might have been Thundrumble—would be so comfortable out in the open if that wasn't the case. "I don't think I've seen it before—"

"That jump weren't half bad, for your first time," came Yarlo's drawling voice from behind her. "Though I'd have preferred if you hadn't strayed *quite* so far from the path."

"Oh, I think you know the answer to that, little miss," said Yarlo, stringing his thumbs through the ropes at his hips. "Don't tell me you haven't felt the icy chill of their big stinkin' palace under the Driff City docks, even from leagues away."

Grit didn't answer.

"This here is Unseelie territory, darlin'," said Yarlo. "Has been for over a century. Probably since the last faerie war, I should think."

The last faerie war that your court lost was his implication. He was trying to get a rise out of her. But Grit, young as she was, had never known faerie war firsthand, which made keeping the past in the past a little easier. She shrugged, but she had to admit she did feel . . . outnumbered.

"You mean there aren't *any* other Seelies here?" Grit asked.

It was Yarlo's turn to shrug. "Oh, I'm sure there're some. But no one's holding any territory, as far as I know," he said. "Rumor used to be there was an old Seelie holed up on Wetherwren Light—used to be a king in the old country, they said. Maybe he thought he'd build a nice reputation here, helping the old lighthouse keepers bring the ships in safe—in exchange for a tithe, of course." Yarlo tipped his hat and winked. "Maybe even wanted to rebuild his own kingdom."

"But?" asked Grit.

"But he weren't countin' on there already bein' a sheriff

Grit looked from Thundrumble, whose fingertips had now sprouted spikes as well, to Yarlo's steely gaze. She took the hint. The Crooked Castle and its mysterious occupant were, for whatever reason, off-limits . . . for now.

Yarlo jerked his head, a motion for Grit to follow him, and turned back the way she had come. She stuck her tongue out at Thundrumble and touched down beside Yarlo, brushing one of the hanging wind chimes in the trees with her fingers on the way down.

"What exactly are we doing here, anyway?" asked Grit, her good mood significantly diminished since the bicycle ride. No one would *dare* stick a spike in her face back home.

"The Trailway's one of the few bits o' nature in the city limits," said Yarlo. "It's where we prefer to stay whenever we're in Driff City. Reminds some of us of home."

Grit must have looked puzzled at that, because Yarlo laughed.

"Just because Free Folk live closer to humans than most don't mean we're not fae," said Yarlo. "'Smatter of fact, there're some'd say the *only* difference between the Wonder Show faeries and you is you live under somebody's thumb, and they don't."

Grit noticed he did not say "we."

"Speaking of that thumb I live under," said Grit, "if this is the only solid stretch of trees for miles, where are the other faeries? Where are the Seelies?"

in town, as the humans say," said Yarlo, chuckling. "And I bet you can guess what happened then."

Grit frowned. The unnaturally green trees suddenly seemed even stranger—their dark, intertwining limbs an endless maze on all sides.

"They say there's nothing but his heart left," said Yarlo, his voice almost a growl. "Ripped out by the Unseelie king himself. And sometimes, on a stormy night, you can still see it glowing, right from the top of the lighthouse, like that old Seelie king's still trying to guide one last ship home."

Grit shivered and bit back a retort. Yarlo had no idea that she had actually seen a faerie heart without a body— several of them, in fact—in the diabolical hands of the Mechanist, the same man who had taken Yarlo's wings. She doubted the cowboy would get as much enjoyment out of his ghost story if he did.

"Of course, that was years ago," continued Yarlo lightly, obviously pleased that he'd unnerved her. "Doesn't matter much, for your purposes, anyway."

"My purposes?"

"Pokin' around in our business and such," said Yarlo bluntly, and Grit had to laugh.

"You know Tinka asked us to look into the *Jasconius* crash," she said.

"I know he asked that Friend of yours."

"Which means he asked us."

Yarlo smirked. "We're happy to help in any way we can," he said. "The Wonder Show is our home, too. But back to—"

"Why should we tell her anything?" interrupted the high-pitched voice of Beamsprout. She touched down beside them in a blur of white and crossed her pearly arms. "She tried to burn down our ship!"

"I did not!" countered Grit. "I *threatened* to burn down your ship. There's a difference."

"Settle down, ladies, settle down," said Yarlo with a chuckle.

Beamsprout sniffed and sat in a hole in a fallen log, daintily crossing her light green–clad legs. She made it look like sitting on a throne.

"Grit's Friend's been tasked with investigatin' the *Jasconius* crash," Yarlo explained.

"That's what I was coming to tell you," said Beamsprout, looking put out that Grit had beaten her to what was sure to have been a dramatic announcement. "*And* I think it's a terrible idea. Whoever is messing with Tinka's ships has nothing to do with us. And ri—"

"And regardless of what you might think, dear heart, it's happenin' anyway, as things tend to do," said Yarlo. "So Grit here will be spendin' some time in Driff City."

A smile of smug realization came over Beamsprout's face at the same time Grit's stomach settled somewhere around her toes.

"And that means, as a Seelie"—Beamsprout scrunched up her nose at Yarlo's mention of the court—"she needs to declare her presence to the Unseelie king."

A shiver ran down the back of Grit's neck at the name. If anyone would be able to spot her for a Seelie princess, it would be the king. And he would most likely *not* be thrilled about her "pokin' around" in his kingdom.

"You should probably bring that Friend of yours along, too," suggested Yarlo. "Just to be safe."

9.
TWO HEADS ARE BETTER THAN ONE

TINKERTON AND CARMER WALKED BACK TO THE airfield proper. White and gold criers' balloons circled the Wonder Show's camp like Edison lightbulbs at the foot of a stage.

"It's only a matter of time before someone else figures out the pattern," said Tinkerton. "Supposedly, the fire destroyed any evidence there was to be found on the *Jasconius*, but if they do trace the problem to the condenser, and the condenser back to me—which I'm confident someone will, as you have—they'll soon find the others."

Tinkerton looked out onto the camp, now bustling with morning activity. A few acrobats stretched in line while they waited for a hot breakfast from the cookhouse;

a balloon shaped like a bumblebee was being checked for holes; painters hung from every height of the hundred-foot model of Jacob's ladder, touching up scrapes with blinding white paint that really did make it look like a stairway to heaven. Someone was waving a broomstick in the air from deep within the mirror maze; Carmer heard one of the balloonists affectionately grumble about "the girls" always getting stuck in there while they swept.

"Unless I can find who's really behind the crash," said Tinkerton, "I'll be ruined. And Rinka Tinka's Roving Wonder Show will be no more."

Carmer, more than anyone, understood the seriousness of Tinkerton's predicament. For all of these people—Tinkerton included—the Wonder Show was their job, yes, but it was also their home. He'd traveled for enough years with Antoine the Amazifier and Kitty to know that. For traveling entertainers, many of whom had left all traces of their old lives behind, your coworkers *became* your family. To lose the Wonder Show would be to lose everything.

But first, Carmer had to know if Tinkerton's family included only those strictly defined as humans.

"Have you noticed anything . . . odd, about the Wonder Show itself, Mr. Tinkerton?" Carmer asked. "Has anything suspicious happened during a performance? Anything no one could explain?"

"Nothing," said Tinkerton, shaking his head. "In fact, we get bigger and more successful every year."

Carmer, of course, had an idea about why that was the case. But if Tinkerton wasn't going to admit he knew about the faeries in his show—or if, quite possibly, he *didn't* really know—Carmer wasn't going to spill the beans just yet. Not if he could help it.

"And all of the accidents have happened in or around Driff City," explained Tinkerton, "where the saboteur would have plenty of access to any number of ships or planes. The Wonder Show company tours all over the world—ten cities a year, sometimes more. Unless one of my pilots has discovered the secret to instantaneous travel, they simply wouldn't have the *time* to get to Driff City and back without anyone noticing."

"Does anyone in the show know about your side business?" Carmer asked. "Especially, um, anyone you might've let go, or something?"

Tinkerton laughed. "Your estimation of the human condition is rather low for someone so young, isn't it?"

Carmer shrugged and looked away.

"That wasn't an insult," Tinkerton said, more gently. "Merely an observation. And it's a fair question to ask. While everyone knows that I'm an active member of the aeronautical community, only a trusted few know the details of my business operations—and they all have financial stakes in my success."

Carmer ran a hand through his hair. "Sir, I'm sorry to ask this, but do you think I could take a look at the designs?

And your models. The ones that have been involved in the accidents, I mean."

If Tinkerton was getting faerie help with his inventions at the show and not realizing it, then it was entirely plausible the same inventions would fail to work *without* such help.

"Carmer," said Tinkerton, "I'm the one who asked *you* to look into the *Jasconius*. You needn't feel badly about doing what any investigator worth his salt would do. And besides, a second set of eyes could only be a good thing, especially from one of the 'great minds of Skemantis.'" Tinkerton tapped his glasses in a little salute.

Carmer was getting the impression that Tinkerton rather enjoyed teasing him. Perhaps Grit was rubbing off on him, because it only made him more determined to do the job well.

"Feel free to look through anything in my office that might be of use," Tinkerton explained. "I've kept detailed reports of every accident, as far back as I could connect them to myself."

To his surprise, Tinkerton led them to the docked *Whale of Tales*, through the whale's mouth and past the hall of myths, and into a small but well-furnished office near the back of the ship.

"Who do you think listens to all the stories?" asked Tinkerton with a raised eyebrow. "They serve as wonderful inspiration. Someday, you'll have to tell me how you defeated that evil mastermind."

Carmer paled, but Tinkerton was already turning to leave.

"Shut the door on your way out, mind," said Tinkerton. He rapped his fingers on the ornately carved dark wood. "But not too hard. It's hollow on the inside, you know!"

To save weight in the air, Carmer realized with a laugh. Of course.

"Oh, and Carmer?" called Tinkerton from down the hall. "You can tell your friend he's got a job!"

GRIT WASN'T SURE her new wing would appreciate—or, if she was being honest, hold up for—the whole flight back to Elysian Field, so she hitched a ride on the gondola of a cargo ship for part of the way. Only a month ago, the mile across her Arboretum would have seemed a great distance to travel on her own. Now, she could cross whole cities in a few hours, even without using her wings. It was incredible how most faeries wouldn't come within feet of an airship, never mind ride one. They were *really* missing out.

She glided over the Wonder Show's camp, gritting her teeth against the pain in her shoulder until it faded into a dull ache, and headed for the open mouth of the *Whale of Tales*. She wasn't surprised when the door shut behind her and the silver curtains in front remained closed. There was enough magic floating around in this place that some of it was bound to rub off on the show itself. That magic didn't seem to care if she was in a hurry—and it would always be hungry for more stories.

"Oh, come on," Grit groaned. "I shouldn't count as a passenger! My feet don't even touch the ground."

But the song came drifting along the hall:

One who seeks
A hint of mystique
Must also be willing to pay
The sum of a story
The tax of a tall tale—

"All right, I get it." She sighed, thinking. "Many years ago, a young knight rode through the woods on his way to meet his bride."

Almost without realizing it, her voice began to slow, slipping into the lilting cadence she'd listened to for hours as a young sprout on her mother's knee.

"A faerie king's daughter saw him riding by. Charmed by his handsomeness and grace, she revealed herself to him and asked him to dance." Grit paused. She couldn't say why she'd picked this story, but now that she'd started, it seemed there was no choice but to finish. "The knight thanked her for her offer, but insisted he must ride on to be married to his true intended. The princess offered him gold and riches beyond his wildest dreams, if he would only come away with her, but he spurned her, and remained loyal to his human bride.

"Incensed by his rejection, the princess cast a curse upon his heart and sent him on his way. By the next morning, he was dead, discovered by none other than his pretty young bride. Consumed by grief, she followed soon after. They are buried side by side, in the same hills where the faerie princess dances still."

Grit's words hung in the air. If she listened closely, she could hear the faint turning of the gramophone's cylinder, hidden somewhere nearby. She wondered if her voice even registered on its recording. She hoped that it did not.

The silver curtain parted.

Grit flew past the Hall of Stories, fighting the chill that had crept into her bones. How silly, scaring herself with her own story!

But Grit could not comfort herself with the idea that it was "just" a story. The very real Unseelie king—and his real daughter—waiting a few miles away were proof enough of that. Nothing was just a story in her world, because stories were a good part of why her world still *existed*. If the power of the fae couldn't even live on in rumors, or old wives' tales, or whispers around a campfire on a dark night . . . what would become of them? What would become of them when no one was left who believed?

Grit shook her head, red and yellow curls springing out of her bun. She was starting to sound like her *mother*, for fae's sake. Best leave the worrying to the old crones back at the Arboretum.

She found Carmer at what she assumed was Tinka's desk, half buried under stacks of notes, reports, and diagrams. He was so absorbed he didn't even notice her land on the edge of the newspaper he was reading until she started to make it smoke from the soles of her feet.

"Hey, what the—" He jumped back, patting at the blackened edges, until he saw her and sighed with relief while she cackled with amusement. "You know better than that! How many times have I told you—"

"No open flames around the airships," she repeated along with him.

He raised an eyebrow into his shock of messy black hair.

"Do you see any flames?" she asked innocently. "Besides, it *would* have taken a small explosion to distract you, anyway. Anything good in there?" She nudged a stack of papers with her foot; Carmer grabbed it before it fell over.

"Not really," he admitted, sighing. "I've been over every accident report from the police, every internal review Mr. Tinkerton—that's Tinka's real name, by the way—has done himself, and so far, I can only come to the same conclusion as he has."

"Sabotage?" Grit asked. It made her feel rather important and grown-up to be slinging words like "sabotage" around.

Carmer nodded. "I can't find any flaws in his inventions. In theory, they should all work without any 'extra help,' if you know what I mean. Bell was right—these designs *are* genius. The modifications to Frost's ornithopter alone—"

Grit cleared her throat.

"Ah, right," said Carmer, blushing. "Not strictly relevant, I guess. I should have Bell take a look at these, though. Admittedly, I don't know as much about aeronautics as I should."

"You should get right on that in all of your spare time," Grit teased.

"I did notice something odd, though," Carmer said, shimmying a few papers out from the bottom of each stack. "It's probably nothing, and I'm probably just over-analyzing things—"

"*Carmer*," Grit said, swatting the paper in his hand.

He flattened out two of the designs in front of him.

"Tinka organizes his notes for each design by date," he explained. "And he keeps *everything*. It's kind of fascinating, actually, to see someone else's progress from the initial sketch of the idea all the way to the finished product." With one finger, he spun the propeller on a model airplane on the edge of the desk.

"But the problem is, his original sketches . . . well, they don't look so original to me." He turned a diagram toward Grit; all she saw was a mess of circles, lines, and indecipherably tiny labels that made her head spin.

"It might help if I knew what I was looking at?"

Carmer waved her off. "That's not the important part. Just *look* at it. I was just thinking . . . when I'm working on a new design, my drafts are, well, messy. Maybe the sketch is incomplete, or I've crossed out original ideas and changed them halfway through drawing . . . or if I've been using a pencil, there're erasure marks all over the page. But Tinkerton . . . he keeps *meticulous* records of every stage of a design's development, but his early drafts are just as pristine as his later ones."

Grit took a closer look at the diagram and saw Carmer was right. There were no scrawled notes in the margins like she'd seen on Carmer's designs, no crossed-out labels or even *creases* in the paper.

"Maybe he only preserves clean copies for his records," Carmer suggested. "Or . . ."

"Or maybe his *copies* are exactly that," Grit finished for him. "And these aren't Tinkerton's designs at all."

Carmer shrugged. "He *could* have made copies to cover up discrepancies in the handwriting. This isn't the same writing as the note that we intercepted." He told Grit about the moment during Bell's audition when he had brought up another inventor's work on ornithopters—and how Tinkerton had seemed a little too eager to skip over the subject.

"That ticket could have been sent by anyone on the show, though, just trying to sneak in a friend," Grit pointed out. "But there's something else as well." She recounted her little chat with the Free Folk on the Trailway—Carmer blanched at the mention of the Unseelie king, but said nothing—and the mysterious hand emerging from the Crooked Castle. "Beamsprout said, 'Whoever is messing with *Tinka's* ships has nothing to do with *us*' . . . almost like the Wonder Show ships and his other projects didn't have anything to do with each other."

Carmer thought for a moment. "If he's got a . . . a 'silent partner,' let's say—"

"Or he's *forcing* someone to do the work for him," Grit suggested darkly, her mind immediately turning to the Mechanist.

Carmer nodded. "Or that. Maybe they're fed up with being taken advantage of, and they want to discredit him . . . but . . ."

"But?" Grit turned to the newspaper she'd burned with her feet, struggling to lift the wide pages open to the full story about the *Jasconius* crash.

"If Tinkerton were stealing someone else's work without their permission," Carmer explained, "wouldn't that person be his number one suspect? Why would he hire us to investigate, when he had the most likely culprit right in front of him? Why risk outsiders finding out?"

"That's . . . a fair point, actually," Grit conceded. "But what do we do now?" She smoothed out the corner of the page with her boot, careful not to singe it this time.

"Actually," said Carmer, shifting in his seat. "I don't think we do anything."

"What?" Grit looked up at him in surprise.

He raised his hands. "At least not until we have more proof. The sketches could mean anything."

"But if he's got someone locked in a tower—"

"Grit," said Carmer, "you saw someone in a ship that *looks* like a tower. Are you going to tell me that the Wonder Show performers who work on the replica of Baba Yaga's house on giant chicken legs are really being cooked in a stew by some old witch?"

Grit pursed her lips and paced along the newspaper on the desk. "Of course not. But something's just not right here, Carmer."

"I agree. But in the meantime, I think we should focus on our job. And also, apparently, on our upcoming visit with the Unseelie king."

"*My* upcoming visit with the Unseelie king," corrected Grit, frowning at how pale Carmer looked at the prospect. "It's no big deal," she said with a wave of her hand. "I just show up, say hi, how are you, promise not to sow any seeds of magical unrest, et cetera—" Grit suddenly stopped short. "And speaking of our job," she said slowly, staring at the newspaper under her feet, "I think I just found something that might make it easier." She scooted the paper toward Carmer.

"I've been leafing through these all day, and I haven't found . . ." Carmer trailed off as he looked at the grainy photograph, clearly taken just moments after the crash. In the flaming chaos, a young man was running away from the ship. Unlike the other bystanders around him, he had not turned back to look at the wreckage. Only a brief stop to catch his breath, or some other distraction at the exact moment the photo was taken, meant his features were in focus. And even then, he was half cut off at the edge of the cluttered frame.

Despite capturing the catastrophic scene, the photograph was admittedly not as striking or as well composed as some of the others Carmer had seen. He wasn't surprised it hadn't made it into the other papers.

He *was* surprised, however, to be looking down at the terrified face of Bell Daisimer.

10.

WITNESS PROTECTION

CARMER AND GRIT HAD HOPED TO FIND BELL still at the Wonder Show camp, but a quick search turned up no sign of him until they ran into Nan Tucket, who seemed sure he'd gone back to the Moto-Manse. Carmer biked to the nearest air-bus station and hopped on.

The universe seemed to sense they were in a hurry, so naturally, the bus hit traffic as soon as it neared Topside. The ship was forced to slow down, penned in between another air-bus and a sightseeing tour. The jam was so bad the ships were trapped end to end, like fish caught in a narrowing stream.

"What's the holdup?" someone yelled from down the line.

The captain of the ship beside them stepped out onto his gondola to see if anything was up ahead. Curious passengers leaned out of the windows despite the bitter cold.

"Police action at the Topside Hotel!" a man's voice shouted from up ahead. "Some nutter's threatening to jump off the roof!"

"Well, I wish he'd make a decision!" a woman snapped. "We're all going to freeze in our ships out here!"

"They say he's wearing costume wings!"

"I heard he's with the circus!"

Carmer's head snapped up. *If Bell was somehow mixed up in all of this . . .*

He ran to the window, ignoring the fluttering in his stomach at the thought of looking down, but there was nothing to see—only the floating hulls of other ships and the occasional balloonist trying to play hopscotch over the congestion. It was twenty minutes before they came within sight of the hotel, and by then, police were already clearing the area. No one seemed to be on the roof.

"Who was it, Ern?" Carmer's air-bus captain shouted to a policeman who was waving ships along.

The officer frowned but called back: "Some Russian fellow from the Wonder Show. I'm just glad I'm not the one scraping brains off the pavement!"

The captain shouted more questions, but "Ern" waved them along. Carmer sank back into his seat, not knowing whether to be relieved or not. Whoever the suicidal ornithopter pilot was, it probably wasn't Bell. But it was someone.

"Carmer," Grit whispered into his ear, "do you think it's the pilot you said Tinkerton kept complaining was a no-show, Mikhail something? The one Bell replaced?"

"Maybe."

The air-bus stop was crowded and noisy as they disembarked, everyone abuzz with gossip about the jumper. It made Carmer feel sick, but he listened anyway.

"*I* heard he was babbling about Rinka Tinka's Roving Wonder Show," a woman's hissing voice declared to her neighbor. She sounded anything but upset. "Said something about that Tinka playing with power that weren't rightfully his. '*Flying too close to the sun,*' and all that."

"And then, SPLAT!" interrupted a sooty-faced boy, sending his friends howling with laughter and the gossiping women tut-tutting.

Carmer pushed through the laughing boys, knocking their leader on the shoulder as he walked away. It was a move that would have normally garnered him a pounding, but something in his face must have warned the boys off.

"Carmer . . ." Grit started.

"Later," he said. "Let's just find Bell, okay?"

Grit sighed. It was a cold, quiet journey back to the Moto-Manse.

BELL DAISIMER SLUMPED in his chair in the tiny kitchen of the Moto-Manse, fingers shaking as he held the newspaper clipping up to the light. He barely registered Carmer and Grit's concerned expressions. He almost wanted to be mad at them—he'd *just* scored the job of a lifetime, in the greatest flying circus on earth!—but he knew it wasn't their fault. They hadn't taken the photo. Someone would have found out eventually, and it could have been someone who would make him pay for it.

"I should've left," he said, trying to fight the lump in his throat. "I should've kept going, busted balloon or not. I should never have come back to Driff City."

The voice echoed in his head: *Run, little boy, and don't look back.*

Carmer nudged the tea closer to Bell, and he took a half-hearted sip. Bell was pretty sure Carmer would make them all tea if the sky were falling.

"Why did you have to leave in the first place?" Grit asked, her voice uncharacteristically soft, but still insistent. "And why didn't you tell us?"

"Because . . ." Bell put his face in his hands. "Because . . ."

"Because he was part of the crew," Carmer said gently. "Even as a cabin boy, he was part of the crew. And that means . . . well . . ."

"It means I deserted," said Bell bluntly. "It means it was my duty to stay with the ship, to protect its passengers with my life, and I ran. I was a coward. I felt it going down, and as soon as I could jump overboard without breaking my legs, I ran. And I didn't look back."

Carmer and Grit were silent. Bell could feel their hesitation, that they didn't know what to say. But there was nothing *to* say. They were disappointed in him, he was sure. He was Bell Daisimer, the aspiring airman—and guaranteed to bolt at the first sign of trouble. They should put that in the advertisements for the Wonder Show.

Except there would be no Wonder Show for him now. He was an Icarus who had fallen before he'd even tested his wings.

"I need to leave," Bell said, standing up. His bony knees clacked against the underside of the table, nearly upsetting it. "It wasn't right of me to accept that job from Tinka, not masquerading as an honest man. And if anyone else from the crew knew—or knows—what I've done, my career'd be finished, and for good reason."

"Bell," Carmer said, "sit down, you're in no shape to—"

"Wait," said Grit. "So no one knows that you did this?"

"It's only a matter of time before they do," said Bell, shaking his head. "I wasn't where I was supposed to be. I was late for my shift, and that's something people notice, and . . . it doesn't matter. I couldn't live with myself here, knowing I'd left those people, knowing I'd left the rest of the men to . . ."

"It wasn't your fault, Bell," said Carmer. "From everything I've read, the ship would've gone down anyway. You were scared, and—"

"So were they!" said Bell harshly. "So were the three crewmen, when they died, and the firefighters, too. And where was I? I ran . . . I ran, and I didn't look back. I ran . . ."

The room tilted.

And suddenly Carmer was there at his side, easing him back into the chair. Grit fluttered nervously in front of his face.

"Bell!" said Carmer. "Bell, are you all right?"

"I . . . I don't know," said Bell, trying to catch his breath. Grit was staring so intently at his face it was making him even more uncomfortable. "I'm sorry, I—"

"Bell," interrupted Grit, "I want you to repeat the last thing you just said to us. Carmer, come around and stand by me, please."

Bell almost laughed. If *Grit* was saying please and thank you, he must be nearly at death's door. Now they were *both* staring at him. Grit turned her faerie light on to brighten the room and hovered close to his face. The edges of her silhouette softened in the light, blurring his vision again, and suddenly Bell knew exactly what she wanted him to say.

"I said . . . I said that I ran," he said. And then, not even sure if he was talking to himself, he remembered. *Run, little boy, and don't look back.*

Bell gasped, sitting straight up and nearly knocking Grit aside with a flailing arm. "I'm sorry . . . I don't know what . . ."

"Bell," said Grit again, in that calm voice that commanded attention. "Do you know that your eyeballs go all funny when you say those words?"

Bell was stumped. "I . . . no."

"Did you see it?" she asked Carmer.

He nodded. "She means your pupils dilate."

"Who said that to you, Bell?" Grit asked, more gently this time. "Who told you to run, and scared you so badly you left your whole life behind?"

The woman's cloak swished around the corner. He blinked, and it was gone.

"I wish I could tell you," Bell said. "But honestly, I don't remember much. I think . . . no, I *know* it was a woman, but after that . . ."

He trailed off, expecting Carmer and Grit to be frustrated with him, but Grit was still staring at his eyes so intensely it was making his stomach even more jittery.

"I'm sorry, but I don't remember. I wish I could tell you . . . Dark hair? Pale? Maybe?" He threw up his hands. "Ugh, I'm worse than useless."

"No, you're not," said Carmer. "You faced someone evil enough to bring down a ship full of people and were smart enough to get out of it alive."

"That," said Grit, "or this mystery woman *made* you run away."

Carmer exchanged a quick, dark look with Grit and went a bit pale himself. "You don't think . . ."

"I think there are enough signs that ignoring them would be pretty dumb," said Grit. "I also think we've been going about this all wrong."

Bell said, "Anytime someone would like to fill me in here . . ."

"What I mean is, what if these accidents aren't about Tinka at all?" Grit asked. "What if they're about the Wonder Show's *faeries?*"

"Grit," Carmer said, sitting back down at the table. "We're talking about cross-continental airships here— in a multimillion dollar industry that we've barely scratched the surface of. Not *everything* traces back to faerie magic—"

"Okay, sure," said Grit. "Let's ignore the fact that the show we're investigating is *full of faeries*. Faeries who haven't exactly been forthcoming about their operation. And there's also that Wonder Show pilot disappearing, and showing up again with his brains scrambled? And now Bell, who just *happens* to get the same job—"

"I did very well on that audition, I'll have you know," Bell protested.

"And who just *happens* to have witnessed the *Jasconius* crash, too?" Grit continued. "It's just too much coincidence, Carmer."

"It still might be that," Carmer insisted.

Grit huffed and turned to face Bell again. "Well, there's one way to find out. Bell, this woman you met. I need you to try as hard as you can to remember this: did she put her hands in your hair?"

Bell saw Carmer's hand drift up to his own hair, but Bell's mind wasn't in the kitchen of the Moto-Manse anymore; it was back on the *Jasconius*, where he was staring into the white, veiny face of someone who shouldn't have been there at all.

"Oh, don't worry," said the young woman. She looked like a girl, really—except for her eyes. There was something older in their gray depths. Something darker. "I'm not a passenger."

Bell staggered back, but her icy hands had already clawed up into his hair, fingers snagging in his short, tight curls.

"Bell!" A spark zapped in front of his nose; the smell of burning hair told him his eyebrows had been singed. He opened his eyes with a start. He hadn't even realized they'd drifted shut.

"Grit!" scolded Carmer, but Bell waved him off.

"Whatever you need to do to bring me back to planet Earth, little miss, you go ahead and do it," Bell said breathlessly. What was *happening* to him? He shook his head. "Though I admit, this'd be a beautiful face to waste."

"Yes, yes, you're gorgeous," said Grit. "Now do you remember? Did the woman put her hands in your hair?"

"As a matter of fact," said Bell, almost not quite believing it himself, "I think she did."

Grit flew back to the teakettle and leaned against the lid, crossing her arms with grim satisfaction. "I knew it."

Carmer looked far from pleased.

"Faerie knots," Grit concluded, as if this explained everything. "It's one of the ways powerful faeries can manipulate humans," she said. "It's much, much easier if you're already asleep or unconscious—"

"Or otherwise not in control of your mental faculties," Carmer muttered, blushing.

"—but it's not *impossible* otherwise," Grit said. "At least, I don't *think* so . . . Anyway, faeries can weave spells into human hair—"

"That is *profoundly* disturbing," said Bell.

Carmer nodded in agreement.

"Would you let me *finish*?" Grit glared at the both of them. She curled her legs underneath her on the teakettle. "They can weave spells into human hair to do all sorts of things. Most of the time it's just mischief—make a human who's offended the fae sleepwalk into a cowpat or some- thing—or make a child forget they've wandered off and spent a night in Faerie. They wake up in the morning none the wiser."

But Bell had already heard enough to make the room feel like it was spinning again. "Just mischief," he said flatly. "Making people do things against their will, making them forget?"

Grit hugged her knees into her chest. "Sometimes it's not."

"And you think a *faerie* did this," Bell said. "Brought down an entire airship, and made me forget? Forced me to abandon my post?"

Bell Daisimer didn't come from a world where faeries *existed*, never mind one where they could get inside his head. It was hard for him to imagine someone the size of Grit—and the woman on the ship most definitely hadn't been—causing so much damage. But a small part of him dared to hope. If it wasn't his fault, if he really wouldn't have run away . . .

"Grit thinks it's a possibility," Carmer answered. "And I do, too. But—"

"Well, how do we prove it?" asked Bell, leaning forward.

"The thing is, Bell," Grit said slowly, "I'm not sure we can."

Bell dropped his head back into his hands.

"Carmer once got his memories back through a lucky encounter with some faerie dust," she explained. "But I can't make any on my own, and I don't trust those Free Folk—especially when they might be knee-deep in all of this. What we really need to know is what that woman looks like. If she took human form long enough, she must be an incredibly powerful fae . . ."

"Or Friend of the Fae," suggested Carmer. "She could still be human. I can't be the only one who's hidden a faerie under their hat when they needed magic close at hand. After Bell blacked out, the real faerie could've done most of the damage, and altered his memory, too."

"So, we keep an eye out for more magic and . . . strange women?" Grit asked skeptically.

"Always happy to help narrow down your list of suspects to only half the population," Bell said, raising his teacup for a weary toast.

"You've narrowed it much more than that," Carmer said. "Before today, I thought Tinkerton's competitors were the most likely suspects."

Grit sniffed, but Carmer plowed on. "And I don't see any reason to *stop* thinking that completely. Maybe one of them is using faerie magic, the same way Grit and I have in the past."

"Excuse me, when have we *killed people*?" Grit protested, then bit her lip.

Carmer looked at his feet.

Bell remained firmly glad these two were on *his* side.

"Anyway," Carmer muttered, "it's worth asking: is there a chance any of Tinkerton's major rivals are women?"

Bell didn't even have to think about his answer. "Actually, yeah," he said. "Much more than a chance. And she lives right here in Driff City."

BELL TAPPED THE picture Grit had just pinned to the wall. "Isla and Robert Blythe," he said.

The Moto-Manse's attic laboratory had changed some since the Amazifier's departure, mostly due to Carmer's organizing influence. Drawers that were previously bursting with gears and cogs were now neatly shut, their contents labeled in Carmer's small but legible hand. Many of the mysterious jars of specimens and other unidentifiable things had left with the Amazifier. The tools were now more likely to be used for crafting model automata than making magicians' linking rings. But the moving model solar system still hung from the ceiling, spinning slowly, and a model train, the very first device that Grit had ever powered with her fire magic, was still mounted on its track that ran all along the walls. She shot a few sparks at it occasionally, just to see it run its circuit around the room.

But now, they'd transformed the lab even further. It had been Grit's idea to put all of their information about the Wonder Show and the *Jasconius* crash on the wall above Carmer's desk, where they could see it all in one place. Newspaper clippings, copied excerpts from the police reports—even Bell's picture—were all mounted on the wall in the best timeline they could cobble together, from the first accident on a small model plane all the way to the disaster on Bell's ship.

"*You* may be able to keep track of everything you've ever read," she'd told Carmer, "but some of us need a little reminding."

They took Carmer's list of Tinkerton's top competitors, along with a few additions from Bell, and mounted their names (and pictures, when they could find them) on the wall with everything else. A studio portrait of Isla and Robert Blythe, cut out of a newspaper clipping about their latest test flight, was now pinned to the very top of their list. Grit gave the pin an extra push, for good measure.

"Look familiar?" she asked Bell.

He squinted at Isla's serious face. She had hair of some medium shade—it was impossible to tell from the black-and-white picture—arranged in becoming waves around her face, but it did little to soften the severity of her cheekbones or the triumphant-looking glint in her eye. The man next to her shared her features, but his hair was darker, his jutting chin covered by the kind of bushy black beard that had gone out of fashion years ago.

It was obvious even from the picture that the Blythes were . . . well, even bigger than most big folk Grit was used to. Their broad shoulders pushed at the edges of the frame, though they were posed quite close to each other. Grit could hardly imagine such a distinctive woman sneaking into a restricted area of an airship without anyone noticing.

"Well, yeah," Bell said, sighing, "but that's because I've seen both of them before. Even before the accident. Blythe Flights, Inc. isn't exactly a secret."

Unlike Tinkerton, Bell had explained earlier, the Blythe siblings made no attempt to disguise their ideas, or their identities. They were determined to be the first aviators to successfully fly a manned airplane, and they made sure everyone knew it. They ran an entire research laboratory in Driff City dedicated to discovering the secrets of motorized flight, and even owned their own stretch of private beach along the coast for testing their machines.

They were also, as Bell attested and Carmer confirmed with some research, expertly aggressive at eliminating their competition. They frequently bought out smaller firms and independent aviators to claim new technology under the Blythe Flights umbrella. They'd never made Tinkerton an offer—or so he claimed when they asked—but there were, of course, less public and less acceptable methods of ensuring his failure.

"Would it help if you saw her in person?" Carmer asked Bell.

Grit held back a sigh of frustration. They wouldn't need to waste time going after human suspects when Grit could just *ask* the closest faeries around about their mystery woman, but Carmer had insisted they give the Wonder Show faeries a wider berth, at least for now, when they couldn't be sure of the faeries' involvement in Mikhail Hunt's death.

"We should be asking both of them a few questions, anyway," added Carmer. "We can pretend to be visiting engineering students from Skemantis here on winter break between terms."

"Look at you," Grit said proudly, "lying and sneaking and willingly talking to people you don't know!" She flitted from one of his shoulders to the other until he affectionately swatted her away.

"It's a Christmas miracle," Carmer said, making Bell laugh for the first time since the night before. "But we've still got to be careful. It's likely *they* might recognize *us*."

Bell's smile fell. "You think so?"

Carmer pointed to the intimidating, bearded figure of Robert Blythe. "It's possible. Because I've never seen Isla, but I recognize him. He was standing behind us in line for the Wonder Show."

BLYTHE FLIGHTS, INC.
will be CLOSED
Thursday, December 21–Tuesday, January 2
Merry Christmas and a Happy New Year

That the sign was posted on the inside of the firm's glass-paned door only added insult to injury, as if to say, *Ha! You can't even reach me to give me a good whack, and I know how much you want to.*

Grit compensated by snapping a spark at it with her fingers. It pinged off the glass and nearly hit Bell in the face.

"Whoa! Contain the rage, little miss," said Bell. "Contain the rage."

"You're going to have to explain to me exactly what Christmas is again," Grit complained to Carmer, "because I still don't understand why the whole human world shuts down for someone's birthday."

Bell chuckled, but the disappointment hung thick in the air around them. The Blythes had been their best human lead, and now they would have to wait.

"Why can't you just count summers, like reasonable people?" she muttered. "What now?"

Carmer stomped his feet in the biting cold. Grit had ridden in his hat on the way there, her warmth staving off the worst of the cold, but now the wind was really picking up. The gray clouds above looked packed with snow. For all of Carmer's insistence that Virginia would make for a milder winter, it didn't feel like it then. Billboards and marquees all around the city had been plastered with warnings for residents to keep their ships firmly on solid ground; a storm was coming.

"Maybe we should check in with Tinkerton again," suggested Carmer halfheartedly. "See if there's anything else he can tell us."

"I vote for that," Bell said, rubbing his hands up and down his arms and looking up at the sky. He had a lumpy knitted scarf of Carmer's wrapped around his neck, but was otherwise unprotected. "Or really, anything that gets us out of Scudside before that Snowpocalypse hits."

The Blythes' office skirted the edge of the neighborhood affectionately (or not so affectionately) known as Scudside. It was dingy, muddy, and home to the few remaining factories that didn't produce airship parts, as well as many Driftsiders too poor to live in the more desirable parts of the city. There were few streetlamps, and the chugging smokestacks made visibility even poorer, despite the brisk wind.

Carmer, Grit, and Bell just managed to get onto one of the last departing air-buses of the afternoon before Driff City suspended service in anticipation of the storm. The ship was nearly empty, and the ticket-taker looked as if he wanted to scold them for even being out at all.

Carmer kept to the middle seats, as was his custom—it was easier that way to pretend that he was on a train, or a regular bus, and not a hundred feet in the air—but Bell took advantage of the empty gondola to look from window to window.

"I can't believe it," Bell said, stopping short. He pressed his face nearly to the glass. "That's not . . ."

"The *Jasconius*, all right," said their air-bus captain over his shoulder. "Feds dropped her in there this morning. Guess they found all they was gonna find."

Carmer sat up straighter, craning his head toward the window, and started at the sight below. "Is that . . ."

Bell nodded, a faraway look in his eyes. "An airship graveyard."

And before Carmer could say another word, Bell pulled the lever to request the next stop.

"I DON'T THINK this is a good idea," Grit said. "And if *I* don't think something is a good idea, chances are, it's a *terrible* idea."

The three of them stood at the entrance of the largest junkyard Carmer had ever seen, on the western edge of Scudside. It stretched as far as his eyes could see. A wrought iron arch overhead, jet-black laced through with crumbling veins of rust, formed the words DRIFTSIDE METALS, INC. Snow flurries were already collecting on the sign like a thick layer of dust.

"Yeah," admitted Bell. "Plus, this place is a dump." He laughed nervously. No one joined in.

"You really think this will help?" Carmer asked for what was probably the third time.

"I just need to see her," said Bell. "If it helps me remember, great. If you guys find some sort of clue in there, even better. But I just need to see that ship. For me."

Carmer nodded. Grit stood with her hand on her hip, still unconvinced.

"You don't have to come with me," Bell insisted. "But if you wanted to take a look around, I can't think of a better time to do it." He looked up at the dark gray sky, snowflakes clinging to his lashes. "I hardly think we'll run into anyone else out here today."

"You're not going in there alone," said Carmer firmly. Grit groaned. "We get in, we find the ship, we look around, and we get out."

"And how do you propose we do any of that?" Grit asked. But she had already flitted to the padlock on the gate. She sent a blast of energy toward it, breaking it with ease.

"Easy," said Bell, starting forward. "We already saw her from the air. Just look for the biggest shipwreck in the sea."

11.

BLOSSOMS
IN A BLIZZARD

THE AIRSHIP GRAVEYARD, CARMER THOUGHT, FELT more like a place for dead things than any cemetery he'd ever set foot in. Perhaps it was because the only sound was the crunching of their shoes over fresh snow, unidentifiable bits of metal, and (real) grit. Perhaps it was because the falling snow made it hard to see more than a few yards ahead of you, and when you did, all you saw were glimpses of the great, hulking frames of airships long past any hope of flight. These were not the ships stored in protected hangars in other parts of the junkyard, carefully preserved to return to service one day—or even to be formally harvested for their most valuable parts. These were the leftovers of the leftovers.

Most had been stripped of their envelopes, leaving only the rigid frames behind, usually half caved in or simply splintering away piece by piece. They lay empty and abandoned, like the skeletons of great beasts.

Bell had been right about two things. The first was that there were no Driftside Metals staff or other scavengers to bother them; there wasn't another human in sight, making the alien landscape of hollowed-out ships feel even stranger. Even the guard's shed by the gate stood empty. Clearly, the native Driftsiders had taken the warnings about the upcoming snowstorm seriously and battened down their hatches. All it took was a frozen envelope to make even the slightest, lightest balloon sink like a stone. There wasn't a single ship in the sky.

The second was that the *Jasconius* was easy to find. Its envelope was still mostly intact, except for various punctures and slashes from the initial collision and general rough handling; no one had had a chance to strip it for everything it was worth yet. Or maybe they just didn't want to risk the bad luck. A ship as large as the *Jasconius* wouldn't normally be dumped in a graveyard like this—the parts were too valuable, and it simply took up far too much space. But it seemed that the *Jasconius*'s owners didn't want to hold on to *any* reminder of their biggest tragedy.

The ship towered over all the other wrecks and scrap piles around it like a great beached whale. The frame was the only thing holding it together, and gravity was already taking its toll. Frames weren't designed to support a ship's full weight on the ground, and the sides bowed out while the underbelly pressed into the dirt. The gondola and the engine cars might be inaccessible, if they hadn't been totally crushed beneath the weight of the ship already. Carmer could hear the supports creaking, even over the rushing wind.

"How do we get inside?" asked Grit, gripping the brim of Carmer's top hat so she didn't blow away.

Bell stood frozen to the spot a few paces behind them, jaw clenched and shoulders tensed.

"What is it?" Carmer asked. "Do you remember something?"

Bell shook his head; Carmer looked away while the other boy brushed tears from his eyes.

"The sad answer to that question, little miss," Bell said to Grit, "is anywhere we like."

Carmer ducked his head against the wind as he followed Bell and tried to ignore the wet seeping into his boots. Bell seized hold of a rip in the envelope and pulled with all his might; Carmer joined in to help, and soon enough, they'd made their own door.

"Is it safe to walk inside this thing?" Grit asked, raising her voice above the wind. The snow was coming down harder now, clumping on Carmer's hat and nestling in the folds of his scarf. The thick flakes melted in a circle around Grit; she did her best to kick the rest off the brim.

"Safe enough, if you're with me!" said Bell, shrugging. "And I'd rather walk in there than out here, if it's all the same to you!"

The sound of the oncoming storm quieted a little as they stepped inside the skeleton of the ship, but the wind still whistled eerily through all the odd cracks and holes. They balanced in near darkness, clinging to the metal frame. Grit turned her light on as bright as she could and hovered over their heads to light the way.

Carmer followed Bell in silence, stopping only to ask him once or twice to slow down. Bell knew this ship inside and out, even gutted and grounded, but Carmer didn't have the same practice, and their progress was slow. Carmer's breath clouded in front of him in the glow of Grit's light. Eventually, they climbed up to a catwalk that Bell said would take them to the engine cars. Carmer's arms trembled from hoisting himself up and over and down and around, steel rung after steel rung.

They seemed to walk forever as the storm raged outside, though Carmer knew only minutes could have passed.

"We're almost there," Bell said, though he didn't sound as certain as Carmer would have liked. "We'll have to go back outside again to get into the engine car, but—"

Squish.

Bell stopped short; Carmer almost walked into him, but steadied himself just in time.

Squish. Squish.

Carmer's ankle rolled under him, and Bell hauled him up by the elbow.

"What the—?" wondered Bell. "Are those . . . ?"

Grit flew closer to the ground, illuminating the source of the mysterious squishing.

They were stepping on mushrooms.

Clusters of colorful fungi bloomed beneath their feet. There were white-capped button mushrooms, flowery chanterelles in shades of cream and orange, and others with caps as big and wide as the palm of Carmer's hand, all covered by a thin layer of frost.

"I know I'm no expert on human transportation," said Grit, "but I'm pretty sure an airship's floor is not supposed to look like that."

"It is *definitely* not," Carmer said.

"Still think this crash had nothing to do with faerie magic?" Grit asked archly.

The mysterious mushrooms *were* decidedly unnatural. Had they been there since the accident? Surely, if the investigators who had taken apart the *Jasconius* had seen them, it would've been front-page news. Carmer's breath hitched. If this *was* some aftereffect of faerie magic, or if the Unseelie fae were still there . . .

"Tuck your pants into your socks, if you haven't already," Grit said, ever practical. "And don't touch them—"

Bell instantly retracted his hand from where he'd been about to poke at a particularly springy-looking specimen.

"—just in case," Grit finished, rolling her eyes.

Bell double-checked his ankles and shoved his hands innocently into his pockets.

They followed the trail of mushrooms onward, ignoring the unpleasant squishing under their feet. The fungi grew in thicker clusters as they went on, even creeping up along the frame of the ship on either side. And it wasn't just mushrooms: thick, spongy moss spread out in a roving carpet of damp. Bubbles of mold and clusters of flowering lichen rippled under any painted fixtures and covered every surface in a layer of putrid fuzz. The smell of decay became so strong that Carmer and Bell covered their noses with their sleeves.

It was as if the *Jasconius* really *was* the dead sea monster it was named after, and now nature was reclaiming the corpse.

Grit's yellow eyes looked unnaturally bright in the darkness of the ship. "I don't like this, Carmer. I don't like this at all."

"Maybe we should turn back," Carmer suggested. His foot got caught in an impossibly sticky cobweb, nearly sending him sprawling.

But Bell shook his head, muttering to himself, and kept walking. He ran his fingers along the wall despite Grit's warnings about the flowering mold, occasionally squinting up into the vastness of the ship above them.

"What is he doing?" Grit whispered, flying to Carmer's shoulder. She looked askance at Bell.

"Counting rings, I think," guessed Carmer. "The frame is made up of over a hundred of them. If Bell can find the ring that the engine car is attached to . . ."

"Gotcha." Bell pounded a fist against the rusted, fungus-ridden wall, sending half a dozen bugs skittering out from under their decaying hiding spots. Carmer jumped back in disgust.

The door would have normally led them out of the ship proper and onto a narrow walkway, where they would enter the engine car via another hatch in its roof. But the weight of the grounded ship had crushed the flimsy walkway entirely, smashing the hull almost directly up against the engine car. Bell and Carmer pushed against the first door with all their might until it gave way with a splintering groan.

Freezing cold air rushed into the ship, bringing snow and flakes of rust and mold along with it. The graveyard outside had transformed into a world of white. Carmer instinctively brought up a hand to the brim of his hat, catching Grit from blowing away just in time. She clutched at his fingers as the wind raged; he scooped her under the hat and held it down with one hand.

They climbed over the remnants of the walkway, now nothing but a tangle of twisted metal. Bell brushed away the snow on the hatch; underneath, the metal was corroded so badly it practically crumbled at his touch. He kicked the door open and jumped in before Carmer could say a word to caution him.

The clawing smell of rot rose up from the open car.

"Bell!" Carmer yelled, trying not to gag at the stench.

Grit rapped furiously on the inside of his hat. She bent down toward his ear. "At least let me out so you can see in there!"

Carmer reached up under his hat and grabbed her around the middle; he knew she didn't like to be held like that, but they had little choice in the present circumstances. With numbing, fumbling fingers, he crunched up the hat—he was sorry to ruin it, but hats, unlike faeries, could be replaced—and jammed it down the front of his coat. The wind and snow bit at his exposed ears.

Grit's glow seemed feeble against the darkened sky as Carmer lowered them into the engine car. The space would be close under normal circumstances, with barely room for two men to stand comfortably, but now it was claustrophobic beyond imagination. Frosted mold and flowering mushrooms covered every surface.

Carmer reached out a hand to steady himself as he climbed in, but the metal railing he grabbed fell apart at his touch, brittle as a spent matchstick. At least two inches of unidentifiable . . . *moisture* oozed under his feet when he stumbled to the floor, seeping into the holes in his shoes and through his socks. The engine was partially submerged in stagnant water, while half-frozen trickles of sludge oozed out of the condenser. The entire thing looked as if it had been out of commission for twenty years, not two weeks, and had been left on a rain forest floor for nature to reclaim until it was barely recognizable. Something that Carmer hoped was sleet dripped softly from the ceiling.

Bell stood with his hands hovering over the controls like a doctor surveying a patient injured beyond hope, unsure of where to even start to repair the damage.

"Bell—" Carmer started to say, but the air was so thick with molding debris and blowing snow that the words caught in his throat and nothing but a retching cough came out.

"Bell, we have to get out of here!" Grit finished for him, slightly less affected by the oppressive atmosphere.

But Bell stayed where he was, transfixed by the moldering machinery—until the entire engine car shifted around them, buffeted by a particularly strong gust of wind. Carmer clutched Grit closer to him and put a hand against the slimy wall for support. Soon, the weight of the ship would crush the engine car entirely.

Bell nodded, his eyes still far away. "There's nothing here," he said, shoulders sagging dejectedly. "Only . . ."

Only the contents of a forest floor, Carmer thought, but they didn't have time to dwell on it just then. He offered his hand to Bell, who took it, and together they climbed out of the reeking car and into the raging storm.

The snow blasted against their faces as they tried to grasp the lay of the land. Carmer cradled Grit protectively against his chest, but she pricked him with the spurred heel of her boot. His numb hands barely felt it.

"At least let me be useful!" she protested, shining her light brightly. But it only bounced off the sheets of snow, blinding them. Carmer shook his head.

"Should we go back into the ship?" Carmer asked Bell.

"I don't think it's a good idea!" Bell shouted over the wind. "Let's try and get out of here. Just hug the edge of the hull—it'll protect us from some of the wind! Stay close!"

Bell took Carmer's hand again. They moved along at a crouch, huddled against whatever protection the graying corpse of the *Jasconius* could offer them. Grit had clawed her way into the folds of Carmer's scarf, where she hung on for dear life and flicked her wings against the accumulating snow. Carmer kept looking down every few seconds to make sure she was still there.

"This was a *terrible* idea!" she scolded as they walked, but Carmer wasn't even sure Bell could hear her.

By the time they reached the nose of the ship, Carmer couldn't tell east from west or north from south in the haze of whipping white that surrounded them. It was getting harder to force his freezing feet through the snow that was now at least six inches deep. He'd traveled all over the country, but he'd never seen a blizzard like this.

"The gate's that way," Bell said, jerking his head toward

the right. "We can probably break into the guard's shed and wait this out. Hang on!"

He took his first step out from behind the shelter of the ship, and the wind wasted no time in wrenching their hands apart.

"Bell! Bell!" The snow stung Carmer's eyes, his nose, his chapped lips.

The wind howled like a wounded animal—like a *pack* of wounded animals, drowning out Carmer's calls. The other boy was probably only feet away, but he might as well have been on the other side of the graveyard.

"It's no use!" Grit shouted into Carmer's ear. She looked impossibly small, covered in snow that melted as it touched her fire faerie skin, but not quickly enough. "I can feel their magic, Carmer. We have to— Ahh!"

Carmer's scarf tore from his neck as easily as if yanked by strong, icy hands. Grit was thrown with it into the wind, spinning away so quickly Carmer barely heard her yelp before she disappeared entirely.

"GRIT!" Carmer screamed, but it was like shouting into a vacuum. Panic clawed at his insides, fiercer than any wind and sharper than any bite of the cold. He'd lost Grit. He'd lost her. He'd lost her he'd lost her he'd—

Something moved in the snow.

It was nothing but a snatch of shadow, but it was the only thing he'd seen in minutes that wasn't blinding white and gray. Carmer raised his arms, trying to shield his face, and took a few tentative steps back toward the side of the *Jasconius.*

He saw it again. Closer, this time. But he wasn't even sure *what* he was seeing.

"Grit?" Carmer called cautiously, though he doubted it was her. ". . . Bell?"

In between the snowflakes, the shadow flickered. It was the edge of a black cloak, whipping around a corner and out of sight. It was the curve of a shoulder shrugged just out of Carmer's reach. It was a hood pulled up quickly enough to hide a quirked, purplish lip. It was all of those things, and none of those things, because when Carmer blinked, the shadow was gone.

A train whistled, long and shrieking and clearer than any sound in the world—and coming straight for him.

Carmer ran.

He ran without thinking or seeing. He stumbled and tripped and once banged his hip so hard on the edge of some jutting thing that he almost gave up and crumpled into a ball, right then and there in the snow. But he kept running. The edges of his vision were filled with moving things: loping animal bodies and churning wheels and a girl's long curtain of dark purple hair, furling and unfurling behind her like some kind of black waterfall.

He tripped and went flying, landing painfully on his side, and stared at a tower of landing wheels, all stacked one on top of the other and so covered in snow they looked like a marble pillar from a Greek temple. Other discarded ship parts were stacked in orderly columns around them. The thin canvas that had been protecting them had snapped off; it flapped loose and wild in the wind like a ghostly flag.

Carmer stood up slowly, his ears ringing, and shuffled into the maze of junk. Better to risk being buried under it than staying exposed out in the snow, running in the open for anyone—or anything—to find him.

Surrounded by the towers of crunched-up metal, his frenzied mind calmed a little. He counted more wheels, propeller blades, steel pipes in every size and length. They shuddered under the snow's fury, the same as he did, but they were things he could make sense of, organized and orderly. He took deep breaths.

He'd imagined the train whistle, he told himself. But outside the towers of junk, he still glimpsed the shadows. Moving and waiting.

He also *smelled* something, but it was different from both the fresh snow and the rotting airship. It smelled like . . . burning rubber?

How could something be burning, all the way out here, in the middle of a *snowstorm*?

Grit. Grit was trying to find him. Or rather, she was calling him to *her*.

"You are one smart faerie," Carmer said, though there was no one to hear it. He resolved to tell her later. Repeatedly. With hugs.

"*Carmer . . .*" Grit's voice called faintly, and despite the wind and the snow and the distance between them, he heard her.

Carmer followed the sound of her voice and the smell of burning rubber, ducking his head against the snow, lungs burning with every breath of icy air and acrid smoke, until he found a huge cluster of tires that were suspiciously snow-free. He crawled inside a bunch of them stacked side by side, like a small tunnel, and waited only a few moments before a glowing, tiny, piping-hot force of nature barreled into him.

"We are *never*. Doing *anything*. This *stupid*. Ever *again*," Grit said, punctuating each syllable with a smack to Carmer's snow-covered head. Water dripped into his eyes.

"Remind me of that if we survive this," Carmer said wearily, suddenly exhausted—and colder than he'd ever been in his life.

"*When* we survive this," Grit corrected him. "Hands. Now."

Carmer didn't even bother to protest. He barely felt her land in his numb palms, but after a few seconds, the feeling began to come back into his fingers, and he almost wished it hadn't. He cradled his hands to his chest and tried not to cry out from the pain. Grit made soothing shushing noises, but even she was starting to shiver a little. She was only one fire faerie in the middle of a snowstorm, after all. Carmer curled as tightly as he could around her, feet nearly over his head inside the ring of tires.

"Where's Bell?" Grit asked, her voice muffled against Carmer's coat.

Carmer touched his forehead to hers and gently shook his head. He didn't need to say anything else.

"This isn't a normal storm," Grit said. "I . . ." She stopped, pushing his hands apart, and listened.

Carmer strained to hear whatever she could, but his ears would never be as good as a faerie's. All he could make out was howling wind.

"There's something outside, just here," Grit said as quietly as she could. "It's circling us."

"*It?*" Carmer whispered back.

And then a howl—a very real one that was not the wind at all—burst through the air. Carmer would have jumped sky-high if he hadn't been crammed into the tire like a sardine in a can.

A wolf's head appeared at the mouth of the rubber tunnel.

"Spirits and *zits*," Carmer exclaimed. Was he really seeing what he thought he was seeing?

"Out," Grit said. "Out out out!"

Yes. Yes he was.

Carmer scrambled in the other direction, willing his stiff, snow-encrusted limbs to move, just *move*, while the wolf pawed at the opening, trying to squeeze its giant furry body through the tires. Grit shot golden sparks at its face as they retreated. It yelped and shook its giant head with a snarl.

Carmer clambered out of the last tire, his entire body recoiling from facing the full blast of the blizzard again, only to come face-to-face with three more wolves. Grit grew even hotter in Carmer's breast pocket; he looked down to see her hands dancing with sparks and the occasional live flame as she muttered whatever dead faerie tongue she called upon in times like these.

"Wait," Carmer said, hardly breathing. He squinted through the snow at the wolves, who seemed surprisingly content to stand there patiently in a circle, instead of leaping forward and tearing Carmer limb from limb. One of them whined, pawing nervously at the snow.

Grit stopped her chanting. Some of the sparks on her fingertips floated away, fizzling with little pops into the air. The wolf barked at them, then looked at Carmer expectantly, and Carmer realized they weren't actually wolves at all: they were huskies. Very, very big ones.

"I think . . . I think they want to help," said Carmer. He could barely speak from the shivers that wracked through him.

He held out a shaking hand palm up, and fought every instinct to snatch his hand away when the leader of the dogs took a few cautious steps forward, sniffed at it with an impossibly large muzzle, and gave his fingers a lick with a pink, sandy tongue.

"I hate to rush a delicate process," said Grit testily, but Carmer could hear the relief in her voice. "But if we don't get you out of here soon, you won't have any hands to lick!"

The husky nudged its head under Carmer's palm. He patted its neck until he found its collar, and grabbed on.

12.

ONE BOY, DEFROSTED

CARMER AND GRIT'S ARRIVAL AT THE IMPOSING
brick mansion at the edge of the graveyard would be forever hazy in Carmer's memory. The fact that there *was*
an imposing brick mansion at the edge of the graveyard
was the least of his concerns. It was all a confusing, frost-
encrusted jumble of sturdy hands ushering him inside;
supportive nudges from the dogs; someone expertly strip-
ping him out of his frozen clothes and into a nightshirt
big enough to fit five Carmers; scratchy homespun blankets and panels of dark wood; a roaring hearth—*where
was Grit?*—and swallowing some liquid that was cool in
the mug they pushed into his hands but burned like fire
going down.

He didn't know how long it was before he finally came to his senses, half dozing in an armchair by the fire. The chair was so big he could nearly lie down in it, and he was wrapped in so many blankets he felt like a swaddled infant. An occasional shiver still rocked through him, though he was already sweating through the nightshirt. His feet were bare and beet red, submerged in a pan of lukewarm water. They hadn't given him any pants.

"Still in the land of the living, eh, boy?" said a booming voice, sounding even louder without the roaring wind to muffle it.

Carmer looked up into the face of the large, bearded man who'd stood behind him at the Wonder Show: Robert Blythe.

Carmer couldn't decide, in that moment, whether he was very, very lucky or very, very cursed. "I think so, sir."

"I don't think Isla and I have seen this much excitement since Jules here had her last litter of pups," the man said, affectionately rubbing the head of the husky standing at his side.

"Thank you for your help, sir," said Carmer. He fidgeted under his cocoon of blankets, feeling around for any sign of Grit. "But I really need to be going—"

"No one's going anywhere." Isla Blythe's voice was surprisingly smooth for such a severe-looking woman. "Not tonight, anyway. Unless you'd like to finish the job that frostbite started."

Isla circled around Carmer's chair to stand next to her brother, and Carmer was even more struck by their size in person than in the picture in the newspaper. They weren't what anyone would call *fat*, exactly; they were just *big*. Both of them stood well over six feet tall—Isla looked even taller, thanks to the height of her waved caramel-colored hair—and they each looked broad enough to balance a park bench on their shoulders with ease. Probably with Carmer on top of it.

This, at least, explained the size of the chair—and the nightshirt Carmer felt like he was swimming in. (No faeries in there, either.) *Everything* was bigger in the Blythes' house: the shelves and the pictures were mounted higher on the walls, the table legs were longer—even the glasses on the drink tray looked more like soup bowls than anything else. Carmer felt like he'd shrunk.

"I didn't think so," said Isla, staring down her large, sculpted nose, a twinkle in her eye.

Was she the same woman who'd terrorized Bell?

Bell.

"You don't understand," Carmer said, "I—I'm ever so grateful for your help, but . . ."

He hesitated. It was entirely possible the Blythes had already captured (Carmer didn't let himself think *and killed*) Bell, especially if Isla had recognized the sole witness to her crime. If Bell *had* managed to elude the dogs and seek shelter from the storm, it was better that the

Blythes never know of his involvement. Carmer could have led all of them into a trap.

But if the Blythes were innocent, and Bell was still out there, freezing . . .

Carmer shivered again and made up his mind. Better to be in trouble in a warm bed than outside in a blizzard.

"Yes, my dear?" asked Isla kindly.

"I didn't come here alone. My friend is still out there."

The Blythes exchanged concerned looks.

"I'm sorry to hear that, son, but my sister's got the right of it," said Robert. "It's not safe for any of us to be going out there again."

"But—"

"I'll send the dogs out again as soon as there's a break in the weather," allowed Robert. "But if your friend's been out there all this time . . ."

Carmer swallowed the lump that had suddenly formed in his throat.

"What the devil were you doing out in our yard on a day like this, anyway?" asked Robert gruffly, sitting back in the chair across from Carmer and stroking his massive beard. "I don't recognize you as one of the manager's boys."

"*Your* yard?" Carmer asked, then wished he hadn't. He probably sounded more like a clueless outsider than ever—though not even Bell had known the Blythes ran Driftside Metals.

Robert smiled, standing up a little straighter. "Allow me to introduce myself," he said. "I'm Robert Blythe, of Blythe Flights, Inc., and this is my sister, Isla."

Carmer extricated his hand from the blankets with some difficulty and limply shook both of theirs. Their grips were unsurprisingly crushing.

"And that," said Isla, gesturing outside, "is our scrap yard." She looked as if she were rather daring Carmer to laugh.

"We started it in the early days," explained Robert, "when Blythe Flights was just a pipe dream, and new parts were beyond the financial reach of green, aspiring aviators like us." He chuckled.

"Now, it's just home," said Isla with a fond, concerned look at the snow piling high outside. "But enough about us. You haven't told us what you were doing out there in the blizzard, young man."

Carmer gulped. He had another decision to make, and no Grit to consult before he made it. What were the chances he could get away with lying to the Blythes, famous experts in aviation, about his business on their own property?

He looked into Isla's flinty eyes and thought, *Not very likely.*

"My name is Felix Cassius Tiberius Carmer III," he said.

To their credit, they did not laugh.

Carmer told them everything.

Well, not *everything*, of course. But he spoke as plainly as he could about being hired by a competitor of theirs to investigate the *Jasconius* crash, and how this had led him to their offices, and then the graveyard, where he and his friend (he didn't mention Bell's name) heard the wreck had been delivered, and it seemed unlikely anyone would be around to catch them snooping. He kept the state of the ship's engine car to himself, too.

The Blythes took it all in without saying a word, only the occasional flash of their dark eyes betraying any hint of interest. Neither did they seem inclined to bash Carmer over the head and bury him in the snow as the only witness to their crimes, but he supposed the night was young.

Robert Blythe surveyed Carmer over steepled fingers the width of sausages.

"And Tinka suspects us, does he?"

Carmer worked very hard to keep his jaw from dropping to the floor. "Sorry, I—"

Robert let out a hearty chuckle. "No need to look like such a gasping fish, my boy. Anyone who looked twice at you coming in, even after we'd scraped all the ice off you, could see you'd walked straight out of the circus."

Carmer thought of his silk top hat and patchwork coat. He supposed the man had a point.

"Well, you needn't worry about us," continued Robert. "We've known about Tinka for years."

Isla explained how they'd replied to the author of an article in an aeronautical journal years ago; the initial letter led to a flurry of regular correspondence between the three inventors, and it wasn't long before the Blythes figured out the identity of their pen pal.

"I always knew he was a private fellow," said Robert, "but I thought something must've been wrong when he wouldn't even see me the other night. It was his first stay in Driftside City in ages, and I thought, since we'd been writing each other for years, exchanging ideas and such . . ." The big man shrugged. "But they turned me away, soon as the show was over, and told me I wasn't even to come to the camp."

Robert huffed, and Isla patted him on the arm.

A private fellow? Carmer thought. Tinka had hardly seemed that way to him. He was secretive about his business, that was certain, but in person, Carmer would even go so far as to call him a bit of a show-off. Those pinstripe pants of his didn't belong to someone who wanted to avoid attention.

"Mr. Tinka has contributed more to the field than most could even imagine," Isla said. "We've no wish to do him harm."

Maybe it was the exhaustion of the day catching up with him, or the effects of whatever engine fuel they'd poured down his throat, but Carmer was quite ready to believe her. The Blythes had taken him in when he was facing certain death, and had fed him and clothed him and offered more information than he'd ever expected to a perfect stranger. He was finding it harder and harder to believe that they would bring down an entire airship of passengers just to ruin someone they'd clearly worked with for years.

Then he saw the plants near the window.

They were displayed in glass boxes on a long table that ran the length of the room, electrical heat lamps filling in the gaps where the sun would be in short supply. Exotic greenery of every kind was on display, from cacti and succulents to a hideous flower that looked suspiciously like an open mouth—complete with teeth.

The Blythes saw him looking. Isla laughed lightly.

"Oh! I see you've spotted my plants," she said. "Aren't they lovely? I was originally a botanist, you know."

Carmer smiled tightly, thinking of mushrooms, and was suddenly a lot less convinced.

THERE WAS NO choice but to spend an uneasy night at the Blythes'. Carmer spared himself further interaction with Isla and Robert by claiming fatigue—which was true enough—and was promptly spirited away to an upstairs bedroom by a portly, red-faced maid. She tucked him into a feather bed so large and lush he wouldn't have felt out of place in *The Princess and the Pea*.

The wind howled as mercilessly as ever, snow still

pounding against the windows. Carmer was glad of the warm bed and the bowl of hot soup he received for supper, even if it meant poisonous fungi were going to start blooming in his intestines while he slept. Anything was better than being out there.

Like Bell.

The maid must have seen Carmer's face, because she patted him on the cheek and assured him the dogs would be out to search the graveyard and fetch news first thing in the morning. As if anyone could survive an entire night out in a blizzard like that.

He didn't finish the soup.

The split second after the door closed behind the maid, a handful of papers flew out from behind the inkwell on the desk, flitted around the bed, and dropped on Carmer's head. He jumped so high he nearly fell out of the bed.

"Look what I found!" said Grit, bobbing around excitedly as Carmer extricated the sheets of paper from his already messy hair. "I thought those giant humans would never leave you alone!"

"Nice to see you, too," he said.

Grit touched down on the blanket over his knees and lay back, letting the cushiony quilt swallow her up before popping up to a sitting position.

"You know, I've been thinking," she said. "If we're going to have heartfelt reunions after every near-death experience, we'll soon run out of time for much else."

"So you propose abolishing the policy entirely?"

Grit flitted to his shoulder and gave one of his unruly locks a friendly tug. "Well, not entirely," she said, voice creaking a little.

Carmer blushed and busied himself with the paper in his hands. "What's this you're so excited about?"

"*That*," said Grit, swiftly drawing her hatpin sword and spearing the first sheet, "is a letter. And not just any letter. I was eavesdropping in the fireplace while you were talking to the Blythes, and when they mentioned writing to Tinkerton, I took the liberty of doing a little exploring."

The paper floated in front of his face, still suspended from her sword. "See anything interesting?"

Carmer grabbed the letter, leafing through the pages. Aside from a fascinating discussion on propulsion, the most notable feature was obvious.

"This isn't Tinkerton's handwriting," said Carmer. "It's the same as the note that came with the golden glider ticket." The Blythes' pen pal and the real Julius Tinkerton were clearly not one and the same.

Grit crossed her arms with a triumphant gesture. "I knew it!" she crowed. "I knew I was right about him not being the brains behind that operation."

"Even if that's the case, do you still think this 'silent partner' is the one behind the attacks?"

"Who else could it be?" Grit asked. "If Tinkerton is claiming their ideas as his own, who else would have as much of a reason to bring him down?" She grimaced. "No pun intended."

Carmer told her about Isla Blythe's gift for plants.

Grit frowned. "I've been around this whole house and haven't seen hide nor hair of anything fae," she said, pacing along Carmer's knees. "So it's unlikely she's working with one. And . . . Carmer, even you must have sensed it out there. This storm isn't natural. Not totally."

Carmer thought of that rippling hair, the upturned lip, the hood of a shining cloak held up against the wind.

"You think they're here, but not for the Blythes," he said. He couldn't help lowering his voice to a whisper. "The Unseelie fae."

The wind suddenly rattled the windows, blowing so hard even the sturdy Blythe mansion seemed to shake around them. Carmer looked out the window; for a moment, all he saw was his own pale, tired reflection, but in the next, mixed in with the swirling clouds of white, he saw . . . turning wheels?

They weren't the monstrous train wheels that had so often haunted his nightmares, or even the tires of a car. Flitting in and out of the shadows, they reminded him of *velocycle* wheels. He could have sworn he even heard the sputtering and roaring of their engines, and recalled Bell's offhand comments about the racing velocycle clubs. Surely, no sane person would be out riding in this weather, and so far from the public road?

SNAP. Something hard flicked against the window, making Carmer jump. A branch being blown about in the storm, that was all, but it broke his focus. When he looked back at the window again, all he saw was snow.

"Carmer?" asked Grit. "Are you all right?" She flew to the window, sparks skittering at the ready between her palms.

Carmer realized he was breathing heavily, the back of his neck slick with sweat.

"I'm fine," he said, running a hand through his hair. "But what was *that*?"

"Specifically?" Grit peered out into the snow. "I don't know. But the Unseelie won't attack us here, not tonight." She landed on the windowsill with her hands on her hips.

"What makes you so sure of that?" Carmer asked.

"Because I'm a Seelie princess," Grit said with a sigh, in the tone of one who was admitting to an embarrassing hobby or youthful history of petty crime. "Their creepy king must've found me out by now. And he knows the law. Any direct Unseelie attack against me would be grounds for war between the courts. No matter *how* miffed he is I haven't handed myself over for inspection."

Carmer, for one, was not sorry about this royal perk. "You don't think . . . did they start this storm because of that? Because we broke the rules?" If Bell was lost and hurt—or worse—because of them . . .

"No," Grit said firmly, flitting back to the bed. "There are easier ways to get our attention. I think they were after something else, this time—and I think they got what they came for."

If the faeries really were behind the attacks on Tinkerton's ships, then they'd just had the chance to take care of the sole witness to their crimes; a young pilot lost in a blizzard was a much easier story to believe than one kidnapped by faeries.

"We made it easy for them," said Carmer bitterly. "We walked right into their trap at the graveyard. All they had to do was separate us—"

"Carmer," started Grit, "it's not your fa—"

She froze, plopping down onto the quilt with a small *oof.*

"That's *it*," she said, her voice nearly swallowed by the covers.

"What?" Carmer asked, pushing down the blankets to find her.

"I think I know why the Unseelie are sabotaging Tinka's ships," she said. "It's a *trap*. The accidents weren't just to hurt humans—although that's always an added plus for the Unseelie. They were *luring* Tinka. They wanted him to bring the Wonder Show to Driff City, closer to their castle."

"But what could the Unseelies want with the Wonder Show?" Carmer asked.

Grit sat up and shook her head. "That's just it. I don't think they care much about the Wonder Show at all. It's the faeries *on* it they're interested in."

"But why?" Carmer leaned forward. "You said yourself, back in Skemantis—street fae and court faeries don't mix. So what do the Unseelies want with a bunch of Free Folk?"

"That's exactly the point," Grit said, bouncing up and down on the quilt. "A *bunch* of Free Folk. Street fae hardly ever band together like the faeries on the Wonder Show. The job we pulled off in Skemantis, getting them all to cooperate like that . . . it doesn't happen often. If it did, the official courts might start to get a little . . . concerned."

"They're worried about the Free Folk challenging their power?" Carmer guessed.

Grit nodded. "So what's an antsy Unseelie king to do without openly acting against his own kind?"

Carmer leaned back against his pillow. "They want to break up the Wonder Show. If the circus disbands because Tinkerton's losing too much money, they've separated the faeries and eliminated the threat."

"Or who they *think* is a threat," corrected Grit. "I don't think Beamsprout has any plans for world domination in that silly onion-shaped head of hers."

Carmer smiled, just a little, but his amusement was quickly replaced with worry. "We have to warn them."

"We do. Tomorrow," Grit insisted. "*You* should get some sleep. I'll keep watch."

"What? No, you don't have to—"

"Someone has to make sure the giants don't use your bones for soup," she said practically. "I can just imagine them ordering that maid of theirs: 'One small boy, lightly defrosted, please.' And I only count one of us who doesn't require sleep."

Carmer sighed, but it turned into a yawn.

Grit snorted.

"I did almost die today," he allowed sleepily, pulling the covers closer.

Grit sprawled out on the pillow next to his face and looked at him, her expression searching. He didn't mind that she saw the few tears that dropped down onto the pillow. At least, not very much.

"We'll find Bell," Grit said softly. "He'll be fine."

"And I'm the greatest magician in the world," Carmer said, finally turning his face into the pillow.

Grit flew up into the mantle of the bedroom lamp, already doused for the night, and sat inside. It wasn't comfortable, but if the lamplighters in her kingdom could sit in their globes all night long, then so could she. She turned on her light, just enough to keep total darkness from swallowing the room, and began her watch.

Outside, around and around the Blythes' house, ghostly wheels churned through the snow until it frothed like waves on the sea.

13.

DEVIL FISH

WHICH CAME FIRST–THE JELLYFISH OR THE SHIP? This was the kind of question Bell Daisimer found himself asking. This was the kind of question he let himself ask, because if he wasn't careful, if he let himself ask the kinds of questions he really wanted to—Where was he? How did he get here? Was it real? Was he . . . dead, and this place his punishment for his sins, for abandoning his passengers?—well, that made the gears in his mind turn pretty sticky, pretty fast. And now, more than ever, he needed his mind. He needed something to hold on to.

The storm was a blur in Bell's memory, nothing left but flashes of bright, cold white. Losing Carmer in the snow.

Skinny, clammy hands at the back of his neck and wrapped around his middle, cold enough to turn his heart into an icy lump in his chest. The caress of black silk against his skin. And flying—flying like he'd never experienced it before, because he wasn't just flying *in* the storm. He *was* the storm. He was as vast as the clouds and as small as a single snowflake and as fast—no, faster—than the wind itself.

And after that? Well, he drowned. But just a little bit, his captor assured him.

She didn't tie his hands, or his feet, or even put bars on his door. She didn't need to. He had the whole ship to himself—the whole ship that had probably sunk well over fifty years ago, if the corpses and the cargo were anything to go by, and was now very firmly at the bottom of the sea.

Only her magic, she said, kept the water from rushing in and crushing him to death in an instant—her magic, he supposed, and the jellyfish. The great, gelatinous dome of the creature encased the entire ship, just one of the countless wrecks around it. It ebbed and flowed with the tides and currents and the sparse marine life that dared traverse these waters. It expanded and contracted at her command.

Had the jellyfish been *born* this big, a magical underwater monster, and simply eaten the ship whole? Had the *ship* and everything in it (including him) been shrunk somehow, and the jellyfish was really no bigger than the palm of his hand?

Which came first—the jellyfish or the ship? In a world with no rules, the possibilities were endless.

Bell had tried to run, at first, and she'd let him get as far as the deck. The fleshy ceiling jiggled overhead, distorting any view he might have had of the sea around them. It was not lost on him that this part of the jellyfish was called, of all things, the bell. By the way the girl giggled, he didn't think it was lost on her, either.

But monsters had been waiting for him there. His brain tried in vain to supply names for the pale, bony creatures with bared teeth—basilisks, dragons, *faeries*?—before the answer came to him. The ivory-and-gray soldiers with wings and webbed talons and wide, sneering faces were as tall as he was now, but he'd seen them before. The sailors in the city called them "Jenny Hanivers"—skeletons of rays and skates carved and manipulated to look like mythical creatures. Except *these* creatures were anything but mythical.

Bell's mother—crickets, how long had it been since he'd thought about *her*?—had been a superstitious woman, and a devout one. She didn't think it was natural, humans trying to fly. The good Lord hadn't given them wings for a reason.

Needless to say, they'd had a bit of a falling-out over the subject.

But memories of her flooded back to him, down there in the wet and the dark. Bell's mother had another name for those skeletal creatures, the Jenny Hanivers, that only made him more certain he'd left the earthly plane for good.

She'd called them devil fish.

14.

A TRAITOR
IN OUR MIDST

CARMER AWOKE TO A WORLD UTTERLY TRANS-
formed. The Driftside Metals graveyard was an unrecogniz-
able landscape of lumpy white masses and frozen towers
of scrap metal. It had been messy before, to be sure, but
now . . . now it looked like someone had placed it in a
snow globe and given the whole thing a good shake *before*
they decided to glue the scenery to the bottom. Scraps of
tarp flew about like strange birds in the wind. Frames that
had been intact on arrival were now bent in impossible
angles, or splayed open down the middle like gutted fish.
Occasionally, a solitary tire would roll past, a rubber tum-
bleweed across the deserted landscape.

And deserted it seemed to be. Robert and Isla's dogs

came back with nothing, snow glittering off their shaggy backs, frothing at the mouths with exertion. They jumped around excitedly, yelping and leaping in the snow, until Robert had to kennel them to calm them down.

"They haven't actually seen much snow," Robert admitted rather sheepishly. "Must be excitin'." He clapped Carmer on the shoulder, hard enough to nearly make Carmer's knees buckle. "We'll get you back into town as soon as we can. Maybe you'll find your friend there. Don't, uh, don't stay out in the cold too long, all right?" Robert trudged back into the house.

Carmer absently flapped the arms of his borrowed jacket. It fell nearly to his ankles. "How much do you want to bet there's nothing left of the *Jasconius*?" he asked. "Who will believe us when we tell them we found an engine full of *mushrooms*?"

"Blurgh." Grit surfaced from his pocket, spitting out lint. "The Wonder Show faeries will, if they know what's good for them."

Robert Blythe offered to drive Carmer to the police station to start his search for Bell, but Carmer politely declined. Though no longer convinced of the Blythes' involvement, he wanted them as far away from his investigation—and any further encounters with the Unseelie fae—as possible. Instead, he let the large man accompany him to the nearest airbus station. The skies, unlike the roads, were already clear, and the no-frills passenger ships that made regular trips from end to end of the city were packed with the few commuters daring (or desperate) enough to try to get to work that day.

Carmer was back in his own clothes, which had dried so stiffly they hung on his skinny frame like chunks of cardboard rather than fabric. The inside of his shirt was stuffed with letters between the Blythes and "Tinkerton" that Grit had stolen. He would make time to study them later.

He'd straightened out his top hat as best he could, wondering if the Blythes had been interested enough to see the squashed faerie balcony on the inside, but it looked more than a little worse for wear. Grit spent most of the trip inside it, sitting on top of Carmer's head with her fingers wrapped in his hair to keep her balance and sighing loudly whenever Carmer took a particularly ungainly step. It wasn't their favorite arrangement, but it would have to do.

It was a cold and tough walk to the camp at Elysian Field from the air-bus stop—snowbanks pushed up along the sides of the road took up most of the sidewalks in their path—but it gave Carmer time to think. The storm had been rough here, that was certain, but the snow reached only eight, maybe ten inches high. It was nowhere near the utter devastation that had been wreaked on the graveyard.

Carmer didn't even bother to go to the police. "My friend was abducted by evil faeries in a magically enhanced snowstorm while we were trespassing in an airship graveyard" did not seem like the kind of thing he could write down on a missing person's report.

"AND SO," GRIT finished. "That's why we think the Unseelies have been sabotaging Tinka's ships. They don't like seeing so many Free Folk working together. They think you're a threat to their authority, so they're trying to break up the show."

The Free Folk assembled in their hidden corner of the *Whale of Tales* did not look very convinced.

"The accidents were just to lure Tinka here," explained Carmer. At a sour look from the pearly-skinned Beamsprout, he added, "Um, that is, we think."

"You *think*?" asked Yarlo, crossing his arms. "Just like you *think* they kidnapped Mikhail and—what did you say—'scrambled his brains' as a warning?"

"I *said* that if the Unseelies got him under their thrall, they could have easily manipulated him with faerie knots," said Grit. "He didn't exactly sound like the sharpest thorn on the rosebush to begin with."

Grit wondered what they would do to Bell—someone who had actually *witnessed* their crimes—if she and Carmer were right.

"Mikhail supposedly warned Tinka about 'using power that wasn't his' before he jumped," Carmer said.

"And yeah, we *think*," Grit added with a pointed look at Yarlo, "that he meant you! And now they've taken a friend of ours, too. But it's not like we can just march up to the Unseelie palace and ask, 'Hey, are you by any chance kidnapping humans because some flying circus is giving you a run for your money?'"

But as soon as the words were out of her mouth, Grit knew that one of them could do exactly that—and it just so happened to be her. She was faerie royalty, and had every right to call a meeting with the Unseelie king. And her visit to declare her presence in his domain—an overdue visit, by now—would be the excuse that got her in the door.

"Are we *really* making those stuffy Fair Folk nervous?" asked Canippy, a long-limbed faerie with green arms and legs like string beans.

Yarlo flicked a vine at her, and she jumped back, scowling.

"I wouldn't be pleased, if I were you," warned Grit. "The Seelie and Unseelie courts have ruled Faerie for thousands of years. If they see the Free Folk as a threat to their power . . ."

"We're not going anywhere," said Beamsprout, and a few of the other faeries nodded. A trio of pixies in the corner made chittering noises of approval. "The Wonder Show is our home, and we're not subject to any court's laws. Unseelie *or* Seelie." Beamsprout narrowed her eyes at Grit.

"Innocent humans have been *killed* because the Unseelies think you *should be*," Grit said. "They haven't attacked you directly—yet. Enough distance and maybe, just maybe, enough respect for fae life has kept them from that. But what happens when they change their minds? What happens when they decide enough is enough?"

Yarlo's rope came out of nowhere, slashing through the air and cracking the ground like a whip. Even the Free Folk jumped.

"Enough *is* enough," he said, stalking toward Grit.

Carmer rushed forward, but she waved him off. This was a matter between fae.

"*I've* had enough of you scarin' my people," Yarlo said roughly. "You come into our territory unannounced, and we let you stick your nose in our business."

"*Tinkerton* asked us to—" Carmer started, but Yarlo kept on.

"You threatened us, and we let you pass unharmed. We didn't ask questions. We never even balked at that *abomination* you call a wing." He spat on the floor.

Grit fought the instinct to fold up her wings, a flush rising up her neck, and extended them instead. So this was what Yarlo really thought of her?

"Now you come in here with your crazy claims to try and scatter us like a bunch of scared rabbits." He stepped so close they were almost touching. "Well, we won't be intimidated by anyone, least of all a nosy little Seelie with ten summers to her name."

Twelve! Twelve summers! Grit bristled, but she knew

he was expecting her to play the brat. He knew exactly what she was, she was sure of it.

Fortunately, Grit had a good guess about what *he* was as well.

"How about an Unseelie?" she asked calmly.

Yarlo blinked. "Excuse me?" he said. "Didn't I just say—"

"I wasn't talking to you," Grit said, stepping around him with more confidence than she felt. It helped—though she would never admit it—that Carmer stood close by, with his abominably large human feet, ready if things got ugly. There weren't many situations where he could be considered the muscle of their operation, but this was one of them. "I was talking to the rest of you. Beamsprout. Canippy. Thundrumble."

They did not look pleased.

"All of you. Would you let an Unseelie scare you, or manipulate you?" she asked them. "Because Yarlo here is doing exactly that. And he *is* an Unseelie."

There was a moment of stunned silence, and then Yarlo laughed. And laughed, and laughed.

"Do you expect them to believe that pile of horse dung?" he asked. "I've been traveling with this show for months and never harmed a soul in the fleet. If I was an Unseelie, why would I do that?"

"To . . . to be their faerie on the inside," Grit said, suddenly less sure of herself. All she had was her gut feeling and a couple of offhand comments.

The only difference between the Wonder Show faeries and you is you live under somebody's thumb, and they *don't.*

"To lead the Wonder Show here," Grit continued, "and help destroy them when the time came." It was more than her gut telling her. It was her heart, the deepest magical part of her, that knew Yarlo had not forsaken his court of birth. But to these faeries, the word of her heart was nothing. Some of them were already retreating into the shadows of the ship. She needed proof.

Yarlo was still smiling.

"Sorry to interrupt," Carmer said, clearing his throat. "But, um, how does that work, exactly? I've been wondering what happens, you know, when a faerie leaves their court. Am I still their Friend? Do they have to tell their king or queen?"

Grit could have kissed him.

Carmer shrugged. "I'm pretty new to all of this."

Yarlo's smile twitched.

"And it ain't none of your business, human," Yarlo said. "When a faerie cuts off ties with his court, that's his business alone. Ain't nobody but him and the wind at his back forever." He smiled smugly, and Grit nearly groaned. She'd never convince them.

But to her surprise, the other faeries looked wary. Thundrumble took a tentative step forward, her round cheeks blushing chestnut. "Um, that's not how it was for me," she offered quietly. (Which was actually quite loudly, as Thundrumble had been aptly named for both thundering and rumbling.) "I had to go up in front of my queen and everyone and there were songs and official banishments and things."

Canippy nodded, as did the fire faerie with bright red wings sitting next to her. Beamsprout was glowing so brightly she looked white-hot.

"Aw, you know what I meant, old girl!" said Yarlo, clapping Thundrumble on the shoulder. He yelped and snatched back his hand; one of her spines had poked him. "And it ain't wise to divulge such know-how to the humans!"

"What were the words?" Beamsprout spoke sharply. "What were the words you had to say to break your oath to the Unseelies?"

Vines started curling and uncurling around Yarlo's arms. He laughed uneasily now.

"I—I don't remember exactly, pretty moonbeam," he said, edging backward until he hit the toes of Carmer's boots.

"Don't 'pretty moonbeam' me!" cried Beamsprout, a milky tear streaming down her face. "You lied to us, Yarlo, this whole time!"

Yarlo must have seen his time was up. Fast enough to be nothing but a brown blur, he skittered around and in between Carmer's boots, his ropes and vines flying.

"Grit, what is he—" Carmer took a panicked step forward, but his boots had been tied together in Yarlo's impossibly complicated knots. He tripped and pitched forward, falling down hard. The other faeries dashed out of the way just in time; their little hammocks and nests in the quarters they'd built in this corner of the ship were ground to bits under Carmer's human-sized elbows and knees.

"Carmer!" Grit hovered over him.

"Yarlo's getting away!" someone called.

"So go get him!" Grit snapped. "Carmer, are you all right?"

Her friend sat up gingerly, poking at Yarlo's knots, and surveyed the damage he'd done.

"I'm fine," he muttered. "Just clumsy as a ton of bricks. I . . . I'm sorry about your things."

Canippy, who had soared all the way up to the ceiling to hide, looked at him like he was one of the gigantic, warmongering Titans engraved on the *Whale of Tales*' walls. Only her red-winged friend, glaring daggers at Carmer all the while, was able to coax her down. Thundrumble, on the other hand, gave him a clumsy (and blessedly spike-free) pat on the shoulder.

Beamsprout flitted back into view. "He's gone," she said, wringing her hands. "I lost him in the Hall of Stories. He knows the ins and outs of this ship better than anyone. He'll probably be halfway to the Unseelie king by morning."

"I'm sorry about all of this," Grit said. "I really am. But I thought you had a right to know."

Beamsprout looked like she couldn't decide whether to smile at Grit or slap her. It was an expression Grit was becoming familiar with.

"How did *you* know?" Beamsprout asked. "How did you figure it out?"

Grit sighed. "I think it's because . . . well, I'm afraid I haven't been entirely honest with you all, either. It's true, I'm a Seelie, and Carmer is a Friend of the Fae. But . . ."

"BUT?" boomed Thundrumble.

They all covered their ears.

"But I think I sensed Yarlo because I'm not just a Seelie," she admitted. "I'm a Seelie princess."

The Wonder Show faeries took a collective step back, Beamsprout's eyes as wide as a panicked frog's. The pixies shrieked so loudly everyone covered their ears again. It was exactly the kind of reaction Grit had been hoping to avoid since she'd left home—but there was no way to bring her cover back now.

"Wait!" she said, holding up her hands. "So, I'm a Seelie princess. And . . . I think that means I can help you."

CARMER AND GRIT left the Wonder Show armed with a lock of a water fae's hair, a vial of faerie dust contributed from each of the Free Folk, and directions to the nearest, clearest body of water (a pond in a neighborhood called Portside, which was, confusingly, not near the port at all).

Grit could tell the free faeries didn't trust her much. Why would a Seelie princess care about their plight? She tried to explain that she did care, that she had Free Folk friends back at home, and that she respected their right to rule themselves. That she had seen faeries of all courts and kinds killed, injured, and enslaved by the Mechanist, and it made her understand more than ever that every single one of her kind was in danger all the time. But the words seemed clumsy and inadequate. She was probably spending too much time around Carmer.

The truth was, princess or not, she doubted her word would make much difference. She couldn't even meet with the king on neutral territory, as was customary for official dealings between the courts, because there was nothing official about it. Humans (those who weren't Friends of the Fae) and Free Folk were outside the bounds of much of faerie law. Other than outright slaughter, there wasn't much that Seelies or Unseelies weren't allowed to do to them. And to the Unseelies, it seemed, the respect for faerie life in general extended only so far. (Humans, naturally, were not considered at all.) Grit's mother, the queen, would never have approved of her using her official status as a Seelie princess to ask for favors for a bunch of "lawless street fae."

So the meeting would be an unofficial one, on the king's territory and in his palace under a rotting, unused section of docks in the bay.

Carmer, needless to say, was far from thrilled. He insisted on accompanying her, a matter they fought about for a solid five minutes while the Wonder Show faeries watched impatiently, until Carmer hit upon a solution. He *would* go with Grit to the Unseelie Court; he'd just leave his body behind.

"Fortunately for you," said their friend Madame Euphemia in the reflection of the pond a few minutes later, "I just started boiling the water for my frog leg stew."

A turnip—or it might have been an onion; it was hard to tell—swam across the surface of the soup pot the old woman was peering down into, hundreds of miles away from Carmer and Grit. Grit spared a quick thought for the poor soon-to-be-boiled frogs as she and Carmer leaned in closer over the edge of the water. Madame Euphemia de Campos had many gifts in addition to being a Friend of the Fae and a recipient of her faerie partner's magic at the time of his death. She was a Seer, and that meant she could scry using almost anything. Including, it seemed, the beginnings of frog leg stew.

"How can I help you two troublemakers?" asked Madame Euphemia, her gravelly voice like rocks scraping along a creek bed. Her rainbow-colored braids were wound around her head in an elaborate updo, and her chandelier earrings stretched her brown, wrinkly earlobes well past her jaw.

"How do you know we're making trouble?" asked Grit indignantly.

Madame Euphemia held up a spread of tarot cards, their backs to Carmer and Grit. "You children know I have my ways," she said, the familiar twinkle in her eye. "Also, if the two of you are involved, anyone with half a head of brains can guess there'll be trouble."

Carmer shrugged. She was probably right.

"We need to teach Carmer how to see through other things," explained Grit, "like you do with your puppets." The old Seer had helped Carmer and Grit out of more than one sticky situation by inhabiting her puppets' bodies, all while *her* physical body remained safe and sound inside her home. Grit could see a few of their creepy faces hanging on the walls of Madame Euphemia's vardo in the background. Though why she needed so very *many* . . .

Madame Euphemia frowned. "That'll be difficult, even as a Friend of the Fae," she said. "My eyes were *made* for Seeing things—and through things—that other eyes don't. That boy doesn't have an extraordinary bone in his body."

"Hey!" Grit protested.

"No offense," Madame Euphemia said.

"None taken," said Carmer, who was perfectly content with his unmagical bones.

"You'll need faerie dust, though how you'll get it is a toughie, since you can't make any on your own . . ."

Grit tried and failed not to blush. Faerie dust was

created with the friction of two faerie wings, and she'd never been able to produce any on her own—not even now that she had her mechanical wing.

Carmer helpfully held up the vial of faerie dust from the Wonder Show. "We thought of that, actually."

"Of course you did," said Madame Euphemia with an affectionate, raspy chuckle. "But the free-floating dust isn't ideal, as I'm sure you know. It can have . . . *unpredictable* results. You'll have to have a strong command of the magic."

Carmer gulped.

Grit nudged him. "You'll be fine. Strongest command ever."

"Might I ask why the both of you are so set on this boy leaving his goddess-given body behind?" Madame Euphemia asked.

Grit could see her raised eyebrow, even through the ripples of the water.

"Um . . ." said Carmer.

"Because we have to go somewhere slightly . . . inaccessible," Grit said.

"And slightly inadvisable," added Carmer.

Grit smacked his hat.

"Like I said." Madame Euphemia shook her head, but she was smiling. "Nothing but trouble." She sighed and fished the turnip out of her pot. "I guess those frogs can count themselves lucky. It's going to be a long night."

CARMER WASN'T SURE if he was doing the right thing.

Just weeks ago, Grit had pulled him into her world. She'd made him a part of it the moment she saved him from those bullies in the alley—the moment he saved her from the Mechanist's terrifying mechanical cats. Even before he was named a Friend of the Fae, he'd accepted the danger that might come from being friends with someone whose very existence seemed impossible.

Or at least, he thought he had. But then a faerie queen manipulated his memories, when his mind was the resource he counted on most in the entire world. And then the Wild Hunt came for Gideon Sharpe and killed the Mechanist, right there on the train tracks, and the true mercilessness of the fae was laid bare before him. It was wild and hungry and as beautiful, even, as it was terrible. He had run, then, and the train ran past him, with one more angry soul screaming from within.

Carmer was no Seer, but he couldn't help but feel that someday, when that train whistle blew again, it would be sounding for him.

Maybe the sad thing was, he would rather know that than *not* know. If something was coming—even a huge, incomprehensible, magical spirit horde—he wanted to know everything he could about it. He wanted to learn, so that when the time came, even if he didn't have a fighting chance, at least he'd understand *why*. At least he'd understand *how*.

He was navigating a world he didn't understand, not yet, but he had help. He had Grit, and Madame Euphemia, and even all of the faeries back in Skemantis. But there was someone out there who didn't have Grit, who probably wasn't a Friend of the Fae, and maybe didn't even know that trouble was coming for them. The whistle was blowing, and they might not even be able to hear it.

The person behind Rinka Tinka's Roving Wonder Show, whoever he or she was, deserved to know the truth.

So later that night, when Carmer stayed up late replacing half of his automaton soldier's metal parts with meticulously carved wooden ones—a device with too much iron wouldn't work as a vessel, Madame Euphemia had warned—the last thing he did was write a letter. He carefully copied the Blythes' handwriting on the outside of it, along with the paw print sign they always sketched in the corner to mark their correspondence, in hopes that it would fall into the hands of whoever usually opened their letters. He squished as many words onto each page as he could, tightly rolled up the paper, and just managed to squeeze it into the right compartment of the other machine he'd been fixing up, little by little, since his arrival in Driff City—the Wonder Show's rogue messenger glider. With a little bit of luck, it would soon return to its owner.

Inside, coding his words with a simple cipher the Blythes and the Wonder Show designer had used in their more sensitive communications, Carmer explained everything. He explained who he was, who Grit was, the faeries on the Wonder Show, the Seelie and Unseelie courts, their theories about the reasons for sabotage—everything. He told them where he and Grit would be going, how he would accompany Grit as far as he could by possessing his own automaton. He told them where to find him if another air accident should happen. He offered to talk, if the letter's recipient wanted to, after their visit to the Unseelie king.

Carmer knew he was breaking his vow as a Friend of the Fae to protect their secrets with his life. But he couldn't help but think that in this case, *more* lives would be protected if he didn't. He explained everything, because it was better knowing than not knowing. The Wonder Show was clearly someone's greatest love, their greatest gift to the world. They had a right to know about any forces, both natural and supernatural, that were conspiring against it, just as much as the Free Folk did. Maybe even more.

What they would do with the information? Well, that was up to them.

15.

UNDER THE SEA

THERE IS AN INLET ON THE SHORES OF DRIFTSIDE City where no ships ever dock.

The reason why varies, depending on the level of superstition of whomever you ask.

Some say the shoreline is too rocky, that ships—the kind that actually sail on water—would dash themselves to pieces before they got close enough to land. The wrecks all around it, sleeping at the bottom of the sea, seem proof enough of that.

"But why even build docks there in the first place?" one might ask, to which someone *else* might answer that those docks had been built long ago, back when the first settlers came. They'd fallen into disrepair with the discovery of more favorable sections of the bay. Or perhaps it was that they'd burned down, years ago, and no one had thought to rebuild them. Whatever the reason, the place has long since been forgotten, and most Driftsiders agree it should stay that way.

Then there are others—the grizzled fishermen or retired naval captains or old, wrinkled women with salt-encrusted hair who can shuck a clam faster than you can blink, who might tell you the *real* reason no one sails in those waters, or wanders too close to that inexplicably rocky shore after the sun goes down: because it is haunted. It is the place where the ghosts of those who don't survive the great Atlantic crossing come to rest their weary hearts, where the spirits from faraway places stop to gather their strength and learn the lay of the land. All manner of strange things have been seen there: women in white, wailing for lost children; sleek, pale horses who gallop straight into the sea foam; lights that float in the fog with no lantern to give them life.

And under the crumbling, barnacle-encrusted docks, if the right set of eyes squints the right way, they can see the castle. They can see that the pilings, half eaten away and riddled with holes, are actually great towers, their decorative crenellations just visible above the water. The stalactites that somehow hang from underneath the wooden boards are chandeliers, both beautiful and potentially deadly to the inhabitants below. The skeletons of fish and small animals—and anything else that comes too close—that accumulate in seaweed-tangled clusters could be sculptures in a white marble garden.

All you have to do is look.

Carmer and Grit looked, from their hiding place on a less rocky section of shoreline, and wondered what kind of reception awaited them in a castle that seemed less like an actual palace and more like a sailor's ghost story incarnate. Carmer half expected an eye patch–wearing pirate skeleton to rattle up next to them and demand all their booty—not that they had any.

Carmer didn't even have his own body. Instead, thanks to a crack lesson in faerie magic from Madame Euphemia, his consciousness inhabited his miniature automaton soldier, affectionately named Lieutenant Axel Hudspeth by Kitty Delphine. The lieutenant was about two feet tall and cut an even stranger figure than usual, as many of his metal parts had been replaced by wooden ones, giving him the look of a slightly demonic, half-finished puppet. Only his stately little uniform—handily crafted by Kitty as well—gave him some air of respectability. Carmer's *actual* body was on his bunk at the Moto-Manse, faerie dust coating his sleeping eyelids, well away from any Unseelie castles.

Seeing through the eyes of something that did not strictly have eyes was a strange experience, to say the least.

He kept tripping over the skinny rods of his puppet legs and being startled by every low-flying bird that hopped along the shore, often much too close to his not-face for his liking. His senses were muted, especially his sense of touch. He could feel the hinges in his knees rock back and forth with every step, or the springs turning in his neck, but other sensations, like the ground beneath his feet, were less vivid than usual. Madame Euphemia had told him to expect this, and in fact encouraged it. The more he could differentiate the automaton's body from his natural body—while still maintaining the mental connection—the less likely he was to forget that they weren't one and the same.

Carmer and Grit crept along in silence, hiding among the jagged rocks around the tide pools, until Grit rapped on his shoulder and told him to stop.

"This is as far as you go," she whispered to Carmer. "Any closer and the mermaids might be able to grab you."

"*Mermaids?*" asked Carmer.

"Some of them have suckers on their fingers, instead of webs," Grit explained. "Like octopi! You'd never see the light of day again."

She sounded a little too excited for someone describing deadly suckers.

"I'll patrol the perimeter, like you showed me," said Carmer as Grit flitted off his shoulder. "I'll see if I can find any entrance they might've taken Bell through and then circle back. Shoot up a spark if you have to meet me somewhere different."

"I know the *plan*, Carmer," Grit said, shifting from foot to foot on the rocks and making a face.

"*What?*" Carmer asked.

"I need you to stop talking wearing that automaton's face," she said with a shudder. "It is so. Creepy."

"But sucker-fingers are totally acceptable."

Grit stuck out her tongue. "Stay safe, Lieutenant Creep. I'll be back before you know it."

And with that, she flew off toward the castle, leaving Carmer alone with nothing but his admittedly unnerving reflection in the tide pools.

Until—seconds later—the calm surface of the water was broken by the flash of a familiar rainbow sheen, and Carmer's world went dark.

THE CLOSER GRIT flew to the Unseelie castle, the more unsettled she became. It was one thing to go adventuring with a handful of Free Folk, or your best friend who was perfectly capable of squishing many of your potential adversaries with his ginormous feet. It was another thing entirely to walk calmly, purposefully, and entirely willingly straight into an Unseelie castle all alone.

She ducked under the docks, her feet skimming the

waves to avoid the pointy stalactites, enchanted spider-webs, and other unknown dangers hanging above. The moist and rotting pilings surrounded her on all sides, pressing close. Only a small part of the castle was above the surface, like the tip of an iceberg. The rest was under the water, inaccessible to humans and many faeries alike. She would have to enter Faerie, the ever-shrinking true realm of the Fae, to see the king—and to survive the trip under the waves.

"Such a brave little faerie," said a familiar, accented voice. "But she has learned, I see, to judge when it is wise to turn on her light."

The waves frothed under her, practically boiling, revealing the long hairs of a mane, the outline of a horse's head, and finally the jet-black eyes of a kelpie staring back at her. She recognized him as the kelpie that had bullied her and her Free Folk friends back in Skemantis—but who had also given Carmer a ride on his back in their plan to defeat the Mechanist.

"Guard duty again?" Grit asked, trying to sound mocking, but she was secretly a little relieved to see him. It wasn't exactly a friendly face, but it would do. "It really doesn't suit you."

"I could go back to seducing young *mademoiselles* from the safety of their shorelines, if you would prefer," said the kelpie.

Grit frowned. She had to keep her wits about her in a place like this. She had to remember that even if the kelpie—and honestly, who had ever heard of a French kelpie?—had helped her once in the past, he was still an Unseelie. And that meant that "drowning people" would always be high on his list of leisure activities, whatever alliances he might make to preserve his own life.

"Are you here to drown me?" Grit asked.

"*Ma chère*," said the kelpie with a wet-sounding chuckle, "if I were here to drown you, you'd be sleeping with the fishes already."

Grit gripped a slime-covered crystal on one of the pilings, as high as she could get from the water as possible.

"I'm taking you to Faerie, of course," the kelpie said with a toss of his mane. "Unless you'd prefer to swim . . . but that wing of yours doesn't look very waterproof."

Grit scowled as she glided down toward him. "Where's an iron bridle when you need one," she muttered, and clambered on the back of the beast's neck. His mane felt like a pile of wriggling worms, but she didn't have much time to dwell on that.

The kelpie dove.

CARMER'S FIRST THOUGHT, when he could see again, was that he was back in the Blythes' junkyard. He was in a damp, muddy place, surrounded by . . . well, junk. An ornate wooden ship's wheel took up the majority of one wall, half of its spokes broken off. A collection of compasses on their chains, their needles going haywire, hung off it like necklaces on a jewelry stand. There were nonaquatic souvenirs as well; a Remington typewriter with a handful of keys missing and little cushions covering the others, as if they were bar stools for thumb-sized patrons; a phonograph with a cluster of black-streaked orchids exploding out of the horn; portraits of serious-faced people in ornate frames leaning up against one another like houses of cards; *actual* houses of cards, so moldy and yellowing their faces and numbers were indistinct; even a mismatched collection of silverware in a velvet display case spattered with mysterious stains. Everywhere he looked, there was just more . . . *stuff.*

Under the dim light that came from—rather impossibly—a cluster of glowworms on the high, greenish ceiling, Carmer also saw an object he would have recognized anywhere, draped over the side of a seashell-framed mirror: the Mechanist's cloak.

Hundreds, if not thousands, of faerie wings had been meticulously sewn onto the silk to make one continuous, rainbow-hued sheet of fabric. The Mechanist had killed or captured scores of faeries to experiment on before he finally discovered the "perfect" method of channeling faerie magic for his own purposes. Those faeries had become nothing but a wearable collection of trophies.

Not for the first time, Carmer wondered what part

Gideon Sharpe had played in the creation of that cloak. Had those long, pale fingers plucked the wings from dead faeries—or live ones like Yarlo—and sewed them together with impossibly tiny, expert stitches?

The most pressing question, though, was what the cloak was doing here—wherever *here* was. The last time Carmer had seen it was in the abandoned underground railroad tunnel where Gideon had lost his freedom and the Mechanist had lost his life.

"Do you like my collection?" asked a soft voice.

Carmer turned his head with some effort—his neck was unusually stiff—and saw a girl. She was sitting in a chipped teacup that had been turned on its side, her legs dangling over the edge. The cup was perched rather perilously on a stack of what must have been an entire tea service—all equally chipped flower-patterned cups and saucers and sugar dishes. The girl's dark purple hair flowed out of the cup like some kind of molten candy, hanging past her feet.

It occurred to Carmer, through the fog that was only just now clearing from his head, that girls did not normally fit inside teacups. It also occurred to him—the moment he tried to sit up to get a better look at her—that he was tied down flat on his back. A strained look downward showed his limbs were tied with what looked like seaweed to pointy, tooth-shaped pegs in the floor. For all he knew, they *were* real teeth.

"It's nothing grand, I know," said the girl. "But most ships know better than to come near here by now, and so many things are just too big. I can't exactly sneak a telephone through the front door . . ." She chuckled at her own joke, then amended, "Not that we have a front door, exactly."

When Carmer didn't respond, her pale face fell.

"You do know what a telephone is, don't you?" she asked, suddenly serious. "Or have I said it wrong again? Oh, goodness, that would be so embarrassing . . ."

It took a great deal of effort for Carmer to get his mouth working. "No, um, that's right," he said. "And yes, I know what a telephone is."

"You *do* talk!" exclaimed the girl, flitting down from her chipped china throne with ease. "I thought you might, but I couldn't be sure." The wings protruding from her back were nearly translucent. She wasn't just a girl; she was a faerie.

Which meant Carmer was in the Unseelie palace.

"You'll have to tell me all about telephones," said the faerie, crouching down near Carmer's head. "And then, I'd like to know about *you*."

Her purplish lips spread into a thin smile.

"But how rude of me," she said, tucking a strand of hair behind her pointed ear. "Badgering you about telephones and asking all sorts of personal questions when I haven't even introduced myself."

She smiled and reached out a hand, edging her fingernail under one of the buttons on Carmer's jacket.

"I'm Princess Purslain Ashenstep, of the Unseelie Court," she said. "But you can call me Pru."

BELL DAISIMER HAD never been so happy to be a disappointment in his life.

At first, the young woman from the *Jasconius*—the Unseelie faerie princess, he knew now—barely let him out of her sight. She barely let him sleep. They would sit in the ruined dining room of the shipwreck—he at one end of an impossibly long table, surrounded by skeletons still in their dinner clothes, and she in the curved fixtures of the chandeliers up above—as she peppered him with an endless stream of questions. Why had he come back to Driff City? Had he told anyone about the day of the crash? Who was that fuzzy-headed little sprout of a faerie he was traveling with? Why was he working for "that buffoon," Julius Tinkerton? And most important—did he know the Roving Wonder Show's secret?

Bell told her about Carmer and Grit. He didn't feel great about it, but they weren't exactly *hiding* who they were or what they were doing in Driff City, and so he didn't see why he should, either—especially when Purslain threatened to constrict the jellyfish dome of his prison around him until he drowned.

But when they got around to the subject of the Wonder Show, Bell obviously knew much less than Pru had hoped.

He confessed he'd never even met the faeries on it—only Carmer and Grit had had that honor—and honestly, all he really wanted out of this whole thing was a new balloon and a fresh start, so could she please, *please* just let him go? *Please.*

The answer was always no, with a toss of her slick, silky hair.

"You should've run when you had the chance," she would say.

As their sessions together grew more infrequent, Bell began to wonder if he was losing his usefulness to her— and what was in store for him if that was the case. But Purslain no longer whispered threats while she twirled his hair around her fingers, and she didn't seem inclined to kill him just yet. Perhaps he had simply been cast aside once he no longer entertained her, like one of the sad, broken dolls in her collection of human things. The secret of the *Jasconius* could never get out if its only witness was trapped at the bottom of the ocean for the rest of eternity, after all, and it wasn't like his prison ship seemed destined for many other uses. For now, he was left alone and unharmed . . . mostly.

And now that she'd stopped trying to get inside his head, Bell began to think a little more clearly—or as clearly as he could in an underwater magical realm he was told made humans inherently loopy. He began to consider his escape.

But if Princess Purslain had lost interest in him, it only seemed to make the *other* inhabitants of the Unseelie kingdom even *more* interested. He would look out of the portholes to see hideous green, gilled faces staring back, or tangles of blue-black tentacles scuttling past. The Jenny Haniver guards—the few that were still stationed outside—had a time of it, poking their sharpened shell swords at the curious fae onlookers who got too close. A few of the mermaids, unfortunately, seemed to enjoy special privileges; they would braid their seaweed hair and wave with their sucker-covered fingers right up against the barrier, smiling with coy grins full of pointed, sharklike teeth. Bell began to avoid the deck and the windows; sitting with the stiffs in the dining room quickly became preferable. How could he even think about making a break for the surface with all of those fishy eyes constantly trained on him?

And then one day—night? How long had he been there?—the waters outside churned with so much activity that Bell was afraid the ship would tilt over. Everywhere he looked, schools of fish skeletons, chatting gaggles of water sprites, and writhing sea serpents were streaming past the ship. And though he knew the fae took pains to keep him in the dark—often literally—he could still make out the whispers that skipped from creature to creature like jumping salmon.

She is coming.

The other princess is coming.

"The other princess?" Bell wondered out loud. Did the Unseelie king have another—hopefully slightly less murderous—daughter?

Whoever this princess was, she was causing quite a stir. And Bell Daisimer had every intention of taking advantage of it.

16.

THE THRONE OF BONES

GRIT PADDED DOWN THE CORRIDOR TO THE throne room alone, though she wasn't naive enough to think she went unobserved. The glittering walls on either side were covered in a hodgepodge of crystals and sea-shells and blooming mushrooms, and—occasionally, if she turned around fast enough to catch them—wide, unblinking eyes.

No, the king knew she was here. And he was waiting for her.

The great stone and mother-of-pearl doors to the throne room opened of their own accord, looking far too much like tombstones for Grit's taste. Even in the magical "sideways-world" of Faerie, as Carmer called it, the infamous throne of the Unseelie king loomed large. It was as pale as the wall of crisscrossing, glittering cave formations behind it, but for quite a different reason. Some said the throne was made out of the bones of the king's enemies; others that it was the ruins of every shipwreck the Unseelie fae had ever caused, bleached white with salt and age. Some said it was merely pale coral. One of the wilder theories was that the throne was actually some kind of special iron alloy that the king exposed himself to on purpose, to build up a resistance and discourage any-one *else* who might have entertained ideas of sitting on the throne of King Roden Bonefisher.

But clearly, the last theory was wrong, because when Grit approached the throne, so tall she had to crane her neck to see the top, there *was* someone sitting in the Unseelie king's throne—and it was not the Unseelie king.

It was Mister Moon, the three-eyed leader of the Wild Hunt.

"Well, if it ain't the little princess of the freaks of Skemantis," Mister Moon said in his jarring cockney accent, leering down at her. He raised two out of three eyebrows at her mechanical wing. "And hoho, the title's more fittin' than before!"

"What are *you* doing here?" Grit asked. "Where's the Unseelie king?"

Mister Moon flicked a lit cigarette between his fingers, like Grit had seen Carmer and the Amazifier do with playing cards. How *any* fire could survive in this damp pit was a mystery to Grit.

"The king's more important matters to attend to than a trespassin' princess," sneered Mister Moon. "Oh yes, we *know* how long you been here. Without announcin' yourself, too. That's downright rude, if you ask me!"

Though she hadn't exactly been excited at the thought, Grit had been counting on the Unseelie king's presence. What sort of king let some lackey hold court for him—and even sit in his throne? Queen Ombrienne didn't have a throne, but Grit tried to picture her allowing someone to sit in it, if she did, and order about the other faeries while she swanned off somewhere else. It was so unthinkable Grit nearly laughed.

Grit had been counting on the king's obligation to give her an audience, one royal faerie to another. Mister Moon, though he *was* the leader of a major fae institution (if you could call a marauding band of criminal fae and spirits an "institution"), had no such obligation.

"Well, I'm here now," Grit said. "Ta-da." She spread her wings and bent one knee in a brief, mocking curtsy. "And I need to talk with the *king*. Not you. It's official court business."

"Is it?" asked Mister Moon with a tilt of his head, taking a drag from his cigarette. "'Cause here I thought you was about to sing us a little song about some filthy street fae scum."

The blood-soaked conductor's hat that marked him as a redcap oozed a fresh droplet onto his shoulder.

And somehow, the Free Folk are the filthy ones here, Grit thought.

"Did your friend Yarlo tell you that?" Grit asked. "I'm afraid he won't be able to feed you information anymore."

"Oh, I've got lots of friends," said Mister Moon. A chill crept into the room, followed by indistinct whispers and the squeaking of what sounded like turning wheels. "And *Friends.* You might even know some of them! Like, oh, what was that little snitch's name . . . Gideon Sharpe?"

Tittering, wheezing laughter cut through the whispers, and Grit forced herself not to flinch at the sound. She hoped, at least, that Carmer was having better luck than she was.

"I KNOW IT'S a strange habit for a faerie—especially an Unseelie princess—but I can't help but be fascinated by the contraptions humans make," Pru said, caressing a few of the items in her collection as she strolled around the room.

"Just think! They can't sing a tree taller, or summon a flame, or whisper to the wind so it takes them where they need to go. But somehow, those silly humans can do all of those things—and more. They can make buildings taller than any tree. They can strike a match and have a flame in their palm in an instant; they make the things that burn work for *them*, to power their machines. They can sail through the air in their ships farther than most faeries could ever hope to fly in one stretch."

Princess Pru's face loomed over Carmer, coming in and out of focus. He couldn't figure out exactly why his eyes—and his whole body, in fact—didn't seem to be working the way they should. Even the proportions of the room seemed off, somehow; the spoons in the velvet case much too big, but the doorways leading to who-knows-where much too short. He supposed it was one of the side effects of being in Faerie; all the magic made humans' brains fuzzy.

Pru's dark purple hair trailed to the floor, leaving a wet smear wherever she moved.

Her skin was so *white*, like paper soaked in water and left out to dry, thin and crinkled—except for her feet. Starting from the knees down, her skin gradually darkened to completely black, gnarled, and callused toes. She wore no shoes.

"Ashenstep," she'd said her name was. He could see why.

"Humans have used their gifts well," she said, pausing a moment to run her fingers along Carmer's arm. "And they've conquered us because of it. Oh, don't look as if I've shocked you, like the faeries at court always do. They *have*.

Why else would we hide here, in the depths of the sea, the only place the humans haven't managed to extend their reach? Why else would we stop demanding their tithes, or luring them to our revels, or making them our sweethearts, if they were young and beautiful enough? Because we're *scared*. Because they've got the upper hand, and have for over a hundred years. Every day their power grows, and ours diminishes."

She stood up, suddenly agitated, and strode away from him; small clusters of lichen sprang up in her wake where the soles of her blackened feet touched the floor.

That explains the mushrooms, Carmer thought.

Pru whipped around to face him. "Is it so amazing, then, that I should want to know more about my enemy?" she asked. "I don't think so. How could I possibly hope to understand them if I shuddered at the mere mention of cold iron? How could I possibly hope to *defeat* them?"

She took a deep breath, as if trying to calm herself, and smiled at Carmer. "Now you . . . you just might be the most priceless addition to my collection I've ever encountered."

Carmer's breath hitched.

"What's the matter?" she asked, eyes wide and innocent, as if the idea that she might vivisect Carmer in her chamber of decaying artifacts wasn't distressing in the least. "Is it the cloak that frightens you?" She turned to the Mechanist's former garment. She seemed quite concerned for Carmer's welfare, for someone who had him staked to her floor. "It's amazing, isn't it? It was a gift from Father. Look!"

Pru scampered over to the cloak, which took up a large portion of the room. The moment she grabbed on to the edge, however, the entire cloak shuddered and shimmered, the multicolored reflections of the wings blurring in Carmer's already unsteady vision. He blinked once as Pru lifted the cloak with a flourish, and it was suddenly half the size. It floated down around her shoulders, a macabre mantle.

He blinked again, and she was gone.

A giggle emanated from the empty space where she'd been standing just seconds before. A moment later, another titter echoed from somewhere near Carmer's head. He looked frantically around, straining against his bonds, glimpsing only the slightest jumping shadows. A link of chains—*iron* chains, Carmer noted—snaked their way across the floor. The typewriter keys clacked up and down, seemingly of their own accord, spelling out nothing but gibberish.

Something nudged him in the side and he flinched. Ten tiny black toes appeared out of nowhere, wriggling right next to his ribs.

"Boo!" There was a *swish* of rainbow fabric and black silk, and Pru came out from under the cloak beside him.

"Isn't it wonderful?" she asked, clearly delighted to be able to show off for someone. "Father reclaimed it from the corpse of one of our enemies, as was his right. Why should such an artifact go unused, left to molder with the dead human's flesh, when so many faeries died to make it whole?"

Or didn't die at all, and might want their wings back, Carmer thought.

"Father imbued it with new power," explained Pru, stroking individual wings in the cloak affectionately, as if she, too, remembered who they belonged to. "And now it serves a higher purpose: me."

Carmer's mind raced. If the Mechanist's cloak had been given more magical properties by the Unseelie king—if it could make its wearer invisible, and even protect a faerie from iron—then suddenly, the idea of a faerie princess sneaking onto an airship and destroying an entire engine car seemed much more feasible.

And so did the idea of the same faerie princess capturing an innocent cabin boy and manipulating his memories.

"*Bell*," Carmer breathed.

Pru's head snapped up, quick as a snake. "What did you say?"

"Bell Daisimer," Carmer said with more confidence than he felt. He tried to imagine how fierce and no-nonsense Grit sounded whenever she confronted an enemy (and sometimes, unfortunately, a friend).

"Where is he?" Carmer demanded.

Pru hung her head until the dark curtain of her hair fell

forward, obscuring her pale face. "That was rather rude, you know."

Somewhere, the soft *drip, drip, drip* of water echoed.

"We barely know each other, and I've done all I can to keep you comfortable here, even though I bet you're a sneak and don't *really* know what a telephone is, and I've shown you my collection and my favorite present and yet you DARE TO MAKE DEMANDS OF ME?"

Pru did not yell so much as her voice seemed to come out of every corner of the room; it blared out of the phonograph horn and echoed from the conch shells framing her mirror. Even the mouths of the serious faces in her stolen pictures opened and closed along with her words.

"I . . . I didn't—" Carmer stammered. The ground started to sink under him, forming a shallow basin. The seaweed around his limbs tightened and flipped him over onto his face before he could even cry out. He struggled against his bonds, but they might as well have been ropes inches thick.

"It's my turn to ask the questions," said Pru as water began to bubble up out of the ground, soaking Carmer through, running into his nose and tickling his lips like a cold, unwanted kiss.

"GIDEON SHARPE IS of no concern to me," said Grit flippantly. She hoped it was flippant enough. "I'm here to discuss another prisoner you've taken. His name is Bell—"

"That boy of yours sure seems concerned," interrupted Mister Moon. "Wailin' into his sheets at night. 'Gideon! Oh, Gideon! Stop, you're hurting him!'" Mister Moon held a fluttering hand to his forehead.

Grit's first instinct was to launch herself at that stupid throne, cursed bones of the king's enemies or not, but she held herself back. If Mister Moon knew Carmer was having nightmares, it meant he'd been spying on them. And though she'd hoped to bargain civilly with the king for Bell's release, the uncomfortable truth was that humans had little protection under faerie law—and Mister Moon would probably sooner bargain with a Seelie unicorn shooting sunbeams out of its eyes than with her. She'd have to come at this from a better angle.

"Sharpe is paying for his crimes," Grit said flatly. "He acted against his court, and you judged him for it. But you know who you *don't* have the right to judge and torture however you want?"

"I'm gettin' an idea," drawled Mister Moon.

"The so-called filthy street fae scum," spat Grit. "The Wonder Show faeries aren't under your power."

"Not yet."

"Not *anymore*. They've forsworn their courts. They haven't broken any laws."

"They've shared their magic with *humans*," sneered Mister Moon.

"So have I!" countered Grit, throwing up her hands. "And it just so happened to help stop a *raving lunatic* from enslaving us all. Want to lock me up for that as well?"

Mister Moon shrugged and whistled through his teeth— the shrieking whistle of the Wild Hunt's train, so loud Grit had to cover her ears.

Well, so that was his opinion on the matter.

"You're forgetting something else, redcap," Grit said. "No one's *noticed* the Wonder Show faeries' magic. No one was panicking in the streets or crying about the end of days and burning Friends as witches. No one was felling forests—"

"No more than usual—"

"No one was noticing anything, and no one was getting hurt, until *you* started bringing down Tinka's ships!"

Mister Moon straightened in his seat on the throne, his black-nailed fingers gripping the armrests.

"Before you start swingin' 'round accusations you know nuffin' about," he said, swinging his own long legs to the floor with a squelching stomp, "you might want to take a second and *remember where you come from*, Princess."

"I don't see what that has to do with—"

"Oy, and that's the problem right there, innit?" Mister Moon slapped his bony knee. "You're the heir to a Seelie *throne*. The future keeper of an entire kingdom. You come from a line of fae that once brought humans to their *knees* in fear and awe of us. And now, you're wastin' your breath on the same fae that would rather sing for their supper from the Big Folk than honor the old ways, who'd forsake their court and kin and stretch thin what power we have left. So I suggest you shut that pretty little trap o' yours until you *remember where your loyalties lie.*"

His words hit Grit like a slap in the face. But what did Mister Moon know about her anyway? She was loyal to her kingdom, wasn't she? She'd nearly sacrificed herself to protect them! She was loyal to Carmer, who'd cemented his own allegiances when he became a Friend of the Fae. What did it matter if she wasn't exactly ready to blindly follow a few rules so old and musty they practically had mothballs?

What did it matter if this wasn't the life she would have chosen, if she'd had the chance, as long as she did her best? She *was* doing her best.

. . . Wasn't she?

"The courts have ruled Faerie since before your grandmother sang her first forest, and probably before *her* grandmother, too," said Mister Moon, easing back a little in the throne. "Seelie and Unseelie: two sides of the same coin, as those humans you're so fond of say." He flicked his cigarette butt away; it spun artfully end over end to the slimy floor. "Ain't no such thing as a third side of a coin."

Grit bit her lip. "Coins have edges, though," she said. "Don't they?"

The Free Folk certainly lived on the edge of faerie

society. The edge of a coin was the in-between, the impartial and seemingly insubstantial line that somehow still balanced the whole thing as it spun.

And boy, was this coin spinning.

"The thing about edges . . ." mused Mister Moon, tapping his long fingers on the arms of the throne. "I'm no engineer, like our Friend Mr. Carmer . . . but they have to stay pretty small, don't they? We can't have edges runnin' 'round, growing as big and powerful as they please. That'd change the shape of the whole thing."

He smiled, revealing a mouthful of teeth filed into deadly points and a forked tongue. "Someone's gotta smooth out the rough edges. Don'tcha think?"

CONTRARY TO WHAT a good many people in his life might've thought, Bell wasn't an idiot. He was an aeronaut and an adventurer and, okay, a bit of a thrill-seeker. He'd never shied away from a good time. But even if he occasionally flirted with the fine line between "a little bit reckless" and "just plain stupid," he prided himself on at least knowing the *difference*.

And that made it a lot harder to resist the urge to take advantage of all the hubbub this "other princess's" arrival was causing, grab whatever sharp implement he could get his hands on inside the shipwreck, climb to the top of the deck, and start hacking his way through meters-thick magical jellyfish gut. How would he outswim his guards all the way to the surface? How could he be sure he was close enough to swim to shore, even if he did? No. *That* escape attempt would have firmly fallen into the stupid category.

But that didn't mean he had to sit there and do nothing. Judging by the chatter in the usually silent waves, these monsters were in the mood for gossip. And Bell was ready to be an all-too-willing listener.

He stayed away from the guards on the foredeck and retreated farther into the ship, to the captain's quarters—a space he'd claimed for himself. (If he had to be imprisoned on a sunken ship, Bell figured, he might as well do it in style.) He knew the fae, especially Pru's mermaid friends, liked to watch him sleep through the window. Usually, he found this incredibly creepy, but today . . . well, today, Bell was about to find out if his most charming smile had cross-species appeal.

Sure enough, it wasn't long before he spotted three familiar-looking mermaids swimming the same way as the rest. *Toward the castle?* he wondered. Surely, that would be where a visiting princess would be headed. Bell waited for them to pass by. He took a deep breath, tried not to be too worried it might be his last, and rapped on the window.

The mermaids' heads swiveled around as one, just a *little* too disconnected from their bodies for Bell's comfort. Bell took in their mottled gray-green skin and seaweed hair filled with squirming parasites and held back a shudder.

"Hello, ladies," he said with a little wave.

The middle one regarded him sourly.

"My apologies," Bell corrected. "Ladies and *gentleman*."

A rocky start, to be sure. But the night was young—or the day, possibly. It was kind of hard to tell down there.

17.

DON'T DROWN
THE MESSENGER

NAN TUCKET WAS STANDING OUTSIDE THE DOOR-
way of the Moto-Manse when she heard a crash.

It was a different crash from the belly-rumbling *gong*
that echoed when she rang the doorbell, of that she was
fairly certain. Which meant that someone was most likely
home, and that she was standing out in the cold for no
good reason.

She blew on her hands, which were cold even through
her gloves, and rapped on the door.

"Hey!" she said. "Felix Cassius Tiberi-something . . . oh,
darn it, I forget. Carmer! It's Nan, from Rinka Tinka's Roving
Wonder Show! Can I come in, please?"

Because my toes are about to fall off? she thought.

There was another sound, like something shuffling along the floor. He probably had a cat or something that was scampering about in there, warm and dry, while here *she'd* been instructed to wait until she could deliver her message in person.

Thud.

Now *that* would have been a very big cat. Nan pressed her ear to the door.

"Carmer?"

She heard more indistinct sounds of movement and looked up; the sound was coming out of an open second-floor window of the moto-mansion.

"Is everything all right up there?" Nan called to the window.

There was no response.

Something was wrong, Nan knew it. It was like being in the air and realizing that her balance was off—that split second when she *felt* the whole thing going south before her mind fully realized it. That split second between adjusting your footing, if you could, or falling.

Nan wasn't an acrobat and a wire walker for nothing. She wedged a foot onto the doorknob, accidentally tapping the ridiculous doorbell—the resulting *booooooiiiinng* sent the whole house shaking again—and vaulted up, grabbing the top of the door casing. Another push and she cleared the door entirely, pulling herself up into the open window.

Really, she thought as she hoisted herself up, *people ought to be more careful. It's lucky I haven't decided to use my talents as a cat burglar.*

All other thoughts were swept away, however, as she entered the sleeping compartment of the moto-mansion. The boy called Carmer lay on the floor, a broken lamp—which must have been the cause of the crash—next to him. His eyes were closed and his limbs thrashed about wildly. Horrible gurgling, gasping sounds came from his throat.

"Carmer!" Nan jumped down from the window and onto the floor. There was barely enough room for the both of them in the narrow hall; two bunk beds and another sleeping berth took up most of the space on either side.

Nan hovered over the boy, unsure of what to do. Was he having a seizure? She didn't even know what a seizure looked like, but she'd heard about people having fits. Was she supposed to protect his head, or turn him on his side? She had no idea.

She grabbed him by his shoulders and shook him, hard.

"Carmer, wake up!"

He opened his eyes, but Nan could tell he was most definitely *not* awake. His eyes were glowing *gold*, the lids covered in a shimmering powder that Nan was wise enough not to touch.

Nan had seen gold dust like that once or twice before, on the Roving Wonder Show, and she had an inkling it meant Carmer wasn't dealing with any normal affliction. No one ever *said* the word "magic," of course, for fear of being laughed right out of the sky, but there was no dismissing the favorable winds that came out of nowhere to push their caravan along when they were running behind, or the doors that opened and closed by themselves, or the cheery music that sometimes echoed through the camp at night when no one was awake to play it.

But something much darker was afoot here, Nan was certain. Carmer's skin was flushing from bright red to practically purple, to deathly pale and back again. He couldn't *breathe*, she realized. Every few moments, in between the horrible gurgling sounds, his chest would heave in a great gasp, like a drowning man breaking his head above the water, only to be sucked back down again. A large bowl of water next to the bed had been overturned in his struggles. Rivulets of it ran across the wooden floor, getting both of them wet. It looked like it came straight from the pond; bits of dirt and plant life still clung to the inside of the bowl.

"What do I do, what do I do?" she asked. She had been told Carmer might be in trouble, but she hadn't expected this *kind* of trouble.

"Grab some iron, girl, and quick!" said the floor.

Nan jumped so high her head nearly hit the ceiling.

"What's the matter, never seen an old lady before?" groused the rough voice again.

Nan grabbed for Carmer's kicking legs, trying to still them, and peered down cautiously at the pooling water on the floor. She could just make out the reflection of a weathered face, blinking in and out of view.

"The fire poker will have to do," muttered the old woman's reflection. "Now go, make sure it's good and hot, and wake him up before the poor boy drowns!"

The water trickled along the slope of the floor, spreading out until it was too thin to make out the old woman's face. Nan looked around desperately, found the stairs, and jumped the whole way down into the kitchen. The fire was nearly burned down to embers, but she pushed in the poker as deep into the heat as she could. The precious seconds waiting for it to heat up seemed interminable; she strained her ears for sounds of continued life from the boy upstairs.

When she could take it no longer, Nan ran back up to the second floor. Carmer was alarmingly still.

"Sorry about this!" Nan apologized to his prone form, and pressed the end of the hot poker into his palm.

With a great gasp, Carmer sat up like a shot.

"Water . . ." he said faintly, coughing and sputtering.

"Haven't you had enough of that?!" Nan exclaimed.

Carmer shook his head and motioned for the bowl.

Nan handed it to him with shaking hands. There was only a little bit left in the bottom of the bowl, but Carmer proceeded to splash it directly onto his face.

It made him cough even harder, but it also cleared the shimmering powder from his eyes. He let the bowl drop with a clang and sagged against the bed frame.

They sat in silence for a few moments. Nan felt just as exhausted as Carmer looked, though *she* hadn't been the one mysteriously drowning on air only moments before.

"Thank you," Carmer said finally. "I can't believe I forgot . . ." He trailed off and stared at Nan, seeming to realize for the first time who he was talking to. "How did you find me?"

Nan was sure *How did you get in here?* would follow close behind.

"I was warned you might be in trouble," Nan said. "So I came to check on you. It's a good thing she got your letter in time."

If it was at all possible, Carmer looked even more gobsmacked than before.

"*She?*"

A DISEMBODIED HAND met Grit on her way out of the throne room. It was Lieutenant Axel Hudspeth's.

Oh, no, she thought. *No no no no no . . .*

A few steps down the hall revealed a small leather boot . . . and then a leg. Grit sped up, following the scattered body parts of the automaton—another hand, a model bayonet, a foot, a shiny brass button from his coat—like a trail of gruesome bread crumbs through the maze of the Unseelie court's halls. The shiny, dripping walls pressed in on her from all sides as she broke out into a run, calling Carmer's name.

She nearly tripped over his head.

The painted eyes stared up at her, unseeing. The face was wet and dirty and chipped at the chin.

A subtle movement in the air caught Grit's attention, distracting her from her panic.

Princess Purslain Ashenstep appeared, wearing—of all things—the Mechanist's cloak around her bony shoulders.

Grit had never met the Unseelie princess—she imagined both of them were discouraged from straying too far from their palaces—but she'd heard a few stories. Fewer of *them* were good.

"I like your Friend," Purslain said in a singsong voice, turning side to side so that the light from the glowworms bounced off the wings in her cloak. "I think I'll keep him."

Grit lunged.

Purslain disappeared, stepping back into nothingness. A laugh echoed in the hall; she reappeared *behind* Grit and waggled her finger.

"Be careful, Grit," said Purslain, pulling down the hood of the cloak. "Some people might think you were about to *strike* me just then. But that's ridiculous, isn't it? Because any direct attack on me, or one of my subjects—especially in my own *house*—would be grounds for war between our courts, wouldn't it?"

Grit seethed. Purslain was right. Grit would have to be insane to attack the Unseelie princess here. Unfortunately, with bits of her best friend scattered all over the floor, she was feeling a little less than sane.

"What have you done to him?" Grit demanded.

"It's clear where that boy is learning his manners from, that's for sure." Purslain sighed. "I assume you mean that *rude* Friend of yours, who had the gall to try and sneak around *my* castle without even wearing his real face. It's impolite not to tell your hostess you're bringing a *plus one*, you know."

Grit clenched her fists so hard that a few of the glow-worms on the ceiling exploded in puffs of spark and smoke, snuffed out like candles. Their charred little bodies fell to the floor and disintegrated into piles of ash.

Purslain swept her hair over them; they disappeared in wet smears.

"I won't hold that one against you," Pru said diplomatically. "When I was as young as you, I had trouble controlling my powers, too. A few more decades of practice should do it." She wiggled her blackened toes.

"I'm not going to ask again," said Grit. "*Where. Is. Carmer.*"

Purslain twirled around in her grisly cloak. "Oh,

everyone's wrong about you, you know. You're no fun at *all*, and neither is your silly Friend. He absolutely *refused* to tell me anything about why you were nosing around my kingdom—as if I didn't already know!—or how he managed such an interesting trick with that puppet of his—"

"It's an automaton," Grit corrected automatically.

Purslain's lips twitched. "You even said it right. *Automaton.* See, under different circumstances, I think we'd get along famously!"

A few more glowworms were zapped out of existence.

"Oh, all right, all right," said Purslain. "Your boy remembered where his real body was . . . eventually. Which is a shame, because we'd just started having fun."

Grit didn't want to know what Purslain's idea of "fun" was.

"I came here to talk to your father," Grit said, forcing down her panic. If Carmer had remembered to leave the puppet, he was alive and safe back at the Moto-Manse . . . probably.

But these were not the words Princess Purslain wanted to hear, apparently, because her teasing expression immediately soured.

"It's about a human he's taken captive, and Rinka Tinka's Roving Wonder Show," Grit said, pressing on. "He needs to leave the Free Faeries alone. They haven't done anything wrong. They—"

"You know what?" Purslain interrupted. "I think I've

had enough of the both of you for one night, our appreciation for *machinery* aside." She wrinkled her nose at Grit's mechanical wing.

"Wait, Princess Purslain—"

"I'll give you and your street fae until the New Year to step aside and hand over Rinka Tinkerton," Purslain said, hands on her hips. "That girl belongs to *me*. She can take the next week to say her good-byes. But keep her after midnight and you can say good-bye to your pilot *and* the entire Wonder Show. Consider it a courtesy, one princess to another."

That girl? Grit wondered, trying to keep the surprise from showing on her face. What girl? Rinka Tinka was just Julius Tinkerton's stage name. Carmer had been certain of that. And if *his* name was Julius . . .

And then it hit her. Rinka Tinka's Roving Wonder Show.

Rinka Tinka had never referred to just one person. It was two—Tinkerton and his "silent partner," just as she and Carmer had suspected. And for some reason, Princess Purslain of the Unseelie Court wanted the other one.

"I heard you're a good swimmer," said Purslain, pulling up the hood of the Mechanist's cloak.

Grit would have to find out how she'd gotten her hands on *that*, and how it seemed to change size for the wearer.

"Let's find out, shall we? Consider your invitation to the Unseelie realm *revoked*." With a stomp of Purslain's foot, Grit was thrust out of Faerie, and everything changed. Black water rushed in from all sides, and Grit had just enough time to take in one last gulp of air before she found herself outside the palace, submerged deep under the docks. Where there had once been a hallway, there was now only murky ocean and a maze of rotting wood.

Grit turned her light on, taking her chances with the murderous mermaid guards, and kicked fiercely in what she hoped was an upward direction. She *was* a good swimmer, this was true, but she could barely see under the water, and the mechanical wing weighed her down, pulling her back toward the shipwrecks and drowned skeletons littering the ocean floor.

When Grit finally heaved herself onto the shoreline, muscles shuddering with exhaustion and gasping for air, she lay back in the rocky sand and let a single, reluctant sob escape her throat.

Carmer was okay. She was okay. Rinka—whoever she was—was okay. For now.

But it was going to be a long flight back to the Moto-Manse.

CARMER HAD JUST finished mopping up the contents of his scrying bowl and building up the fire in the stove downstairs when Grit flew in through the kitchen window, careening off the walls.

Carmer grabbed her straight out of the air; she collapsed in his palms, icicles and bits of frozen seaweed clinging to her hair. She hadn't even taken the time to dry herself—or she simply hadn't had the energy.

"It's all right," Carmer said. "You're all right." He opened the stove door and deposited her straight onto the burning coals. She sank all the way into them, soaking up their heat. He waited until she surfaced, her face soot-blackened but looking a little calmer, before he spoke.

"I assume your visit to the Unseelie Court went about as well as mine did?" He held up a bandaged palm.

Grit closed her eyes, took a deep breath, and nodded. "Probably," she said, and relayed to him her encounter with Mister Moon.

Carmer had to sit down at the mention of the conductor of the Wild Hunt on the Unseelie Throne, and hoped Grit didn't notice.

He ran a hand through his hair and explained his own capture by Pru.

"Only *I* could forget I wasn't in my own body," he said, sighing.

"Madame Euphemia did warn us," allowed Grit, scooting to the edge of the stove and hanging her feet over the side. "But you must have remembered eventually. How else would you have gotten out?"

Carmer looked down at his feet. "There's something

you should know," he said. "I . . . I fixed the messenger glider and reached out to the real designer behind the Wonder Show, in a letter I pretended was from the Blythes. I knew it would probably get into the right hands."

The flames in the stove shot up to the roof. Carmer scooted back.

"You *what?*" Grit exclaimed.

Carmer held up his hands. "Just wait," he said. "And fortunately for me, she sent help just in time." He fished in his pockets for the note that had come with Nan. His burned hand throbbed with every movement of his fingers.

"I cannot *believe*—" Grit stopped and took a deep breath; steam rushed out of her nostrils as she exhaled. "The faeries trusted you to protect our secrets. *I* trusted you. You took a *vow*, Carmer."

Mister Moon's threats echoed in her head. *Remember where your loyalties lie.*

"Well, so did you," Carmer snapped, "and that didn't stop you from dragging Bell into all of this."

Grit's face went pale beneath the soot.

Carmer took a shaky breath. "I'm sorry," he said. "I didn't mean it like that. If anyone's to blame for Bell . . . I only meant that you weighed the risks of breaking your secrecy and revealing your magic when someone needed your help, and you made the decision you thought was best. Well . . . so did I."

Grit nodded; Carmer looked away as she wiped a stray tear from her face. She sniffed and pointed to the piece of paper in his hand.

"What is that?"

Carmer unfurled the note and held it up to the firelight. It read:

I have captured a small cowboy. Please come at once.
—Rinka

18.

THE CROOKED CASTLE

THE OTHER PRINCESS, THEY'D SAID. THE SEELIE queen's daughter. The one with the iron wing.

"The iron wing?" Bell had asked, his heart skipping a beat in his chest before his mind even made the connection.

Human-made, the merman clarified, scrunching up the snakelike slits in his face where his nose should have been.

"Ah," said Bell, looking politely interested. "That's certainly . . . unusual." Bell hadn't met many faeries, but the mermaids seemed to agree.

It was only after the last of their tails had flicked completely out of sight that he let himself say her name.

"Grit," he whispered, staring out into the inky blackness

beyond his jellyfish prison. Bell had never wanted to be right about something so badly in his life. "Come and get me, little lady." Grit was the princess. She had to be. Grit knew he was here, and she was coming for him. Bell Daisimer would see the sky again. He was sure of it.

He had to be.

She is coming.

THE CROOKED CASTLE was now docked with the rest of the Wonder Show camp. It was lit up when they arrived, despite the late hour. Nan met Carmer at a rear hatchway and hurried him up and inside before anyone could see him.

"You're not coming?" Carmer asked her, leaning out of the ship.

Nan shook her head. "More than one person at a time is a bit . . . much, for her."

Carmer had no idea what to make of that.

"And I'm thinking the less I know about all this foolishness, the better," she said. "Now go in and don't speak too loudly . . . and don't make any sudden movements, and don't stare right into her eyes, she hates that—"

"Is this a girl or a tiger?" Carmer asked.

Nan shooed him on and scampered off into the darkness.

"I've got a smoke bomb up here with me, just in case," said Grit under Carmer's hat.

"Are you *insane?*" Carmer hissed. The smoke bombs from their magic act weren't exactly the most dependable distractions *or* weapons, even enhanced with faerie magic, and bringing one onto an *airship* . . .

"You'll thank me if it's a tiger," said Grit, though Carmer felt her tuck the small cylinder away onto the balcony he'd just rebuilt inside his hat.

He cleared the last few steps into Rinka's airship.

It was one long, narrow room, with loft space built into the ceiling. Paper-covered lanterns hung every few feet from a ceiling covered by a large, light-colored wooden sculpture; it was intertwining tree branches, Carmer realized, each piece intricately carved and sanded to a pine-colored sheen, as if they'd been chopped off the real thing and stripped of their bark that very morning.

All sorts of objects hung from the branches along with the lanterns: colored strips of fabric, glass terrariums full of exotic plants, model airships, and most of all—drawings. The sheets of paper hung everywhere. There were sketches of fantastical beasts, and elements of the Wonder Show—Carmer spotted a diagram of the *Whale of Tales* hanging near a potted spider plant—as well as more practical designs. Most of them, Carmer saw, were of winged things—gliders and balloons and even the airplanes that Tinkerton had been so desperate to keep secret.

Carmer took a tentative step forward, carefully brushing aside the drawing in front of him.

"Hello?"

There was no reply, but it seemed to him the fabric ribbons in the air shifted, just a little.

"Rinka, my name is Carmer. I, um, I'm here with my friend Grit, to . . . well, as you may have read in my letter . . ." He trailed off. Carmer wasn't used to dealing with someone even shier than he was.

Grit snorted and scooted out from underneath his hat. "Oh, for fae's sake," she grumbled, and called to the other end of the ship. "Do you have the wingless cowboy faerie or not?"

Carmer sighed.

Another rustle, this time farther away.

"You've really got to work on the soft sell, Grit," Carmer muttered.

"If I left the two of you weirdos to sort this out, we'd be here till next Tuesday."

Carmer shushed her and took another step into the hanging maze. Grit fluttered along next to his shoulder, using her hatpin to bat away ribbons and papers with a little too much enthusiasm.

"Are these your designs?" Carmer asked the still-hidden Rinka, taking a closer look at a rough sketch of an ornithopter. It reminded him of Bell, so excited in his pilot's suit. Carmer had to look away. "They're amazing."

"Th-thank you," said a soft voice, so quiet it was almost inaudible.

Carmer looked at the drawing, pointedly avoiding the direction he thought the voice came from. "You're the real architect of the Wonder Show, aren't you, Rinka?"

There was another stretch of silence, and Carmer was afraid he'd spoken too rashly too fast.

"I . . . I help my father with his work," corrected Rinka.

"If by 'help' she means 'lets him steal her ideas,'" Grit whispered into Carmer's ear.

"Could you tell us more about the Wonder Show?" Carmer asked Rinka. "We need to know more if we're going to help you . . . and the faeries."

Grit glared at him, but there was nothing to be done. He'd already written about them in his letter.

"They haven't done anything wrong!" Rinka said, louder this time. "They've only been . . . helping me. They've always been with me. Ever since I was a little girl."

There was a flash of movement from the other end of the ship; the swaying of a skirt, perhaps, but it was hard to tell.

"All of them?" Grit piped up.

". . . No," Rinka said. "Not all of them. A-and especially not *him*."

There was a sound like a fishing line being reeled in, and an object was lowered from the ceiling, coming to a stop to hang right in front of Carmer and Grit.

It was a glass jar. And Yarlo was in it.

"This here is cruel and unusual punishment, this is!"

Yarlo's voice was hard to make out through the glass, but his fury was not. The vines sprouting from his wrists pushed fruitlessly at the top of the jar, trying to find any small opening to widen, but except for a few tiny airholes, Rinka had reinforced the lid. He wasn't going anywhere.

"I suspected something was wrong with my little friends . . . with the *faeries*, you called them, months ago." Rinka spoke more confidently now, though she still hadn't shown her face. "And then, when I caught him running away . . ."

Carmer wondered what to make of a girl who couldn't stand the thought of looking someone in the eye but had also somehow managed to lure and capture a powerful earth faerie with her bare hands.

"What has he told you?" Carmer asked warily.

"Oh, just that the Unseelies'll be comin' to break up your merry band of misfits any day now," said Yarlo with a poorly aimed kick at his glass prison.

"So jack *squat*, basically," said Grit. She glared at Yarlo. "I should've told the others the second I sensed something off about you, Unseelie."

"And why didn't ya, then?" Yarlo asked.

"Maybe because I felt *sorry* for you," Grit shot back. "Maybe I thought you had your reasons. I don't know. But whatever reason you have, I hope it's a good one, because I assume you know that your own princess is *wearing your wings as a coat*."

Yarlo stopped struggling against the jar.

"Oh, you didn't know?" asked Grit acidly. "*She* has the Mechanist's cloak of faerie wings now. The king enchanted it to grant its wearer invisibility—among other tricks we haven't had the pleasure of seeing yet, I'm sure. It's how she's been sneaking onto all the airships."

"A *faerie's* been behind the attacks?" asked Rinka, her already soft voice cracking a little.

The hanging diagrams ahead swayed, as if someone was pushing through them. Carmer caught another glimpse of a bare brown foot, the edge of a skirt, and a hand pushing a lantern to the side.

Yarlo was still staring at Grit, his eyes hard, as if he couldn't quite believe what he was hearing.

"And she's not going to stop until she's broken up the Wonder Show," insisted Grit. "And until she has—"

"Then the faeries here need to run," interrupted Rinka, voice panicked. "They need to leave, before—"

"We're not going anywhere," said a determined little voice, and Beamsprout appeared from out of one of the lantern shades.

Rinka gasped, and Carmer was willing to bet this was the first time she was actually *seeing* some of the faeries on her ship, even if they'd been lending her their magic for a while.

"We're gonna stand up to those Unseelies and FIGHT," said Thundrumble, scooting over the edge of her lantern with a little difficulty. A few of the nearest hanging objects shook at her booming voice, and everyone cringed. "Well, if we absolutely have to," she added, looking glum at the prospect.

At that, a few of the other Free Folk came out of their lanterns as well—though it was just as likely they'd been scared out by Thundrumble as it was a show of solidarity.

"No one's fighting anyone," said Grit. "At least not yet. They've given us until the New Year. Which should be plenty of time for one of you to tell us why what they really want is *you*." Grit crossed her arms and glared in Rinka's general direction.

"Grit," Carmer warned.

"Next Tuesday . . ." Grit reminded him.

"Me?" asked Rinka.

Somewhere on the ship, a door opened.

"Rinka!" called Tinkerton. "What's going on in there?"

The faeries scattered at once, some hiding up in the sculpted tree branches while others made straight for the few windows cracked open to the chilly night air. The absence of their light left the ship in almost total darkness.

"Oh, for fae's sake!" said Grit, alighting on Carmer's shoulder. He scooped her up under his hat in what was becoming a smooth and practiced movement.

"Rinka?" Footsteps sounded at the front of the ship.

"H-hello, Father."

Carmer backed away, slowly and silently. The same reeling sound he'd heard earlier probably meant that Yarlo was being yanked up toward the ceiling.

"Why are we standing in the dark?" Tinkerton asked.

There was another sound, like a lever being pulled, and several real lights—Carmer could only guess which of Rinka's inventions powered *them*—sprang to life from the ceiling.

"It sounded like you were having a party in here." He chuckled at the likelihood of such an event.

Carmer took a few more steps back—and collided with a terrarium with a solid *clank*.

"What was that?" Tinkerton asked. "Who's there?"

"It's nothing, Father . . ."

Faster than Carmer imagined he could, Tinkerton strode across the airship, parted the curtain-like strings of fabric, and stood face-to-face with Carmer. A girl who must have been Rinka clutched feebly at his arm, trying to pull him back.

"You," Tinkerton said, staring wide-eyed at Carmer. "What are you doing here? Who gave you permission to enter this ship?"

"Sir, please, I never meant—"

"My daughter is ill, do you understand?" said Tinkerton. "This is a family matter, and my family is none of your concern."

"Father, it's all right," pleaded Rinka. She was older

than Carmer had expected—nearly Bell's age, sixteen or seventeen—with light brown skin and thick, waist-length dark hair that stuck out in all directions and, as Kitty Delphine might say, hadn't seen a brush in a good long while. She was frightfully thin, her arms as skinny as some of the smaller branches crisscrossing her ceiling, and her plain green dress hung loosely on her frame.

"I'm sorry, sir," Carmer apologized again. "But you asked me to look into the Wonder Show—"

"I never asked you to pry into my private—"

"And she's what I found." *Well, one of the things I found*, Carmer thought. But he was suddenly angry, seeing Tinkerton towering over his daughter like that. Maybe Grit had been right. Maybe Tinka *was* forcing his daughter to make his money for him. "How long, exactly, have you been claiming her ideas as your own?"

Grit gasped inside his hat—she clearly hadn't expected Carmer to speak to anyone like that—but Tinkerton didn't notice.

"You know *nothing* about me, or my daughter," said Tinka with a furious swipe of his hand. Carmer jumped back. "And you will *say* nothing, boy, or—"

"Father, stop!" said Rinka. "I . . . I *asked* Carmer to come here."

Tinka slowly turned around. "You what?"

Rinka looked as if she hadn't realized that making such a declaration would require any further explanation. She fiddled with one of her hanging ribbons, twirling it nervously around her finger.

"I asked him to come here," she said again. "I found out that he . . . he likes to make things, too. Like me."

Tinkerton's face softened so swiftly that Carmer was forced to reassess his snap evaluation of who was controlling who in this strange family dynamic.

"Rinka." Tinkerton sighed and took her thin hands; they were curiously knobbly, like an old woman's. "We've talked about this. You can't let just anyone into your life. They wouldn't understand you. They wouldn't be able to keep you *safe*."

Rinka seemed to fold in on herself then, as if she'd used up all her rebelliousness in two sentences. But Carmer had no time for backtracking.

"Mr. Tinkerton, I'm sorry I . . . disturbed the two of you," he said. "But . . . I found something else as well."

Rinka's head snapped up; she shook it silently behind her father's back. But Carmer had no choice.

"Mr. Tinkerton," said Carmer, "do you believe in faeries?"

19.

AN IMPOSSIBLE THING

IN THE MOMENT OF TENSE SILENCE THAT FOL-
lowed, Carmer half expected Tinkerton to laugh at him.

He didn't expect to be grabbed by the collar and
shoved against the wall so hard that several model planes
fell down from their perches and smashed to pieces on
the floor.

"Father!" cried Rinka.

"Why," snarled Tinkerton into Carmer's face, "would
you ask me such a ridiculous question?"

It seemed he'd struck a nerve.

Carmer was about to reply when his hat tossed itself off
his head. Or rather, a furious faerie *shoved* it off.

Grit hovered between Tinkerton and Carmer, a glowing smoke bomb held aloft.

"Lay a hand on my friend again," she warned. "And I will throw this in your stupid mustached face, hydrogen balloon or not."

Tinkerton jumped back, flailing into hanging diagrams and sending a paper lantern crashing to the floor.

"What . . ." Tinkerton blinked. "Is that . . ."

"Now, that really *was* threatening our ship," Yarlo noted from wherever his jar was hidden.

Tinkerton whipped around, searching for the voice, and then pointed a shaking hand at Carmer.

"Out," he said.

"Mr. Tinkerton," Carmer said, holding up his hands, though the glowing smoke bomb Grit held probably negated the peaceful gesture. He glared sideways at her. "Rinka is in danger. People have already died. *Your* people have already died—"

"OUT," repeated Tinkerton, spit flying from his mouth and sweat breaking out on his forehead. "We'll have no more part in this . . . this sorcery! This lunacy!" He dragged Rinka behind him once more.

"Rinka, please, you have to tell him—" Carmer pleaded, but Rinka was still fiercely shaking her head, not meeting Carmer's eyes. "We have to figure out why they want you—"

"OUT. NOW," roared Tinkerton. "Or I will call the police, I swear I will!"

Grit raised the smoke bomb higher, but Carmer shook his head.

"But—" Grit protested.

"Enough people have already gotten hurt," Carmer said, slowly backing out toward the exit hatch.

Grit huffed and followed suit, pausing only to stick out her tongue at Tinkerton.

"And that's why I hope you'll listen to what I have to say," Carmer continued as he dodged around the remaining ribbons and plants and models. "Because people will *keep* getting hurt if you ignore the Unseelie fae."

It was harder to see Rinka and Tinkerton through the hanging objects in the ship, but Carmer thought he saw Rinka start forward, just for a moment.

Carmer opened the hatch and started climbing backward down the stairs. Just before he hit the ground, he called up into the ship: "Did you forget about Mikhail Hunt?"

"The police, Mr. Carmer!" roared Tinkerton, but Carmer walked along the side of the ship to one of the windows, close enough so that Rinka would hear him.

"What are you doing?" Grit whispered to Carmer.

"He *was* one of your ornithopter pilots," Carmer called through the window. "But he was taken by the Unseelie fae. They kidnapped him and filled his head full of faerie knots and used him as a warning, and now he's dead."

Grit alighted on Carmer's shoulder and gave it a

squeeze. Someone—Carmer assumed it was Tinkerton—slammed the window shut.

"And now," Carmer said, practically shouting, but he couldn't keep his voice from breaking, "they've taken my friend Bell, your *new* pilot, because he was in the wrong place at the wrong time. How many more people have to die, Rinka?"

Carmer thought he knew Tinkerton well enough to bet on the man's stubbornness—and his greed. He would never admit to anything that might take Rinka—or the business she brought him—away. But Rinka . . . Carmer was counting on her to be better. He was counting on her to help them pick away at the truth. Only then could they hope to understand how they might all survive.

But there was no reply. Grit's glow and the fog of his breath in the cold night air were his only company. Carmer sniffed.

"It was worth a shot," Grit said softly.

Carmer turned to leave, boots crunching in the snow with every step away from the Crooked Castle. They'd done everything they could for the Free Folk. They'd solved the mystery—the parts of it that were theirs to solve. They'd have to find another way to get Bell back. If Rinka and her father weren't willing to meet them halfway, then what else could they do?

How could they save someone who didn't want to be saved?

"Wait!"

Carmer waited. Took a deep breath, and turned around.

Rinka ran toward him from the ship, her father close behind, skinny brown limbs flying, wearing nothing but her dress against the chill. She didn't even flinch when her bare feet hit the snow.

"Rinka, no!" cried Tinkerton.

But Rinka kept running—until she couldn't. Something was slowing her down, like someone had put stones in her shoes—if she'd been wearing any at all. It was almost like the ground was pulling at her, holding her back.

Carmer stepped toward her, and it took his brain a second to comprehend what he was seeing.

The ground *was* pulling her back. Roots sprouted from Rinka's toes and the backs of her ankles, and her legs took on the texture of brown tree bark. Smaller roots pushed themselves up from underneath the snow, trying to snag on to the shoots that came from her feet. She tried to shake them off, but every time she took a step, her legs became less girl, and more *tree*.

More fae.

Tinkerton finally caught up to her, and with one great yank from under her knees, managed to separate her feet from where they'd been planting themselves—*actually* planting themselves—into the ground. Rinka yelped in pain as her roots left the earth and reluctantly shrank back into her gnarled feet, as if parts of her had been left under the earth.

"I—I'm sorry," she said, panting slightly as she leaned into her father's chest. "That happens sometimes."

Carmer had a pretty good idea why the Unseelie fae were so interested in Rinka Tinkerton even before Grit said it, her eyes as wide as he'd ever seen them:

"You're a changeling."

RINKA'S FEET, STILL looking more like the limbs of a tree than the limbs of a human, dangled over the side of her loft bed. Tinkerton tucked a blanket over her lap to hide them from view, but there was no unseeing what they'd seen. For all that she looked like a normal human girl—or at least, *mostly* normal—she was something else entirely.

Carmer busied himself with tidying up one of the terrariums that had been knocked over, to give Rinka and her father a moment of privacy, but Grit was, as usual, in no mood to wait until "next Tuesday," as she put it, for answers. She perched on the top of one of the hanging lanterns near Rinka's bed.

"How long have you known?" Grit asked, but her question wasn't directed at Rinka; it was for Tinkerton.

The man sighed and ran a hand over his face, disrupting the perfect mold of his mustache so one side pointed up and the other down. No one bothered to tell him about it.

"If I'm being honest," he said, and Grit nearly snorted; it was clearly a first for him. "I had my suspicions since the very night it happened."

Tinkerton looked exhausted, as if he could barely stand up, and scanned the room halfheartedly for a chair. Rinka reached up somewhere by her head and yanked on one of her many levers with surprising strength. A bundle of branches swung out from the wall, wide enough to make a small bench, and Rinka plopped one of the pillows from her bed onto it. Tinkerton sank into the seat with a grateful nod.

"Rinka's mother," Tinkerton explained, "well, my . . . first daughter's mother, died just after she was born. But my daughter was . . . fine. She was . . ."

"A perfectly healthy baby?" Grit guessed.

Tinkerton nodded with an apologetic glance at Rinka, who pulled her blankets up to her chin and looked away.

"Until one night, there was a storm," Tinkerton said. "I was a traveling actor at the time—that's how I met my wife, in the theater—and my troupe had made camp en route to the next town. I'd never seen anything like it, and I hope never to again. The rain broke *through* our canvas tents. Trees were uprooted all around us; the horses ran off into the woods, and we never found them again. And in the morning . . . Rinka was sick."

"Except it wasn't really her," finished Grit. It was a rare thing, these days, for the fac to risk detection by swapping a human child with a sickly one of their own, but it wasn't unheard of. The existence of Gideon Sharpe, a human boy raised by the Unseelies, was proof enough of that. "It was an Unseelie faerie, born sick or powerless or otherwise *imperfect*"—she couldn't keep herself from spitting the word out—"glamoured and spelled to look human for the presumably short time until it died."

Carmer looked at her sharply, a warning glance to watch her tone, but Grit couldn't help it. She'd been a seedling, yes, but still old enough to know what was going on around her when the other faeries of the court were *still* suggesting to her mother that really, wouldn't it be kinder, in the end, to leave little, weak, and flightless Grettifrida with the humans and let nature take its course? To have a bright, lively child they could groom as one of their own, at least for a little while, instead?

Grit knew what kind of odds Rinka had been up against.

"Except you didn't die when you were supposed to, did you?" she asked Rinka, who hid even farther under the covers and shrugged. Grit sighed. Some day, she would make a friend who knew how to take a compliment. Where was Bell Daisimer when you needed him?

Oh, right.

"I couldn't travel anymore, of course," said Tinkerton, placing a hand on Rinka's knee. "So I returned to my mother's clock-making shop in New York. Rinka's . . . gifts became apparent before she was four. By the time she was nine, she was doing half the work in the store, at twice the speed I was, and eager for more." Tinkerton reached out to stroke Rinka's hair; she shrugged him off, blushing.

"But it was growing harder to ignore the things about her that were . . . different," continued Tinkerton.

"Her glamour was wearing off," Grit said. She looked at Rinka's toes peeking out from under the blanket, and wondered how she hadn't seen it before. "It still is."

Tinkerton nodded. "Even the city itself started to make her sick. She was better out in the country, out in the open air. That's where we saw our first air show."

Rinka smiled a little at the memory.

Tinkerton patted her hand. "And the rest, as they say, is history."

Grit, for one, saw the necessity for secrecy, even if she wasn't thrilled about Tinkerton claiming all the credit—and the money—for his daughter's inventions.

"What a charmin' story," drawled Yarlo, and everyone jumped.

Carmer nearly dropped the terrarium. Rinka narrowed her eyes, just visible above the covers, and pulled the lever to reel his jar over to them. At first glance, it appeared empty, but Grit knew Yarlo was just playing with Tinkerton.

"Father," said Rinka, easing out of bed to catch hold of the swinging jar. "This is Yarlo. He's a faerie, too." She wrapped her bony hands around the jar; the glass vibrated as if from some invisible pressure.

"Granted," said Yarlo, appearing instantly before them, "most of us have wings. I'm a special delivery."

"Well, aren't we all special snowflakes," groused Grit. "You forgot to mention the part where you're *evil*, and we're not."

"I take great offense at that," sniffed Yarlo.

"Rinka, who is this?" Tinkerton demanded. "And *what* is going on?"

"Well, I . . . Father . . ." Rinka trailed off helplessly.

Carmer was at her side in an instant, holding a broken glider model he'd rescued from the floor. "Can you help me with this?" he asked, extending the model out to her.

"Carmer," said Grit, rolling her eyes, "we're a little *busy* here!"

"The lady has a point," Yarlo conceded.

Carmer ignored them and turned back to Rinka, gesturing to the glider. "I don't think I could get this wing back into alignment . . ."

Rinka grabbed the model from his hands, hunched over it, and beckoned for a tool set lying at her desk a few feet away.

"Wire clippers, please," she said, not looking at Carmer. He happily obliged, and Rinka set to work.

Slowly, at first, but growing more confident as she worked, Rinka explained to him—to all of them—how the faeries had nearly always been with the Wonder Show. Rinka hardly noticed them when she was young; they would give her gliders an extra boost or sing to her as she fell asleep, or tend to her terrariums when she was too busy working on another invention. But as she got older, she started to recognize that her "little helpers" were everywhere; they'd made the show theirs as much as it was hers.

"You being a changeling explains why the faeries were attracted to you—even if none of you realized it," Grit said, after Rinka was done. "But the Unseelie Court"—she gestured to Yarlo—"that's where this fool is from, by the way—don't like faeries without a court gathering together, and gathering power, outside of their control. There's a pretty big taboo against killing other faeries—even faeries outside your own court—which is why they haven't attacked directly before now. But I don't think they'll stop until they force the Wonder Show apart . . . and get *you* under their thumb." She nodded to Rinka.

Grit realized she had practically echoed Yarlo's earlier speech against the courts, but it was too late to take the words back now. He looked at her with a smug expression.

"It's simple, then," said Tinkerton. "We disband the Wonder Show. Your little friends go their own way, sad as it may be. We lie low for a while, perhaps return to New York—"

"No."

Surprisingly, it was Carmer who had spoken. He looked just as surprised as any of them.

"I mean, it won't work," he clarified, shuffling his feet.

"If the Unseelie faeries really want Rinka back, they won't stop. They won't stop hurting people, won't stop sabotaging anything you make. And . . . and if you were never supposed to exist in the first place . . ."

"You're worried they'll just kill me," said Rinka, calmly setting aside the model glider. The wing looked as good as new.

"Carmer's right to be *concerned*," Grit said, "that it won't be the warm and fuzzy homecoming you'd imagined."

Yarlo laughed. Everyone glared at him.

"Warm and fuzzy," he said, "ain't words I would normally associate with the Unseelie *vocabulary*." He enunciated each syllable of the last word with relish. "Do you know what they'll do to me, for failing them, if I ever get out of this jar?" He pressed his hands up against the glass until his finger pads were white. "They'll make me *glad* I've no wings left to pluck. They'll flay the skin off me with a stingray's barb. They'll bleach my bones for that throne—"

"Shut up, Yarlo!" Grit shot a spark at his jar, and he leapt back.

"But I guess there's no reason why the same fate should be waitin' for you," said Yarlo with a shrug. "Why don't you ask little miss *Seelie princess* over here to help you?"

It was exactly the question Grit had been avoiding. If only that glass were soundproof, too.

"*You're* a princess?" Tinkerton asked, taking in all four inches of Grit's height.

"No need to sound *so* shocked," said Grit. "And I am. But a *Seelie* one. Which means—"

"Jack *squat*, basically," teased Yarlo.

Grit shot another spark at the jar. "It means I can't help you," she said, hovering above Rinka's bed. "I can't act directly against the Unseelie Court. If they want one of their subjects back—and you *are* still one of their subjects, raised by humans or not—I can't stand in their way. If I protect you . . . it could be grounds for faerie war."

"*Faerie* war?" asked Tinkerton, looking at Grit with the same expression of disbelief as when she'd announced her royal status. For a man with a changeling for a daughter, he was rather slow to catch on.

"Remember that storm, the night your human daughter was taken? Remember the blizzard that hammered this city two days ago?" Grit snapped. "If the fae go to war, those will seem like a strong but charming summer breeze."

"Now, listen here—" Tinkerton said, standing from his bench.

"Father, wait," said Rinka, putting a hand on his arm. "We can't ask any more of Carmer and Grit. They've already risked too much for us. They've *lost* too much for us."

Rinka stood up, her brown eyes filling with tears. They trailed down her face like dewdrops—which they probably were, if Grit's guess about Rinka being a dryad or an earth faerie was correct.

"If I'm an Unseelie, then I'm an Unseelie," said Rinka. "At least I *know* what I am. And . . . and that's worth something to me, even if there's nothing I can do about it."

She smiled wetly, shrugging her hair in front of her face, and suddenly, the idea that struck Grit was as obvious as Rinka being a changeling in the first place.

"Rinka," said Grit. "What if there *was* something you could do about it?"

Just because Rinka Tinkerton was born an Unseelie fae didn't mean she had to *stay* one, after all.

20.

REACHING TOWARD THE SUN

HOLDING ON TO AN AIRSHIP WHILE IT FLEW WAS a lot harder than holding on to a bicycle, so it was with great trepidation that Grit allowed Yarlo to secure the both of them to the gondola with his vines. Now more than ever, she half expected him to toss her over the side with her wings tied together. Her mistrust must have shown on her face, because the next thing he did was tie the rope around his waist to her own. They could move only six inches apart at most.

He gave the rope a tug and smirked when Grit flinched, her back pressed up against a rail.

"If you go, I go, Princess," he said with a mocking bow, and settled down for the ride.

Their destination was Wetherwren Light—or at least what was left of it. Grit tried not to think too hard about that. If the old Seelie king's heart really was still there, as Yarlo's story said, that made it the closest center of royal Seelie power—power they desperately needed. The ship wouldn't take them all the way there; the remains of the abandoned lighthouse were located on a small tidal island in the bay just big enough to fit the lighthouse and not much else. It hadn't been a frequent destination when it was inhabited. Now most airships had no reason to go there at all— which was why Yarlo and Grit needed to cross to it on foot. There would already be another ship flying to the island that night, and they couldn't afford to attract more attention than strictly necessary. Plus, Princess Pru and her Unseelie entourage would surely spot a giant snail sailing through the air toward the last local bastion of Seelie resistance.

Their journey also depended on Yarlo keeping his end of the bargain. As he was a failed spy—and now a seemingly willing turncoat—the Unseelies would be after him just as much as they were Rinka. He had no choice but to officially switch his allegiance if he wanted Seelie protection. But first, he had to escort Grit through Unseelie territory: along the shoreline, and across the bay to the island. Yarlo wasn't exactly her first choice of travel companion, but he *was* an Unseelie who knew the lay of the land.

"Tell me more about Wetherwren Light," Grit said, nudging him with her foot. She might as well use their unwilling proximity to needle him more effectively. "I want to know more about the old Seelie king, if we're going to use his . . . what's left of his royal magic."

Grit couldn't make herself say *his heart*, an omission that Yarlo, judging by his raised eyebrow, definitely noticed. Faerie hearts weren't for *using*, for wielding as tools. Most of the time, when a faerie died peacefully, their heart's magic flowed back into the magic of all things fae. That was how it *should* be. But sometimes, when . . . extracted . . . by force, the heart's magic lived on, even after the faerie's body had died. The Mechanist had manipulated stolen faerie hearts to do his bidding, most notably to animate his evil mechanical cats—likely the same cats that had snatched Yarlo's wings.

And now, to use a faerie's heart—a faerie *king*'s heart—for their own ends, even if those ends were noble ones . . . it made Grit wonder if she was being loyal to the fae after all.

"There're some folks who said no ship ever ran aground while Wetherwren Light was in fightin' form." Yarlo looked toward the approaching shoreline. "That the waters around it for miles were always calm, even if there was a storm ragin' out at sea, and the light was so bright and warm it made all the rest look dinky as a candle."

Grit thought about all the years the faerie king must have worked with humans—the cooperation between him and the lighthouse keeper, and whether they were friends, like her and Carmer. How many people they brought safely home. She smiled to herself. Maybe he wouldn't mind using his magic this way, after all.

"Could never seem to hold a lighthouse keeper for very long, though," said Yarlo, with his own nastier smile. "Some of them went mad, I heard. Some went missing. One just jumped, one year, right from the top of the light—"

"I get it," Grit said. Her flash of good feeling disappeared at Yarlo's knowing look.

"Well, you know," said Yarlo, "no human ever fared too well after spendin' too much time with the fae."

"THIS," CARMER SAID, hoping he didn't sound as ridiculous as he felt, "is a good faerie."

"Don't-poke-the-puppy-don't-poke-the-puppy-don't-poke-the-puppy," Thundrumble muttered in a continuous stream as Carmer held her up to the nose of Jules the husky.

Every inch of Thundrumble's round frame was fraught with tension, her eyes scrunched up so tightly it barely looked like she had eyes at all. She was clearly fighting the instinct to break out in her porcupine spikes at the appearance of any perceived threat—and a giant, slobbering, wolflike dog was definitely on the list of Things That Could Eat Faeries in a Single Bite.

But Jules merely sniffed Thundrumble for a few seconds, her dark, wet nose twitching, before sitting back on her haunches and staring at Carmer as if to say, "Well, that doesn't look very appetizing. What else have you got?"

Thundrumble let out a sigh of relief so big it lifted her right out of Carmer's hand.

"Wait a minute," Carmer told her. "We've still got a few more."

And they proceeded down the line of waiting dogs, each one of which, fortunately, decided that the prickly faerie wouldn't make much of a snack, either.

If Robert and Isla Blythe thought it odd that the personality they knew as "Tinka" had requested in his most recent letter to borrow their dogs for an evening, they never let on, and cheerfully offered the services of Jules and the rest of the huskies. Grit had nearly laughed until she cried at the sight of Carmer with five leashes in hand, struggling to wrangle all of them across the Wonder Show camp.

"There you are," said Rinka, kneeling down next to Carmer. A shivering Canippy crouched in her outstretched hand; the faerie shrieked when the dog's pink tongue lapped up the side of her face in a friendly lick. Rinka chuckled. "See, they're not so bad."

The idea was to keep the dogs stationed around various parts of the Wonder Show's New Year's Eve Spectacular, the performance right on the harbor where Driftsiders would ring in the New Year. If they could sniff out any invading Unseelie faeries, it would be one less thing for

Carmer and company to worry about. Of course, that meant getting the dogs acquainted with the smell of the *friendly* faeries first.

The second dog whined when Rinka approached it, though it sniffed Canippy happily enough. Rinka blushed and handed the faerie to Carmer.

"Maybe you should do this," she muttered, not looking at Carmer's eyes. "I—I don't think they like me very much. They know there's something . . . wrong . . . with me." She brushed her hands on her skirt and backed away.

Carmer started to protest, but then stopped himself. It was true that the dogs were more skittish around Rinka than with Thundrumble or Canippy, like they could tell she wasn't entirely as she seemed. The full extent of Rinka's magic was still hidden beneath the surface, still camouflaged by powerful faerie glamour.

Carmer supervised the rest of the Free Faeries as they flew up to the dogs directly, since they no longer seemed to need his help. When it was clear no one was going to eat anyone else, he left them to it.

He found Rinka drafting at her pull-down desk—which, like most other furniture in her ship, was a light, polished wood. She looked small behind it; in fact, it seemed like she'd been getting smaller every day this week, as if the magic holding her human form together was growing feebler by the hour, sensing its time was coming to an end—for better or worse.

"There's nothing wrong with you," Carmer said, shoving his hands in his pockets. "You're just . . . different."

It was so wholly inadequate that when Rinka finally smiled, Carmer did, too.

"I wasn't fit to be a faerie," Rinka said, staring down at her drawing, "but I'm not fit to be a human, either."

"I think an entire flying circus full of people *and* faeries might disagree," Carmer said. He looked around and wondered if she realized how incredible she was. How every single ship and balloon in the circus, every performer living their dream, every child filled with wonder and awe at the sight of their first airship, and everyone else affected by each invention she'd ever built, would never be the same without Rinka Tinkerton. "I think they'd all say you're pretty amazing, if they knew what you could do."

Carmer blushed and looked down at his feet, fiddling with his top hat. He half expected a teasing remark from Grit before remembering she was off on a journey of her own.

"I always used to wonder why I loved balloons so much," said Rinka quietly, still looking at her drawing. "Why I kept making things whose entire purpose was to go higher, and faster, and higher and faster still." She looked around at her ship full of hanging drawings and stretching sculpted branches. "But now I know. I was like a tree, reaching toward the sun. Like I knew, somehow, the sky was where I belonged."

Rinka's expression darkened, looking at the faeries and the dogs, now cheerfully playing with one another at the other end of the ship. "But I don't belong. Not really," she said. "No one *can* know what I can do, because they'd never accept me as I am. That's what Father's always said, and he's right. I can't even go *outside*, Carmer. I'm just . . . I'm too impossible."

Carmer sighed. He knew Rinka loved her father, and that Tinkerton loved her, but he couldn't help but think that locking someone in a tower—even a fancy sideways one—wasn't exactly a recipe for a well-adjusted individual, faerie *or* human.

"That's funny," was all Carmer said. "I know someone else who was supposed to be impossible, and she's doing just fine."

MERMAIDS WAITED FOR Grit and Yarlo at the shoreline. Both faeries had used their magic to deflect as much attention away from themselves as they could, but their scent on the wind was enough for all wild things to know that two faeries were trying to cross the exposed passage to Wetherwren Light—and they were doing so on foot. A falcon soared overhead, and Grit thought she could feel its beady eyes turn to them, even hundreds of feet in the air.

Yarlo and Grit had barely taken three steps onto the thin, shelly strip of beach when a dozen armored ghost crabs scuttled into view, cutting off their path with interlocking white claws. The mermaids were out of sight, just beneath the gently lapping waves. Perhaps they hadn't decided if the intruders were worth surfacing for.

Grit immediately rubbed her hands together, summoning the energy to call a flame to life to launch at the crabs, but she didn't have the chance to shoot off as much as a spark before one of Yarlo's ropes snapped around her wrists.

"Hey!" Grit gaped at him. Well, *that* had been a short-lived bargain.

"What did I say?" Yarlo demanded of her. He yanked on the rope, forcing her to her knees. "No funny business, or we walk like this the whole way there." He gave the rope another tug, and her knees scraped on the rocks through her trousers.

"What do you think you're—"

"Howdy, boys," said Yarlo to the ghost crabs. One of them clicked its claws menacingly, and Yarlo tipped his tiny hat. "Fine evenin', ain't it?"

We do not get many visitors around these parts. What interesting company you keep, faerie.

The voice—voices?—came both from beneath the waves and inside Grit's head, though the mermaids themselves never surfaced. She wasn't sure if they were talking to her, or Yarlo, or both. She stayed silent, her mind racing, with no clue how she was going to get out of the clutches of those webbed fingers, should they decide to drag her straight down to Princess Pru. Yarlo, on the other hand, spoke up right away.

"This little Seelie freak, you mean?" asked Yarlo. He flicked the toe of his boot against Grit's metal wing, just hard enough to jar her shoulder. She glared at him and focused on generating enough heat, just enough to get those ropes smoking . . .

"She's my prisoner," Yarlo said confidently.

She is fae, said the mermaids, sounding even more skeptical. The waves on either side of Grit and Yarlo lapped higher. *And all things fae belong to themselves. Only the king may keep prisoners in this kingdom, and he has not told us of any Seelie girl with a metal wing.*

Grit paused in her struggle. What did these mermaids mean, the Unseelie king hadn't told them about her? When she'd approached the palace before, it was like she'd been expected. She'd assumed Yarlo had snitched and the king knew everything about her. Princess Pru and Mister Moon certainly did. Perhaps the rumors of her tumultuous visit hadn't yet reached this side of the bay.

Grit peered over the edge of the rocks, searching for a glimpse of wet, flowing hair or filmy gray eyes underneath the water.

Yarlo corrected himself: "Ah, of course not, ladies. I should've rephrased; she's my *enemy*." He looked sideways at Grit, his eyes steel. "She dishonored me, and I captured her."

Grit stopped trying to set the ropes on fire. Was Yarlo . . . lying?

Dishonored you? asked the mermaids. *How could one so small and young manage that?*

Yarlo ground his teeth together. "She worked with the monster who took my wings," he snarled. "A human inventor, up north. She helped him capture faeries to steal their magic, in exchange for that mechanical wing."

He *was* lying. And the strange thing was, judging by the fact that the mermaids hadn't dragged them straight down to Princess Pru, the mermaids didn't seem to know it.

Even though she knew it was best to play along, Grit could barely force down her protest to such a blazing falsehood. As if she would *ever* have helped the Mechanist! Still, she tried to look downcast and defeated.

The water churned, rising higher, but the mermaids were silent.

"I'm taking her to the lighthouse to summon the Wild Hunt," explained Yarlo, and Grit remembered her own mother explaining to Carmer, what felt like so long ago, the rules for official dealings between faeries of different courts.

They had to meet on neutral ground. *Where the fae do not tread*, Queen Ombrienne had said. *The crossroads between realms.*

Wetherwren Light, she supposed, could be either—or both—of those things, depending on how you looked at it. A guide from one land to another, abandoned by the Seelies but avoided by the Unseelies; it could have been years since any living fae had set foot there.

"Then *they'll* decide her fate," Yarlo finished.

Grit held her breath, listening to the waves licking the rocks. The setting sun glinted across the ghost crabs' shells.

You may pass, said the mermaids, and this time, a few curious heads broke the surface, clammy foreheads and squinting eyes unaccustomed to being above water. *We will send a message to the Hunt to expect your arrival.*

It seemed that slipping past the local Unseelies unnoticed had been a bit too much to hope for. If Grit's guess was correct, though, and Princess Pru did intend to attack the Wonder Show tonight, she had a feeling the Hunt would be otherwise engaged.

Yarlo tipped his hat again. "We'll be on our way, then." He tugged Grit to her feet so she could stagger alongside him. "No more funny business from you, ya hear?"

Grit shook her head, still glaring daggers. She had no delusions that the mermaids would let them go the rest of the way unobserved; it seemed she was Yarlo's prisoner for the rest of the evening.

The crabs scuttled away to let the faeries pass, but their beady eyes watched Grit much too attentively for her liking. She waited until they were at least a dozen human paces away before muttering to Yarlo, "That was some quick thinking." It seemed odd that these Unseelies hadn't recognized her, but perhaps word of her visit to the palace hadn't yet reached all of the fae.

Yarlo looked at the angle of the sun and the waves on either side of them.

"You've gotta be quick in these parts, little lady," he replied, and Grit understood his meaning. They'd wasted time in their dance with the mermaids—time they didn't have. The walkway to the lighthouse was exposed only during low tide. If they didn't make it to Wetherwren before the water started to rise again, they'd be out of luck.

And Grit doubted very much that the mermaids would be inclined to help.

21.

TOO MANY TINKERTONS

Come forth, fine friends.
The old year ends.
Its candle is burning low.
A new day is dawning,
So come, join the revel
At the Roving Wonder Show.

THE WHALE OF TALES ROSE FIRST, LEADING THE fleet for the first time. Much to the disappointment of the wealthy Driftsiders, there were no golden tickets for sale for Rinka Tinka's Roving Wonder Show's New Year's Eve Spectacular. There would be no guests on board that evening, they were told, though all were welcome to join them for a reception at the Topside Hotel after the city fireworks display. It would be magical, they were assured. The performers would be there. Even Rinka Tinka himself would be there, if the gossip was true.

It was to be a masquerade.

But first, the spectacular itself: a sunset parade through the city's skyways, culminating with a final show right on the pier. Giant floodlights had been set up to point at the sky and illuminate the show once the sun had set; the whole pier was strung up with lanterns and filled to bursting with vendors and food carts taking advantage of the crowds. After the show, at the stroke of midnight, the ships would retreat for a finale of fireworks as the city rang in the New Year.

Almost every ship in the parade had a crier leaning out of its gondola, waving to the crowds. Curiously—perhaps to enhance the masquerade theme—they were all dressed exactly the same, with long, full black hair, smart silver jackets and caps, and black or white gloves. Each one wore an intricately carved mask in silver, white, black, and gold.

At the city center in Topside, the ships spread out, reaching out over the city as they had when they first arrived, spreading the invitation to the night's performance not just to Topside, but over every district—Portside, Scudside, Downside, and beyond. Their song rang out over the whole city in the chilly afternoon air.

Unbeknownst to the public, each crier also had company—a faerie tucked into the fake sandbags at their waists that usually held the golden gliders.

Well, every crier except one.

If one ship took a more circuitous route around the city, its crier waving rather shyly—if the ship was a little plainer than the others, not as brightly colored, and slowly broke off from the rest as it neared the coast and struck out over the ocean, well, no one could be expected to notice that, could they?

IN THE CROOKED Castle, Rinka and Mr. Tinkerton were having an argument. A very *loud* argument.

"You can't make me stay here, Father!" shouted Rinka, striding carelessly through her ship of hanging curiosities. "And you can't make me go to some stupid masquerade! You can't make me do anything!"

"Rinka," came Mr. Tinkerton's voice, "listen to me. You *will* do what I say. I've given you an opportunity—a chance for a lovely evening!"

"Oh yes," said Rinka. "A chance to hide in the crowds behind a silly mask, not telling anyone who I really am!"

"I've told you time and time again, Rinka, it's not safe for you out there!"

Something was dashed to the ground with a splintering sound.

"No, Father!" cried Rinka. "Carmer was right! You're

just selfish, and greedy, and you want to keep my inventions all for yourself! Well, I just can't take it anymore!"

The hatchway flew open, and a girl with thick black hair ran out, rubbing her tears on her sleeve. "Leave me alone!" she sobbed, and ran, shoulders hunched and hair falling in her face, until she reached a steam car parked at the edge of the camp. The engine was already running as the newest Wonder Show employee futzed around with something under the hood. Word around camp was the boy had a knack for all things mechanical and Tinkerton had asked him to do a quick checkup on all of their ground transportation.

The girl yanked the car door open, threw herself into the passenger seat, and sat sobbing with her head in her hands.

A moment later, the driver's side door opened.

"Rinka, what's the matter?" Carmer asked.

"Just drive," said Rinka. "I can't stay here another minute."

A small, light green head poked out of Rinka's pocket, and Beamsprout whispered, "You nearly squished me!"

And the girl dressed as Rinka looked up and muttered, "Pipe down, will you? My wig nearly fell off. We've all got problems."

Nan gave the wig an aggressive pat, disguised with another round of wracking sobs.

Carmer drove.

MILES AWAY, the real Rinka Tinkerton made her way toward Wetherwren Light.

At least, Carmer hoped that she did. It had been his idea to dress up the Rinka decoys under cover of the Wonder Show and Driff City's annual New Year's carnival. Rinka needed to get to Wetherwren Light, along with Grit, but the Unseelies were clearly watching her movements closely. If they figured out what she and Grit were planning, they would surely try to intercept her on the way.

Then, there was the matter of her . . . well, complicated magical existence. Grit had explained that faeries could sense the presence of one another's magic, even if it was just a general, inexplicable feeling; it was part of the reason why so many Free Folk had been attracted to the Wonder Show in the first place. They knew Rinka was magical, but they couldn't quite put their finger on how. This complicated the ruse further, as they couldn't just dress a bunch of Wonder Show employees like Rinka and hope for the best. No, each Rinka decoy had to be paired with a faerie, to at least create the illusion of something magically "off" about them.

At the insistence of the faeries, most of the decoys didn't know about the magical guests on their ships. Carmer had protested that people dressing up like Rinka had a right to know they might be attacked, but he was voted down with the promise that the faeries would abandon their ships at the first sign of any real trouble and lead the Unseelies away from the show. And this time, Grit hung around to make sure he didn't write any letters.

Nan Tucket, despite knowing something of the danger ahead, had volunteered right away.

"I like that little girl," she'd said, as though that settled everything, and though Nan couldn't have been more than two years older than Rinka. "And I've always wanted to try going brunette."

Now, Nan's teeth chattered in the open cab of the steam car as the frigid winter wind rushed past them. It appeared that, like other aeronauts, Tinkerton's obsession with light-ness had extended to eliminating any excess weight on his vehicle—even if that meant freezing to death.

"Where are we going?" she asked Carmer as he drove farther and farther away from Elysian Field, down the muddy back roads, until the ships above Driff City began to shrink into specks in the distance.

"As far away from the shore as we can get," he said with a quick glance behind them. He had hoped that causing such a ruckus back at the camp would attract the attention of the faerie they wanted to keep the most occupied and farthest away from the Wonder Show and its spectators—Princess Purslain Ashenstep.

Of course, that also meant there was every possibility they'd bring the wrath of the entire Unseelie Court down on their heads. Carmer thought of Grit's comment about faerie war making the other day's blizzard seem like a summer breeze. He tucked his scarf more snugly around his neck and would not—*could not*, for Nan's sake—think of train whistles. Or dripping red caps. Or creaking wheels and gunning, wheezing engines. Or tunnels filled with smoke.

He would not think of any of those things.

"Carmer . . ." said Nan quietly, pulling her fake hair farther around her face. "I think we're being followed."

The road they were driving down was deserted, but Carmer knew what she meant. Nan didn't *think* they were being followed. She *felt* it, and so did Carmer. He pressed his foot into the accelerator and willed the car to go faster.

It was the sheer flatness of the landscape that disturbed him the most. There were no mountains, no trees, no buildings to give them any sort of cover—just miles of increasingly muddy reeds and cordgrass bent into swirling patterns by the wind, and giant puddles of melted snow. Eventually, the roads weren't roads so much as infrequently traveled paths the odd traveler on horseback or a tractor from the city's outlying farms might occasionally trundle over. The tree line of a swampy, scrubby forest popped up some distance ahead, a forgotten corner of wilderness no one had bothered to clear and wring out to dry. In Carmer's nervous haste to get away from the city, he'd driven them right into a swamp.

When the sound of revving engines surrounded them, it was like another part of the wind itself. Carmer was barely surprised, though Nan squinted into the distance and twisted around in her seat, searching for whoever was tailing them. *Whatever* was tailing them.

Carmer remembered Bell Daisimer's warning, the first morning they'd approached Driff City.

You'll want to steer clear of gangs like that, traveling on your own.

The steam car's wheels carved deep grooves in the sodden ground as Carmer fruitlessly tried to drive it forward. Specks of mud flew up from underneath, spattering Carmer and Nan every time he gunned the engine.

"Stop!" Nan cried, flinging her arm up to her face to protect it against more flying muck. "Carmer, just stop! We're stuck!"

Carmer sank back against the driver's seat, clenching and unclenching his gloved fingers on the steering wheel. His burned hand stung.

It was getting colder—colder and darker. Overhead, the overcast sky swirled, clouds shifting in and out of one another and changing color like a graying bruise. The tall brown cordgrass was whipped into a frenzy by the wind, rippling this way and that like the very ocean waves they were running from.

The sound of the engines came closer, and then Carmer saw them—the ghostly velocycles of the Wild Hunt. They circled the car, closer and closer, wicking up mud that froze rock hard at the touch of their wheels. Their riders flickered in and out of view, never entirely solid, never really altogether there. There were skeletons with artificial, empty grins and black oil leaking out of the hollows of their eyes; human-sized faeries strapped to their bikes, their blistering skin wrapped in iron chains, pointed ears perked up in the wind; ancient-looking men in full suits of armor whose velocycles seemed to morph from machine to horse and back to machine again. Their jeering calls and ululations echoed even over the cacophony of the engines.

"Run," Carmer told Nan. The girl was frozen in fear, her back pressed up against the seat as though if she leaned far enough away from the Hunt, they wouldn't be able to chase her. She fished a necklace with a cross charm on it from underneath her blouse and held it up with a shaking hand. She whispered something to herself, barely audible above the noise around them; it took Carmer a second to realize she was praying.

A gust of wind whipped the necklace out of her hand.

Nan shrieked. Carmer grabbed her empty hand and pulled her toward him.

"RUN!" he said again, kicking open the door. Nan's boots scrambled against the car as she clambered out and nearly fell. Carmer helped her to her feet, noting a flash of polka dots among her skirts; even under all the layers of Rinka's plain clothes, Nan still couldn't resist her signature pattern. He would have laughed if they hadn't been about to be run down by a roving supernatural band of lost souls.

Still firmly gripping Nan's hand, Carmer ran away from the car and farther into the grass, ignoring the way the squelching mud pulled at his feet like grasping hands. Nan staggered behind him.

Beamsprout forced her way out of Nan's pocket. She looked impossibly small.

"We should separate!" she insisted. "It'll confuse them!"

"No," said Carmer, barely looking back.

"Not you two, *obviously*," said Beamsprout. "Just me! I'll keep my light off and see if I can't lead some of them away!"

Her little white head dimmed, no longer glowing with its usual pearlescence. She shot out of Nan's pocket and into the air before either of them could protest, a blur of green and white against the deadened landscape.

Carmer pushed aside the reeds slapping at his face. If only they could reach the tree line, they might find some sort of shelter, somewhere to hide. But the cackling laughter and trail of broken reeds on either side of them told Carmer the Wild Hunt could catch him and Nan any time they liked. They were simply enjoying the chase.

But then—it might have been Beamsprout's promised distraction, it might not—a few of the cyclists veered away, back toward the road. Carmer and Nan reached the tree line, gasping for breath as they clutched at the slippery trunks of the bald cypress trees around them. The swollen, pale "knees" of the trees that rose up from the watery soil reminded Carmer too much of the skeletons in the Hunt.

Nan's wig had fallen almost totally off, and her dress was torn and sodden with mud nearly to her waist. A long scratch across her cheek looked red and smarting. Carmer imagined he must look equally bedraggled, but they didn't have time to stop. He reached for Nan's hand again.

"We have to keep—"

Moving, he wanted to say, but his words were drowned out by a gust of wind that blew the standing water on the swamp into freezing waves that hissed and steamed as they came crashing back down. Carmer ducked, pulling Nan between the nearest tree and his own crouched body. A thin layer of fog crept along the ground. Carmer peered out from under his arm.

The wind had brought with it a rider from the Hunt. He sat upon his velocycle like a warrior knight would upon his faithful steed. The bike was all mud-spattered, peeling white paint and tarnished steel, but flickering beneath it, under the glamour meant to suit the modern age, Carmer could almost see the red-eyed white horse, eager to charge. The rider tossed his long blond braid over his shoulder as he leaned to one side and touched his toes to the ground, bringing the velocycle to a stop. He pushed up his fogged riding goggles with red-gloved hands, and Carmer saw the tip of a pale ear that looked much more pointed than the last time Carmer had seen it.

The rider was Gideon Sharpe.

Carmer didn't loosen his grip on Nan, but she must

have heard his breath hitch, because she squirmed out from under his arms just enough to turn around and see Gideon. Carmer wondered what this boy—this young man, really—looked like to Nan. Did she see something inhuman, a monster in a gray riding jacket and blood-red leather gloves? Did she see his pointed ears—his fine, thin features and the sharp lines they cut? Did she see the dark circles under his wide eyes, the lines around his mouth that looked out of place for someone so young?

Gideon looked just as surprised to see Carmer as Carmer was to see him. What had the rank-and-file members of the Hunt been told about who they were chasing?

The encroaching fog rippled around Carmer and Nan; it was bitingly cold, numbing their skin as soon as it touched them. Carmer felt as if his blood was freezing in his veins, rooting him to the spot. He looked for something else in Gideon's eyes, beyond surprise—a burning hatred, maybe, or his old disgust at Carmer's mere existence. But even though he would never win any awards for reading people, Carmer didn't see any of those things behind Gideon's hard stare.

He saw fear. Helplessness and fear.

Gideon moved his arm in a swift, graceful arc, and the freezing fog was swept back from Carmer and Nan—though it still hovered inches from their toes. The feeling returned to Carmer's feet like a thousand pins and needles; it was almost as bad as the day he'd been caught in the storm. Beside him, Nan gasped as the magic loosened its hold on her, too.

"P-please," Nan said. "D-don't—"

"Shut up," said Gideon.

Ah. *There* was the Gideon Sharpe that Carmer remembered.

"You're not her," Gideon continued, glaring at Nan and the brilliant red hair plainly visible under her skewed wig. He spoke stiffly, like one of his master's old automata might have. "You're not the one we're supposed to find."

Nan gulped and shook her head.

Carmer tried to find his voice, but the words felt stuck in his throat, just as frozen as his feet had been moments before.

"Gideon, I—" *I'm sorry*, Carmer wanted to say, but the other boy had already looked away, his head cocked toward some sound only his not-so-human ears could hear.

"You have to go," Gideon said, his voice low and rough.

It took Carmer a moment to realize Gideon was speaking to *him*. "What?"

"I can only lead them away for so long," Gideon explained, his eyes already darting around the trees.

Lead them away? Was Gideon Sharpe . . . helping them escape?

"*Go*, Felix Carmer III," said Gideon. "And consider us even."

He righted the velocycle, revved the engine, and sped off before Carmer could utter another word.

Nan leaned back against the tree, clearly trying not to sob. "Who . . . who *was* that? Do you know him?"

"Sort of," Carmer breathed, his own heart hammering.

"'Consider us even'?" she quoted Gideon, her voice high-pitched. "What does that mean?!"

"I have no idea," said Carmer truthfully, getting unsteadily to his feet. He offered Nan his hand to help her up. "Come on, we've got to keep moving."

"But *where*?" Nan asked. "Carmer, we can't outrun those velocycles or . . . *whatever* they are. And I am *not* going farther in there." She pointed into the thickening trees.

Nan was probably right. Heading farther into the wood would only bring them closer to the kinds of magical creatures that would do them harm; that much he *did* remember from his lessons with Grit.

Carmer hoped Rinka had gotten a head start on her journey to Wetherwren Light, because their time was running out. He and Nan needed to get back to the Wonder Show and the (slightly) safer realm of human civilization. But they were still miles away from the city . . .

He had a very, very stupid idea.

"Make a run for the car," Carmer said. "Don't stop for anything, okay?"

Nan looked at him like he had three heads, but Carmer was already running.

If they couldn't get back to civilization, he'd just have to make civilization come to them.

IT WAS LIKE the swamp didn't want to let them go. Carmer looked down as he ran and was convinced he saw the mud under his feet take on the form of clawing hands, just as it had in the subway tunnel the first time he'd seen the Wild Hunt. But then he would blink and shake his head, and the ground would be simply ground once more. He stomped a little harder, just to be sure.

Their jog back to the car was eerily quiet. It seemed Gideon had succeeded in leading the Hunt away, at least for a little while.

Consider us even, he'd said. Was he looking to pay Carmer back for leading him right into the Hunt's hands the night he'd been imprisoned? Was he right now planning a more sinister or painful plan of attack?

"Keep your eyes peeled," Carmer whispered to Nan as he unlatched the hood of the car and threw it open. They'd left it running in their flight.

"What are you *doing*?" hissed Nan.

"Um, calling the police," said Carmer. "Sort of. You might want to step back."

"Oh, sure thing, *Mr.* Carmer," muttered Nan, but she backed away all the same. "I'll just stand here and leave my fate in the hands of a *twelve-year-old boy* . . ."

"I'm thirteen, actually," Carmer corrected. He handed

her a large, rusted-over wrench he'd found in the trunk. She took it without comment; any iron weapon against faeries was better than none at all. "Let's hope you don't have to use it."

Nan continued her fuming while her eyes darted around the cordgrass; she jumped at any sign of movement. Carmer forced himself to be calm, though his hands were shaking so badly he could barely grip the hood. He stared into the engine of the car and all he saw was a maze of metal; mysterious compartments and springs and tubes and turning knobs. Carmer normally knew a steam engine inside and out, but he couldn't make sense of anything through the pounding of his own blood through his ears and the echo of the Wild Hunt's cries and—

He took a deep breath and refocused, remembering something he'd told Grit when they'd been working against Titus Archer:

Everything is less scary when you know how it works.

Carmer knew how this engine worked. The Moto-Manse worked on a similar principle, if on a larger scale. This was just another day at home in his workshop, focused on the task at hand, or an afternoon spent in the Moto-Manse's engine compartment. And this—this was even easier, because he was trying to foul up on purpose.

He hoped Mr. Tinkerton wasn't too attached to his car.

He worked quickly but calmly, his hands moving of their own accord, trusting Nan to alert him to any danger.

When the wind picked up again and the cordgrass around them was frosted over and pressed flat from the freezing gusts, he knew he didn't have much time, but he kept going. He didn't have a choice.

"Carmer . . ." Nan warned.

The same fog from earlier appeared, creeping inches closer every second. The laughter and the banging of weapons and the war cries cut through the still air.

The velocycles burst out of the ether, riding around Nan and Carmer over and over again in a dizzying, ever-tightening circle. It was impossible to tell if they knew Nan was a decoy or not; perhaps they did, and they were just *angry*.

"Carmer . . ."

"I know, I know!"

Carmer fumbled through his pockets until his fingers closed around the small, round object he was looking for. "Run!" he said again, and grabbed Nan's hand.

She planted her feet. "I am *not* running toward those things—"

"You don't want to stay back here," warned Carmer, and to the great surprise of everyone there, he led them *toward* the menacing circle of velocycles.

Five paces, ten paces, fifteen paces—how was he going to aim for *anything* with his heart pounding like this? The cyclists parted before them, surprised, stirring up more clouds of dust and frozen mud. Carmer turned to Nan.

"How's your throwing arm?" he asked her.

"*What?*"

He pressed the glowing, Grit-enhanced smoke bomb into her hand. "What are the odds you can hit the boiler from here?"

"Probably better than yours," said Nan, with a quick, panicked glance down at the bomb. She threw it with all her might.

Nan's aim was true. A second after the bomb pinged against the already overheating boiler—Carmer had disabled the safety valve—the engine exploded. Carmer fell forward, trying to shield Nan as best he could. He looked back and saw a great black plume of smoke rising from the car, which was now engulfed in flames. He willed it to rise higher and higher.

Please work, he thought. *Please, please work.*

One of the riders, on a large black velocycle that emitted a strange red glow, slowed to a stop in front of Carmer and Nan. His bike belched black smoke into their faces until they coughed.

"Oy, what do we have here? The princess of the freaks' little Friend, is it?" asked Mister Moon, dismounting. He had left his train conductor's uniform behind for a set of black riding leathers. The red cap, though, was still as red as ever.

"We're not who you're looking for," said Carmer. "We haven't done anything wrong."

"Speakin' up today, are we?" said Mister Moon. "I think I liked it better when you cowered in the corner." Jeering laughter from the other riders. "You've led me and my boys on a merry chase, that's for sure. Their blood's up. Who am I to deny them two lonely souls lost in the swamp?"

Some of the riders howled.

"I don't think you want to do that," said Carmer slowly, spotting the approaching shapes behind Mister Moon with relief.

The leader of the Hunt laughed. "And why's that, little Friend? I don't see your pet princess around to protect you. No, you were foolish enough to come here *alone*."

"What do I look like?" Nan piped up. "Chopped liver?"

"But we're not alone," said Carmer. "Not for long."

The airship approaching from the city was a small fire-ship, one of the first on the scene for rooftop or upper-story blazes. Two more ships—probably police—followed behind, racing toward the tower of flame Carmer had created. Their sirens blared, cutting through even the sound of the wind and the Hunt's engines.

The Hunt could materialize only in certain places—in the wilderness, or in the dead of night, in spaces unfrequented by most humans. They were a ghost story, and so they lived like one. Shrieking sirens and ships crawling with humans from big cities were *not* their area of expertise.

"Ain't you a clever one," sneered Mister Moon, but even then, he seemed less substantial, somehow. Like

Carmer could see through him if he tried. "I'll be seeing you again some day, boy. You can be sure of that."

The leader flicked his forked tongue at Carmer and swung a leg over his velocycle.

"Come on, boys!" cried Mister Moon. "The night is young! And tonight, we ride!"

The Wild Hunt sped off as quickly as they had come, until all that was left were fading tire tracks in the mud.

The firefighters' siren was the most welcome sound Carmer had ever heard.

22.

NOTHING TO SEE HERE

JUDGING BY THE MOON, IT WAS AFTER TEN o'clock at night. Grit and Yarlo were a little over halfway to Wetherwren Light, and walking slower every minute. The water was up to their knees, the waves regularly sloshing into their faces and occasionally bubbling up over their heads. Grit gasped, nearly inhaling a mouthful of seawater, as another freezing cold wave slapped her in the face.

High tide was at ten thirty. By then, the rocky sand-bar would be completely submerged again. Grit had always boasted that she'd been a good swimmer—but she'd learned in the tranquil frog ponds of the Oldtown Arboretum, not the churning depths of the Atlantic Ocean.

If she wasn't careful, she and Yarlo would be riding in the belly of a *real* whale instead of the *Whale of Tales.*

Yarlo had clearly chosen to meet their fate with the stoic strategy of Firmly Not Talking About It, but Grit wasn't about to drown without at least complaining about it first.

"We're not going to make it!" Grit shouted to him over the spray. He pressed onward as if he hadn't heard her. "Hey, are you listening to—"

Thwack. A wave knocked her completely off her feet, tossing her aside like she was just another jellyfish in the sea. Grit reached out blindly, scrambling to grab on to the slippery rocks, but her hands only pushed against more water—until a vine shot out of nowhere and snapped around her wrist, pulling her back to the sandbar.

She crashed into a sopping wet Yarlo.

"Thanks," she gasped, black spots blooming across her vision. The pain in her shoulder made her shudder, almost as badly as when she'd gotten trapped under Bell's balloon. Yarlo wedged them between the tops of two rocks at the edge of the path. Their feet slipped against the wet stone. "What are we going to do?"

Yarlo squinted up at the sky, reaching up to tip his hat, but it had long since been lost to the waves. "Well, little lady, I'd say one of us is going to use those two good wings of hers and fly away."

Grit stared at him and flexed her mechanical wing, clutching his arm as pain and dizziness washed over her.

Her wing barely extended all the way. The winds were probably too strong, the waves too high for her to even dare to finish crossing on her own.

It also hadn't even occurred to her to leave Yarlo behind.

"No," she said, shaking her head. Drops of water flew from her hair. "No way. You're supposed to be my guide through Unseelie territory, remember?" She didn't much care if any of the Unseelie guards were listening. Their story had been thin to begin with, and the Unseelies surely knew that if the mermaids didn't get them, the sea definitely would. What a nice, built-in security system.

"And ain't I just doing a wonderful job?" said Yarlo, spitting out a mouthful of seawater. "Now get outta here before I toss you up myself!"

But Grit couldn't. She couldn't leave another faerie behind, even an Unseelie who'd spied on her and worked to kidnap Rinka, because she'd promised to see him through this. She'd promised him another way.

Grit looked up at the sky, pleading with the very stars for help—even that beady-eyed falcon would do, at this point—when she saw the silhouette moving toward them, buffeted slightly by the wind.

"Sorry, but you'll just have to throw me off something another time!" She risked her grip on the rock to point up for a moment. "Do you trust me?"

"Not as far as I can throw you," joked Yarlo, though he

nodded at the approaching shape in the air. The water was up to their chins.

"Wait here—"

"As if I've gotta choice—"

"—and after a few seconds, turn your light on as bright as you can! Okay?"

Murderous mermaids be darned. They'd just have to risk it.

Rinka's ship flew closer toward the lighthouse; in a few moments she would pass right over them. Grit felt the vine uncurl from her wrist.

"Get goin', then!" groused Yarlo, and she launched herself into the air.

Grit dodged a crashing wave just in time. The wind snatched and bit at her almost as badly as the waves below. Between the sea spray and the pain blackening the edges of her vision, she could barely even see where she was going. She kept listing to one side, falling much too close to the water below, and having to beat her wings with agonizing effort to regain the height. A moment before she finally, *finally* landed, she heard something snap, and it was all she could do to grab on to the edge of the ship without passing out.

Rinka shrieked at the sight of an unexpected, bedraggled faerie boarding her ship and nearly let go of the tiller.

"Relax!" cried Grit, panting as she heaved herself onto the gondola. "It's me, Grit!"

This didn't seem to relieve the changeling girl as much as it should have. Rinka still looked out at the night sky as if the clouds themselves were about to transform into demons and rip her from this earthly plane—which, admittedly, was not entirely out of the realm of possibility, depending on who they were dealing with.

Grit rushed through her explanation of her and Yarlo's predicament and looked down at the disappearing walkway with dismay. Below, she could have picked out her and Yarlo's rock in a lineup. But all the way up here, in the dark, with the crashing waves . . .

And then she saw it—the flickering golden light, just a pinprick from Rinka's ship, dipping in and out as merciless waves pounded the pathway.

"There!" She pointed the spot out to Rinka, before realizing, "Can you get us that close?"

Rinka may have been a girl of few words, but her reaction to being questioned about her ability to fly her own ship was clear enough.

"Of course you can," corrected Grit. "Of course."

Grit never would have thought she'd be so glad to see a smarmy Unseelie cowboy faerie. Neither she nor Rinka missed the webbed hand that reached out of the water, snatching at his heels as they hauled him aboard.

IT WAS THE last thing Grit had to be glad about.

Landing the ship took far too long without a crew or

mooring mast on the ground—and there wasn't a lot of ground to land on to begin with. Rinka had to lower the ship as much as she dared, release her magnetic docking cables in a complicated web they could only hope would latch on to enough rocks on the shore, and climb the rest of the way to ground herself. Rinka froze up more than once, and it was only Yarlo and Grit's encouragement that finally got her down safely, her poor hands rubbed raw from the rope—even through her gloves—and her arms shaking from the effort.

They tied the rope to the biggest, sturdiest rock on the shore they could find and hoped it would be enough to keep the wind from snatching the ship away.

Rinka clutched her coat around her as she climbed the steep, rocky hill that led to the lighthouse, Yarlo and Grit riding on her shoulders. Yarlo would have preferred to scamper along the ground, as usual, but they'd both taken a good thrashing from the waves. Some of his ropes were torn or frayed, and he looked so exhausted and water-logged, Grit thought another dunk in the ocean would surely finish him off. She kept her wings folded against her back, wincing with every step that jarred her side.

Yarlo had warned her the lighthouse had mostly fallen to pieces years ago, and so she hadn't panicked when they weren't able to see a tower from the air. Ruins could still be powerful; the many old landmarks even the humans revered were proof enough of that. What mattered was that the Seelie king's heart—and the power it contained—was still there.

But as they climbed, Grit couldn't help but feel a distinct *lack* of power. This wasn't like walking into the Arboretum, which thrived on her mother's magic, lit by faerie lanterns and made beautiful by the faeries for hundreds of years until it was almost a magical creature itself. It wasn't even like walking into the airship graveyard, where the weight of the blizzard and the forces hiding behind it had made her hair stand on end and sent chills up her spine.

There were no chills. No shimmers of faerie dust in the air. No doors that opened themselves, or faces appearing where no faces should be. No telltale silvery-blue glow to lead them to a faerie's heart.

And when they reached the top of the hill, Grit knew, deep down in her bones, that it was because there *was* no magic here, and hadn't been for quite some time. There was just a big, sad crater in the ground, filled with water from years of rain and high waves and crumbling chunks of what had once been the lighthouse. One bit of the circular wall was still standing, but it looked like a stiff wind would blow it over.

Somehow, a single wooden staircase had survived, spiraling up through the center of the former lighthouse before breaking off, splintered and twisted, into the ether.

"There's nothing here," Grit said hollowly. Rinka and Yarlo were silent. Grit turned to the cowboy faerie. "You told me the stories. You *told me* the old king's heart was still here."

"I, well, that I did," said Yarlo, with a tired scramble down Rinka's arm. He jumped down onto another rock. Maybe he thought being so close to Rinka wasn't a good idea, at the moment; *Grit* certainly felt like punching him in the face. She grabbed a lock of Rinka's hair, ignoring the girl's yelp of surprise, and rappelled down to waist height before jumping onto one of the piles of crumbling stone. She stumbled on the landing.

"You *said* there was Seelie magic here," Grit continued, stepping toward him. "You told me it was the last 'bastion of their power' or whatever!"

"I told you that *one old Seelie* lived here for a few years until he finally decided to take his chances against us and *lost*," countered Yarlo. "Maybe he wasn't even a king. Maybe his magic died when he did. Maybe a few will-o'-the-wisps play around up here when they're feelin' frisky, and that's it. I told you there were stories. And maybe . . ." His voice broke a little. "Maybe that's all they were."

No, Grit thought. There was no such thing as "just stories" for faeries. They were living, breathing stories themselves. That was what she had always been taught—that their magic could never really die, not if they lived on in the whispers in the trees, or the stories mothers told to get their children to behave (or *else*), or the tales of some friend of a friend who met a weeping faerie maiden or saw a strange glowing light in the forest. These were the spaces where the fae lived—in the streak of movement in the underbrush you couldn't quite make out, in the land still unconquered by human machines, in bedtime stories.

But the Seelie king's heart—the king or queen's magic they *needed* to open a portal to Faerie, to change Rinka and Yarlo's allegiances for good—wasn't here. Of that much, Grit was certain. So even if Wetherwren Light ever blinked on and off on a foggy night—despite the fact that its tower had been destroyed—or the passageway to the island grew or shrunk, ever so slightly, without explanation, or if the black rocks rearranged *themselves* into pleasing little stacks along the shoreline . . . maybe it didn't even matter. Not if no one was looking now but the fae and the waves. The story was exactly that—a story, and nothing more.

Grit almost laughed. They had come all this way, had braved Princess Pru and murderous mermaids and nearly drowned, and now . . . there was nothing. A bunch of rocks and a broken staircase, to go with her broken wing.

"Well, that's just fabulous," she said to Yarlo, furiously blinking away tears. "Maybe the fact that this place is *absolutely boring and worthless* will keep the Wild Hunt from showing up and carrying us all away." The mermaids had probably known they'd just drown or get stuck. She'd been so silly to think she and Yarlo could outsmart them. She turned toward the sea and cupped her hands around her mouth, shouting, "Hey, no need to worry about us! Nothing to see here!" Grit kicked a pebble down the steep hill.

"What am I going to do?" Rinka whispered, staring down at her chafed hands.

Grit looked back at the changeling, embarrassed at her own outburst. *She* wasn't the one giving up her life as she knew it, or trusting her fate to complete strangers—Rinka was. Rinka, and even Yarlo, had much more to lose than Grit did because of their failure.

"I'm so sorry, Rinka," said Grit. She shuffled over to the edge of the ruins and looked down into the pool of water at the bottom. Her own reflection greeted her, the stars in the night sky blurry spots of bright in the dark water.

"I hate to interrupt a good pity party," drawled Yarlo, breaking the silence, "but aren't y'all forgetting something?"

"And what is that?" Grit snapped, still glaring at the water.

"You said we needed a center of Seelie power to have this shindig—"

"Ceremony," corrected Grit.

"Hootenanny, whatever," said Yarlo.

She looked up at him, finally, and he winked; he was holding up a wet, dripping clump of something that looked alarmingly like hair.

"I picked up this from my little encounter with the mermaids down on the rocks," he explained. "You never know when you'll need a bit of water fae."

"What's your *point*, Yarlo?"

"In case *you* forgot, little miss, we've got a Seelie princess in our midst—whether she likes it or not."

Grit bit her lip. Sure, she was a princess. So what? How was she supposed to help them now, when their one slim chance at escape hadn't ever even existed? When she couldn't even fly back to the Wonder Show to warn the others?

Yarlo walked over to the bottom of crumbling stones and held up his grisly souvenir. Grit looked at it, and at the water, and suddenly understood.

"If you need a powerful place," Yarlo said, "you might just have to make your own."

23.

SEAS BETWEEN US

IN THE END, THE POLICE ONLY AGREED TO LET them go when Mr. Tinkerton showed up, dressed to the nines in his rainbow-striped New Year's suit and with an attitude big enough to match. After much bluster and a repeated insistence that no, he did *not* want to press charges against his employees, even if they did blow up his car—in addition to an invented story from Nan that she'd been in disguise and "borrowed" Tinkerton's car so that she and Carmer could *elope* together—they were finally released with a flurry of rushed paperwork and shoves from behind by Tinkerton.

"They're just kids, Deputy Oliver," Tinkerton said with a shrug. "Besides, it's not like they blew up that car on *purpose*."

Carmer gulped.

"Good luck," said the young officer behind the desk to Carmer, with an appreciative look at Nan's flaming red hair, as they hurried out. "I'd do anything for a woman like *that*."

Carmer nodded. "We're very much in love."

Nan yanked him out the door with a little more force than necessary.

TINKERTON STALKED THROUGH the streets like one of the Blythes' dogs on the hunt, whipping his head around every few moments to snarl at Nan and Carmer to keep up, even as the carnival crowds pressed thicker and thicker around them. Nan was using her matted wig as a muff to keep her hands warm; there wasn't much point in keeping up the ruse now.

"Mr. Tinkerton, wait!" Carmer finally called to him. "Where are you going?"

"Where do you think?" Tinkerton rounded on him. "To find the fastest ship that will take me to my daughter. I should have never trusted our lives to a mere *boy*."

Carmer flinched. The revelers around them scurried about, marveling at the hanging lanterns and eating sweets, laughing and talking excitedly about the show, utterly oblivious to the argument in their midst.

"Mr. Tinkerton," said Nan, "I know you're my boss and all, but I've gotta say, you might be wrong there. Carmer saved my life, blowing up that car like he did, and just because we got caught doesn't mean the diversion didn't work. Rinka could be—"

Carmer held up a hand and shook his head. They never knew who was listening out here on the open pier.

Nan lowered her voice. "Rinka could be just fine. It's just too early to say."

"Thanks," said Carmer, looking at Nan in surprise. He didn't think she was his biggest fan.

"Well, I *am* madly in love with you," she joked.

"When will we know?" Tinkerton interrupted them, his face still grave. "When will we know for sure?"

"Not until midnight, sir," said Carmer. "That's the official deadline. Until then . . . the most we can do is keep the Wonder Show safe."

Carmer considered his hodgepodge of lessons about the Unseelies and his new status as Friend of the Fae. Hadn't he been able to sense *something* off, the first time he'd seen the Wonder Show, and again during the snowstorm? They had the dogs sniffing around for unfamiliar faeries. They had their own faeries, returning now from crier duty, who would patrol the ships as best they could. And even if it wouldn't be much help, they also had him.

He couldn't afford to stay on the ground, hidden and hampered by the crowds. He needed to be able to see the big picture. With a sinking feeling in his stomach, he looked at the gold and white balloons tied to the pier, ready to ascend during the spectacular's finale. The balloons would be tethered to the docks—no one wanted to chance them drifting out into open water—but if he got high enough, he'd be able to see the whole carnival below. And maybe, this time, he'd be able to sense something was wrong before it hit.

Carmer pointed to the balloons, proud that his hand shook only a little. "How do I get up in one of those?"

NEARLY THE ENTIRE fleet of Rinka Tinka's Roving Wonder Show spread out before him, every floating bumblebee and swordfish and dragonfly glider. The sprawling coast of Driftside City was below, glowing with the light from the hundreds of lanterns that had been strung up for the carnival like candles on a big and lopsided birthday cake. He could see the spectators on the pier, pointing at the daring acrobats and waving to the masked criers and other crew. Here and there, a wolflike dog paced through the crowds, pausing occasionally to take a lick from an inattentive child's snack.

Carmer could see everything from up there, but he needed to see more. He closed his eyes, willing his mind toward stillness. He needed to forget the hustle and bustle of the crowd, the whooshing of the other ships sweeping by—and how very, very high up he was. He needed to stop seeing and hearing what he was expecting to see and hear and start recognizing things that he didn't. He remembered the feel of the freezing water, that night in the bog, and looking sideways through the glowing lights. He opened his eyes slowly—so slowly, in fact, that it took him a moment to register the faerie sitting on the edge of the balloon's basket.

It was amazing, really, how the magic of the Mechanist's cloak allowed Princess Pru to change her size like that. She was as big as a full-grown human, a feat Carmer hadn't thought possible outside of the realm of Faerie. Her hair was still long enough to pool around her feet. Carmer could just imagine what Grit would say about the impracticality of *that*, but it didn't seem to get in her way; it was an extension of her, like the tails of the mermaids who guarded her palace. Her wings were folded against her back, underneath the cloak. Sitting there like that, she could almost pass for human.

Almost, but not quite.

Pru's milky-gray eyes fixed themselves on Carmer. "I think I *do* like you better this way," she said, her gaze trailing up and down his body. "People nearly always look better wearing their real faces." She said this as if she spent a lot of time around people who didn't—which he supposed was entirely possible.

"Where is the changeling?" Pru asked it casually, but Carmer wasn't fooled. He was familiar with how quickly the Unseelie princess's methods of questioning escalated. He did, however, need to stall for time—for all of them.

"We have until midnight," was all Carmer said.

Pru cocked her head and made a clicking, *ticktock* noise with her tongue, but otherwise made no move toward him.

Carmer looked down at the pier below. He didn't see any signs of distress there, which wasn't what he'd expected. Where were the other Unseelies? After all her threats, had Princess Pru . . . come alone?

"Why do you want Rinka so badly?" Carmer asked her. "Why can't you just leave the Free Folk on the Wonder Show be?"

"Ah, but those are two very different questions, Carmer," said Pru, twirling a pale finger through her hair. He hated the sound of his name on her lips. "The textbook answer—is that how you say it?—to your first question is this: as an Unseelie subject, Rinka belongs to us."

"Nobody belongs to anybody," said Carmer, crossing his arms.

"Says the boy who bonded his soul to the fae with his own blood," countered Pru.

Carmer couldn't help staring at his hands, where Queen Ombrienne's apple blossom staff had drawn blood as he'd gripped it, all a part of the ceremony to make him a Friend of the Fae.

"You didn't want her. You gave her up."

Pru shrugged and hopped up onto the edge of the basket. "And now we want her back." They were a hundred feet in the air, but the balloon didn't even sway with her weight.

"Why?" Carmer resisted the urge to reach out and help steady Pru as she walked along the edge of the basket, evil faerie princess or not. "Because she's got such a head for figures?" He'd been joking, but Pru swerved on her bare, black feet to face him.

"Precisely," she said, jumping back down into the basket. "I thought *you*—a man of science, they say—would understand. Don't you see? Look at what that girl has done, trapped in a human body not meant to last a fortnight, abandoned by her own kind, constantly sickened by the iron around her. That mind—that *beautiful* mind—created all of this, and more."

Pru gestured to the fleet of ships around them, the meticulously crafted gliders, the towering lantern giants, even the glowing lights of the carnival below. Carmer thought of all of "Tinkerton's" supposed inventions, of the airplanes he'd stumbled across that first night in Elysian Field. Who better to design the future of flight than a faerie genius herself?

And *that's* what Pru wanted—Rinka's mind. Rinka's mind in service of the Unseelie Court.

"Don't you understand what we could do, Rinka and I?" Pru asked, taking a step closer to Carmer. Her pale eyes were wide and shining with excitement. "I wouldn't need to sneak around anymore, messing about with silly typewriters and *telephones* in my palace. With Rinka in her rightful place in my court, we could finally stand a chance at regaining the fae's former glory."

"You'd use her technology against the humans," Carmer guessed.

"Some of us would prefer to hide, it's true," Pru said. "To cling to the old ways and sink deeper and deeper into the sea, hoping the iron world daren't touch us there. But not me."

Carmer was suddenly reminded of Grit, rebelling against her mother's inaction against the Mechanist back in Skemantis.

This isn't the time to hide in our trees or burrow into the ground like mice in winter, she'd said to the queen. *The world outside is changing, and it won't be long before it reaches our gates. It already has.*

"There is no 'iron world' to be separated from any longer," said Pru with a bitter tinge to her voice, as if she'd known a time when there still was. "There's just the world, exactly as it is. It's up to us to survive in it or not." Pru looked out at the bustling shoreline.

Somewhere, a clock tower struck twelve.

The airships would soon spread out and land elsewhere on the shore. The balloons would be reeled in. The barges below would let loose with fireworks to entertain the Driftsiders on the shore—and woe befall any balloon that was still in range.

Carmer supposed he had better start getting used to woe.

Between each chime of the clock, he heard the Driftsiders below cheering and singing. A slightly drunken chorus of "Auld Lang Syne" floated up from the shore, snatches of each line getting carried away with the wind.

> *Should old acquaintance be forgot,*
> *And never brought to mind?*
> *Should old acquaintance be forgot,*
> *And auld lang syne?*

"Where is the changeling?" Pru asked again with a flourish of the Mechanist's cape.

"Hopefully," Carmer said, trying not to look in the direction of Wetherwren Light, "far away from here."

Pru seemed to grow taller, more willowy, the veins on her face popping out as the skin was pulled taut. Carmer inched backward.

"They say fire is the first enemy of these flying machines you humans are so proud of," said Pru quietly, though it came out like a snarl. "But you know what the second is?"

Memories of the frozen shell of the *Jasconius* flooded Carmer's mind.

"*Ice*," she said with a sneer. "I wonder how fast I can freeze every envelope of every ship in this fleet?" The ends of her hair, usually dripping wet, had sharpened into frosted spikes of ice. "When people think of water magic, that's what they think of, isn't it? It's not usually my style— I prefer all the things that can take *root*, where there's water to give them life—"

A few mushrooms sprouted from between her toes. "But I'll be obvious if I have to."

Carmer didn't give her the dignity of a response. Instead, he did the thing he'd been hoping to avoid, and whipped out the knife he'd stashed in his pocket. He took one more step back, to the rope he'd already frayed almost to the breaking point—the rope that was tethering his balloon to the docks—and slashed at it with all his might.

The balloon started to drift away.

Pru did not look pleased.

"What are you doing?" she demanded, but Carmer had already cut loose all of the ballast as well. They had nowhere to go but up—until they couldn't. Pru watched the retreating ground with narrowed eyes. He was counting on her to want Rinka—and him and Grit—more than she wanted the rest of the Wonder Show.

"Seeing how high faeries can fly," said Carmer. He comforted himself with the small sense of satisfaction the quip brought him—and so well timed, too. Grit would have been proud.

The singing grew fainter the higher they rose.

We two have paddled in the stream,
from morning sun till dine;
But seas between us broad have roared
since auld lang syne.

But Pru seemed determined to have the last word on any subject.

"I don't know," she said just as cheekily. "How high can humans breathe?"

The balloon climbed, the ships and buildings and people on the shore becoming smaller and smaller. It was absolutely freezing; Carmer tried not to shudder in the cold, thin air. Pru stood there as if the winter wind were nothing but a refreshing breeze.

The truth was, Carmer didn't know the answer to either of those questions—but a brilliant ray of light, breaking across the night sky like a beacon, told him he might not have to.

In the distance, Wetherwren Light was shining once more.

It blinked like a new star in the sky, brighter than any real lighthouse had ever glowed. Carmer felt a wave of magic, the same as when he'd entered Seelie Faerie the first time—like the very fabric of the world was curling up and rippling around him. It nearly knocked him off his feet.

"What was that?" Pru asked, her voice low and growling. She lunged forward and grabbed Carmer's jaw, her hands like ice. "What have you *done*?"

> *For auld lang syne, my dear,*
> *For auld lang syne,*
> *We'll take a cup o' kindness yet,*
> *For auld lang syne.*

Carmer couldn't help but smile, even with his jaw clamped in Pru's bony hands. Grit had succeeded. Rinka was safe—well, safer. Relief flooded through him, almost enough to make him forget that he was stranded up in a drifting balloon with a psychopath of a faerie princess.

The Wild Hunt's train wasn't coming for anyone else tonight. Not if he could help it.

Pru didn't wait for an answer. With a swirl of her cloak, she shrank down to something more closely resembling faerie size; another flicker of shimmering fabric, and she disappeared altogether.

Her only parting gift was the ice slowly creeping down from the top of the balloon—a slick, thick shell that added more weight with every passing second.

The balloon sank like a stone, losing height so quickly it made Carmer dizzy. The gasbag, and then the envelope, crumpled and cracked like broken slate as the whole thing hit the water. Carmer gasped, plunged into icy water that seeped through the basket and up to his knees. He shoved the envelope to the side as it fell and tried to cut it loose—he had to get what remained of the balloon to float for as long as he could—but the whole basket tilted to the side and dipped into the sea.

Carmer shifted to the other end of the basket as quickly as he could, hoping to tilt it upright. But the water had already gotten in, weighing the basket down even more. It sloshed up through the wicker floor, inching higher and higher, each little wave like a blazing, icy knife slashing against his skin.

He could just make out the outline of a ship—he hoped it was Rinka's—leaving Wetherwren Light. He thought about calling out, but he knew it was useless. Rinka and Grit had little reason to sail in his direction, and even if they did, he would be well underwater by the time they reached him.

Or frozen to death. One or the other was a certainty at this point. At any rate, he was alone, in enemy territory, in a decidedly unseaworthy vessel that was about to be swallowed up by the frigid Atlantic.

He thought back to the brief moment, during their conversation, when he'd wondered if Pru had come alone as well. How the Unseelie terrors she'd promised to rain down on them had never materialized. How she had complained about "some of" her people resisting her more active stance against humanity. How many was "some"?

Was it possible—just maybe—that the Unseelie king shared his Seelie counterpart's aversion to open conflict with humans?

His life depended on the answer. Because in the next moment, as the water rose up to his chest, he remembered a boy with long blond hair and his arm in a sling, running into the Oldtown Arboretum with his hands held up in surrender.

As a Friend of the Fae, I claim sanctuary in this place from those who would do me harm, Gideon Sharpe had said.

Carmer had never been so thankful to be in enemy territory in his life.

He repeated the words, straining his chin above the water, and took one last gulp of air before the ocean closed over his head.

24.

DO NOT LEAVE
CHILDREN UNATTENDED

FAERIE FIREWORKS, GRIT DECIDED, WERE MUCH better than human ones. They were brighter and less noisy and much less likely to blow anyone up by accident. As it was, Rinka's ship had to very carefully edge around the New Year's celebration currently exploding off the Driftside City pier.

At least staring at the popping and sparkling—if slightly lackluster—show made for a distraction. Grit had tried to prepare herself for the moment when Princess Purslain Ashenstep landed on Rinka's airship, but the second those tiny, inky footprints appeared on the deck—their owner presumably choosing to remain invisible for dramatic effect—anxiety clawed at her already frayed nerves. The fight would soon be over, one way or the other, and Grit had done everything in her power to prepare for it.

The bone-chilling wind whipped across Grit's face, sending her dandelion cloud of hair flying in all directions, but she barely felt it. She was still touched by the magic of Faerie; her light, which had cast out every shadow on the island and beyond, still glowed from somewhere under her heart. If she closed her eyes, she saw flames dancing behind her eyelids. She wondered if the others could see them, too.

But there had been no time for the customary revels or displays of magic, not with so many other lives at risk, so Grit kept her power in check, though she could feel the energy thrumming from the top of her head to her fingertips, her power waiting and *wanting* to be used. It did nothing to ease the tension inside her, coiled in her gut like a snake.

Grit thought Pru might try to sink the ship first, so she stuck close to the engine car while Yarlo patrolled the area around the gas cells. Rinka had insisted on remaining out in the open to steer the ship herself. Grit had to admit, the girl was braver—and more stubborn—than she looked.

Not that Rinka looked much like a girl anymore. The magic that had kept her looking relatively human for so many years was peeling off like strips of old paint. Her bird's nest of long hair was turning into *actual* bird feathers—still long, but in shiny, healthy shades of black and brown. Her skin was a warm chestnut color with a texture more like bark than skin, but it didn't seem to hamper her movements. There was no sign of wings—at least not yet—but Grit suspected the girl was some sort of dryad or other tree-centered fae, anyway, and not technically a winged faerie at all.

But Pru made no move for the envelope or the engine car, or even a direct attack against Rinka. When Pru finally swept back the hood of the Mechanist's cloak, standing nearly as tall as a human, she even took a few steps *away* from the girl.

Perhaps Grit wasn't the only one who could sense where a faerie's loyalties lay.

"It's well past midnight, Rinka," said Pru, as if she were chiding a child who had refused to go to bed, but Grit heard the faint quiver of uncertainty in her voice. Pru took a step toward Rinka, who gripped the tiller tightly. "It's time to come home."

Grit ran down to one of the railings behind Pru, careful to keep her back facing away from the Unseelie princess. Rinka had splinted her wing, but the last thing Grit needed in this showdown was the Unseelie princess knowing Grit couldn't fly.

"Sorry, Princess," Grit said. "Not gonna happen." It felt gratifying to be able to hurl "princess" as an insult at someone else for a change.

"I don't believe you have any say in the matter, Grettifrida," said Pru, not even turning around to face Grit.

Grit knew Pru was only trying to needle her, but for fae's sake, she *really* hated that name.

"Rinka is a member of the Unseelie Court, and one of my subjects," Pru said with a haughty tilt of her chin. "She will do as I command her."

Rinka looked like she was trying to hide (unsuccessfully) behind her hair, hunched over and backed against the rail. She snuck terrified glances up at Pru.

"N-no," she breathed. It was barely a whisper. "No, I won't . . . b-because I'm not."

"Excuse me?" asked Pru quietly.

"You heard her," Grit said. "It shouldn't come as too much of a surprise, since you can probably feel the change in her magic already. Rinka Tinkerton is no longer a member of the Unseelie Court. She doesn't have to go anywhere she doesn't want to, because she *isn't* one of your subjects anymore."

Grit paused for a breath, trying to sound as confident and imposing as the hundred-year-old Pru: "She's one of mine."

Pru whipped around to face Grit so fast the Mechanist's cloak slashed through the air around her, edges hard as cut glass. Grit jumped back to avoid it.

"Getting a little ahead of ourselves, are we, *Princess*?" asked Pru, her bony white fingers flexing and curling at her sides. "Only a king or queen's magic can change a fae's court."

"Well, that's right," said Yarlo, taking the opportunity to swing down from the ceiling. His eyes immediately went to the cloak hanging off Pru's shoulders; this was probably the first time he'd ever seen it. "So, we had ourselves a little scrying session with Ombrienne Lightbringer. Lovely lady. Tall, hair as close to the color of dried blood as *I've* ever seen, Seelie Queen of the Oldtown Arboretum?"

Pru's eyes shifted from their usual whitish gray to a deep purple as Yarlo spoke.

"But she wasn't really here," Pru insisted. "She couldn't have been. She wouldn't leave that silly *garden* of hers for a minute . . ."

"She didn't have to," said Grit.

"But we did need a queen," said Yarlo. "And fortunately, she named us one."

He bowed to Grit with a fancy flourish of his wrist. She was never, ever going to live this down.

"Meet Queen Grettifrida Goldenwing," Yarlo announced, "Seelie ruler of Wetherwren Light."

"No . . ." said Pru, her eyes darkening almost to black. "No, this land is *Unseelie territory*! That rock hasn't *seen* a faerie since before I was born!" She stomped her foot, and a creeping black moss exploded from under her heel, snaking out over the deck of the ship in seconds. Rinka jumped out of its way and up onto the railing, losing her grip on the till. The ship banked slightly to one side.

"Which means Wetherwren Light was *neutral* territory," Grit corrected her. "And now it's not, and I'd really appreciate it if you would stop terrorizing my subjects and *back off.*"

Pru flew straight at Grit, stopping so close their noses nearly touched.

"Because as you so kindly reminded me the other night," Grit said, "a direct attack against a member of the opposite court is—how did you put it?—oh, right, 'grounds for war.'"

Pru's eyes were filled with black, her chest rising and falling with each ragged breath of barely contained rage.

"This isn't the end," Pru said, her voice shaking with anger. She flitted over to Rinka's side faster than Grit would have thought possible.

"You may be *technically* out of my reach, little frail one," sneered Pru. "But those you love are not. Faerie rules do not apply to humans and Free Folk, as you may have noticed these past few months . . ."

Rinka's lip quivered. The ship was veering farther off course; tendrils of smoke wafted over from the fireworks, much too close for Grit's liking.

"What will your answer be, then?" asked Pru. "What about your little faerie friends? What about all those people on your ships? What about your *father?*"

Rinka looked out to Driftside City with terrified eyes, coughing a little as more smoke from the fireworks show drifted toward them.

Grit's eyes followed Rinka's, and with her keen faerie vision, she could just make out the carnival on the shore. The lanterns were still lit, the pier still packed with revelers, the songs of brass bands still toot-tooting through the air.

Princess Pru had given them until midnight to give up Rinka—and it was well past. So where was the great display of Unseelie might that had been promised? Where was the great storm sweeping in from the sea to destroy everything in its path? Where was the chaos engulfing the carnival and bringing the Wonder Show crashing down in flames?

Either Carmer and Mr. Tinkerton had done an absolutely *flawless* job of defending the entire Driftside City coastline, or that onslaught wasn't coming because it never would. Because a certain faerie princess couldn't afford to draw too much attention to herself.

"What about *yours?*" Grit asked Pru pointedly.

"What?" Pru was inching her pale hand forward, reaching for the ends of Rinka's hair.

Grit wanted nothing more than to shoot forward and slap it out of the way. "I said, what about *your* father? If Rinka's so important, where's the Unseelie king?"

Pru's hand froze, and that was all Grit needed.

"Unless," Grit mused, "he doesn't actually know."

Pru bristled. "My father is far too busy to—"

"*Maybe,*" Grit interrupted with a shrug, "he had some idea about Rinka's existence. Maybe he even thought it would be a good idea to check up on her. But I wonder . . .

no one's seen the king in ages. He's got a reputation as a very secretive, very cautious kind of guy."

Grit plunked herself down on the railing, letting her feet dangle over the edge. "I can sympathize. My own mother's a bit stuck in the dark ages herself."

"You have *no* idea—"

"But I wonder," Grit said, knowing she was pushing her luck, "does he know about his daughter using his generous gift"—she gestured to the Mechanist's cloak—"to sneak onto filthy, smoking, *human* machines? Does he know she's interfered with human affairs so much she's made every newspaper in the country and gotten the attention of whole teams of people dedicated to solving the mystery of the airship she crashed?"

Pru lunged at Grit, who dodged her clawing fingers just in time.

"Rinka, the ship," Grit said between her teeth, scurrying away from Pru.

Rinka turned and yanked at the tiller while Pru rose into the air, shrinking until she wasn't that much bigger than Grit.

"Shut up," Pru spat.

The wind picked up around them, flinging Grit backward. She grabbed on to a rope to steady herself.

"Be queen of your stupid, crumbling rock for all I care. My water fae and I will drag it into the sea before you can say 'Seelie.'"

"Fine by me," said Grit, gripping the rope tighter. She still wasn't quite keen on being the queen of anywhere, even an uninhabited tidal island hundreds of miles from her real home. "It's not a very nice rock, anyway."

"Laugh if you want, Grettifrida," said Pru with a smirk. "It's too bad that fine wit of yours won't be enough to save your Friend."

Grit nearly let go of the rope.

"Oh, did I forget to mention that Carmer and I met again?" asked Pru. Her eyes flicked to the fast-approaching shoreline and back to Grit. Pru turned to fly away, but a vine edged with sharp, pointy thorns snapped up from below. It snagged onto the clasp at her neck.

"Oh no you don't," said Yarlo. "I believe you've got something that's rightfully mine."

"Yarlo, wait—" said Grit, barely aware of what was happening over the pounding in her ears and the words that kept repeating, over and over again, in her mind.

Did I forget to mention that Carmer and I met again?

Yarlo gave the vine a mighty tug. The clasp came unhooked; the cloak fell from Pru's shoulders and landed in a heap on the deck of the ship below.

Pru made a straight shot for the cloak, and Grit had just enough presence of mind to shoot a stream of sparks to cut her off. The wind was so strong Grit could barely hold on to her rope.

"Maybe I'll add his *real* head to my collection, too,"

snapped Pru, just before she let the wind carry her away with a snap of her purple wings.

This time, Grit almost did blow up the ship.

CARMER WOKE UP spitting seawater onto the cold, damp floor of the throne room, face-to-face with the Unseelie king.

The "throne of bones" Grit had described to Carmer was empty, but the wall behind it was not. It was made entirely of pointed spikes of limestone crystals—some as thick as tree trunks, others as thin as well-sharpened pencils. They fit together like an uneven jigsaw puzzle, or a broken jawline with pointed teeth. It reminded Carmer of the gaping maw of the *Whale of Tales*. He just hoped this one wouldn't swallow him whole.

As Carmer looked closer, he saw that it really *was* a mouth, nearly ten feet across. The rock formation morphed into the sculpted face of an old man, each feature carved in jagged crystal that stretched to accommodate the outlines of his face. The spikes became the flowing locks of his long beard, stretching out over the entire length of the wall. Clusters of glowworms filled the holes where his eyes should have been.

Carmer knew he should probably bow or something, but he was already on the ground, and it had been a very long evening. Before he could stop himself, he said the first thing that came to his mind: "Where were you the other day?"

Because if the king had been here—in that wall, behind it, or in whatever form he chose—when Grit came to the castle and spoke with Mister Moon, then the king probably *did* know about Pru's plans and her use of the Wild Hunt. And that meant Carmer was in even greater danger than he'd been in a sinking balloon.

Fortunately, King Roden Bonefisher didn't seem bothered by Carmer's lack of formality. But it was a few moments before he answered, his voice low enough to send a rumble through Carmer's stomach. Carmer bet that voice could cause earthquakes, if it wanted to.

"Sleeping," said the king slowly, each syllable reverberating with a low hum. "As I often am, these days. But I am always here."

Sleeping, thought Carmer numbly. He and Grit had been fighting for their lives in these very halls, and the Unseelie king—the unnamed terror behind Carmer's nightmares—had been taking a nap. In fact, he looked about ready to go back to sleep then and there; his heavily lidded stone eyes looked like he could barely keep them open.

"Thank you for saving me," said Carmer. He supposed he should say *something* about the fact that the Unseelies had just pulled him from a watery grave.

The King inclined his massive head. "You may stay for as long as you need. The mermaids have taken a liking to you."

Carmer tried not to visibly recoil at the thought.

"I'm sorry, I can't stay. And I don't want to take too much of your time," said Carmer, "but I need to ask you something else. Your daughter—Princess Purslain—took a friend of mine . . . another human, but not a Friend of the Fae. His name is Bell. And, um, she kind of kidnapped him and I was just wondering . . ."

Carmer had half been expecting the king to cut him off, but he had underestimated the patience (or lack of interest) of his listener. The king merely blinked.

"I was wondering if he was still alive," said Carmer, hating the finality of saying those words aloud—and wondering if he really wanted to know the answer. "And if he is, and if he's *here* . . . if you could give him back."

For a moment, there was nothing but the sound of the water dripping from the crystals in the king's face.

"Why?" asked the great stone lips. The word seemed to echo back to Carmer from all sides of the room.

Carmer coughed up another burning mouthful of seawater. "Sorry, *what?*"

The king sighed, sending a whispering wind through every crevice of the cavern. The breeze fluttered Carmer's hair.

"Why should I intervene, if my daughter chooses to take a human for her own?" the king asked. He *definitely* sounded bored.

"Because . . . because you can't just go around 'taking'

people you don't like!" exclaimed Carmer, rising unsteadily to his feet. "Bell didn't do anything!"

"It has been many years since I spoke to a human," mused the king. "I am starting to remember why . . ." The massive head began to turn, features blurring back to the natural formation of the cave.

"Wait," said Carmer. He might have expected refusal, or even mockery—as Mister Moon would have surely done—but this . . . indifference? How did he hold the attention of someone so ancient that a boy like Carmer must seem like an ant under his shoe? What could he possibly have to offer the Unseelie king, a guy who made a throne out of his enemies just for fun?

"Wait!"

Maybe it wasn't about what he could offer the Unseelie king. Maybe it was about what the king should offer *him*.

"You owe me a life!" Carmer shouted after the king. "You owe me for bringing you the traitor, Gideon Sharpe!"

The rocks paused, flowing back into the shape of the king's face.

"Gideon Sharpe was responsible for the deaths of scores of faeries," Carmer went on. "And I stopped him. I brought him to the Wild Hunt, back in Skemantis, to face Unseelie justice. So . . . I'd say you owe me one."

Those two-foot-tall eyes didn't look so sleepy anymore.

"A life for a life," Carmer said. "Gideon Sharpe for Bell Daisimer. The princess will get over it."

Eventually, he added silently. One shining, limestone eyebrow lifted in what Carmer thought might have been amusement.

"A life for a life," the king repeated. "And you are sure this is the one you choose?"

Carmer nodded. The king closed his eyes; one of the long tendrils of his beard snaked out even farther, circling the room and prying open the mother-of-pearl doors. The other stones rippled in response.

"He is here," said the king, opening his eyes.

"How do you know?" asked Carmer.

"Because I am everywhere."

Fair enough, thought Carmer.

"It's too bad you can't stay, Felix Carmer III," said the king, his eyes already drifting shut again. "Though I suppose, as it's unlikely *you'll* take a liking to the mermaids . . ."

And just like that, a giant whirlpool crashed through the throne room doors and swept Carmer off his feet.

THE NEXT THING Carmer knew, he was washing up onto the shore of Driftside City, a curiously helpful wave shoving him up under his rear end until he stood and wobbled the rest of the way to dry land. Only after he had taken a few gasping, blessedly water-free breaths of air and collapsed in the sand did he notice the figure flopped down next to him.

Bell Daisimer sat up and dug his fingers into the sand as if he'd never felt anything so terrific in his life.

"I never thought I'd say this," said Bell. "But boy, am I glad to have two feet on solid ground again."

He clapped Carmer, who was already starting to turn into a human icicle, on the back. Carmer took a quick stock of their surroundings: the beach was deserted, but the lights of Driftside City's carnival weren't that far off. Carmer took a few shaky steps and held on to the tall lifeguard's chair—empty now, naturally, in the dead of winter—for support.

A few feet away, a tilted sign for swimmers read, *DO NOT LEAVE CHILDREN UNATTENDED.*

Carmer snorted and pointed the sign out to Bell. When Tinkerton's search party from the Wonder Show finally found them, half frozen and covered in sand, they were *still* laughing at it.

25.

LONG LIVE THE QUEEN

PRINCESS PURSLAIN ASHENSTEP FLEW THROUGH the bowels of the Unseelie palace and straight to her private chambers with every intention of smashing the room to bits. She didn't care that she'd spent nearly a hundred years building that collection. She almost laughed at how stupid she had been. What did it matter that she knew how a protractor worked, or how to play chess, or that she could make sense of the silly scribbles the humans used to record their (far inferior) stories? She would never know enough to truly understand them.

With the changeling girl in her possession, everything would have been different. Rinka's inventions could have brought an entire fleet of airships down in flames. Pru could have driven the humans back from the wild places they hadn't yet managed to bring fully to heel. They would learn to fear the fae again, because the fae would learn to fight back.

Pru had heard about Princess Grettifrida Lonewing, the little one-winged Seelie who could use her fire magic as no other fae could, to manipulate the humans' own electricity against them—who had rebelled against her own ineffective sovereign and forged alliances among all the fae of her city to defeat their common enemy. Pru had been *excited* to meet such a girl.

But then, Grit had not *only* broken every rule of etiquette by not declaring herself to the king, but had fallen in with the biggest group of street fae she could find within hours of setting foot inside the city. Alliances of convenience to preserve the fate of the fae were one thing; willingly associating with the lawless vagabonds who would dilute faerie power, serve at the humans' beck and call, and ignore thousands of years of faerie tradition was another.

Pru flew faster, trying to shake off every memory of the horrid girl. What a *disappointment* the entire affair had been. She would summon Mister Moon right away, no matter what desolate corner of the globe he was supposed to be prowling tonight. She would have him and his warrior prisoners hound that stupid flying circus to the ends of the earth if she had to. Rinka's gentle heart would soon give in—and Pru's father need never know.

The curtain of hanging vines cordoning off her rooms separated as she approached, as it always did. But the room inside was nothing like she'd left it. Pru had been dead set on destroying her collection in her fury—but it was already destroyed.

Her playing cards and photographs were ripped to shreds. Her phonograph horn looked as if a giant shoe had stomped on it. The needles from her hanging compass collection had been torn free and jabbed into the wall like arrows in some sort of target practice. Her pens and quills had been snapped, the spoons and forks bent backward into angles so awful they looked like tangles of broken limbs. Her china tower—the beautifully crafted cups and bowls and sugar dishes she'd spent ages foraging the ocean floor for—was nothing but a pile of porcelain shards, some pieces ground to less than dust.

Fear trickled down Pru's spine; it wasn't an emotion she was used to feeling, and it was much more unpleasant than her anger, or even her disappointment.

"Is something the matter, my daughter?" Her father spoke from the single remaining undamaged photograph, a pale old man with a grizzled beard so long it trailed down to the floor and looped all the way back up again over his shoulder.

Pru couldn't remember the last time she'd spoken to her father face-to-face; perhaps he was so ancient, he just didn't feel the need to have a face at all. She sat in front of the frame, gingerly avoiding the shards of her smashed possessions. "No, Father," said Pru, but she couldn't bring herself to look into the old man's piercing eyes. Come to think of it, she could hardly remember the last time they'd *spoken*.

"I had an interesting visitor tonight," mused the king. "A young boy. A Friend of the Fae."

Pru silently cursed Felix Cassius Tiberius Carmer III with every fiber of her being. If someone didn't stop that little upstart soon, he was going to turn into someone important enough to have all of those names.

"Really?" Pru asked with a tone of perfectly mild interest.

"He asked me to release one of your prisoners," her father said, "so I did."

Pru clenched her hands into fists at her sides; feathers of grayish lichen oozed out between her fingers. She sat on her hands to hide them from her father.

As if she could hide anything from him for long.

"He seemed concerned about you," continued the king, "as did some of the guards I questioned after bidding him farewell."

So he'd "questioned" the mermaids loyal to her. Pru wondered if they still had tails.

"Should *I* be concerned about you?" asked the king, his voice so deep the floor shook. Pieces of broken crockery and glass danced across the ground in a nervous jitter.

"No, Father," said Pru again. She picked up the ends of her hair and ran her fingers through it, still not meeting his eyes, surreptitiously smoothing out the jagged, icy locks into their usual silky strands.

"The Seelie Court gained two new members tonight," the king said, as nonchalantly as if he were commenting on the weather, "and . . . a queen."

But Pru had seen her father in action enough to know the weather was more likely to comment on *him*.

And what are you going to do about it? Pru wanted to scream, but the problem with arguing with a father who was *also* basically the castle you lived in was that he was *also the castle you lived in.* Those watchful walls could get awfully close, awfully fast.

"Wetherwren Light is nothing, Father," said Pru. "I'll toss that crumbling rock into the sea before first light. But if you would just let me—"

"That girl is gaining followers, Purslain," said the king. Pru didn't have to guess very hard at who "that girl" was. "Fae from all corners of our world whisper about the brave princess with the human-forged wing who nearly gave her life for us all."

Pru crossed her arms and finally met her father's gaze. She didn't bother to hide her glare.

"What do they whisper about you?" he asked.

The glass in the picture frame shattered.

CARMER STARED OVER his steaming mug of hot chocolate at Rinka Tinkerton. He was probably being rude, but it was kind of hard *not* to stare.

Since her initiation into the Seelie Court, Rinka had become decidedly more faerie-like. She had already shrunk to about four feet tall and was getting so much shorter every day that Tinkerton couldn't buy her new clothes fast enough.

"When do I tell him I probably won't be wearing clothes at all, as soon as I find my tree to live in?" Rinka had whispered conspiratorially to Carmer. He'd blushed so red Grit had nearly choked with laughter.

"That's, well . . . that's a very personal choice," Carmer said. He advised her to keep the decision to herself for now.

The Wonder Show would head north to escort Rinka to Queen Ombrienne's kingdom in the Oldtown Arboretum. Rinka wasn't sure if she wanted to stay in the park, but there wasn't a better place for a crash course in all things faerie; it was also a good idea for her to lie low in relative safety from the Unseelies while all the excitement they'd caused died down.

The faeries of the Wonder Show were free to go or stay as they pleased; Carmer thought Beamsprout, in particular, might enjoy the chance to meet the Free Folk of Skemantis. Tinkerton was keeping the Wonder Show open, at least for the time being, though he'd had to accept it might not be quite as *literally* magical as before. Even if he couldn't be with his daughter—or the girl he'd thought of as his daughter for sixteen years—he could be closer to her through the creation they'd built together. (Also, since there wasn't much point in denying it, he still wanted the money.)

Carmer didn't know what Rinka really thought of being used for her intellect for so many years, sheltered from the outside world to a degree that had shaped every part of her. Rinka loved her father, it was true. But she was also taking the first chance she got to live in a tree and possibly never speak to another human being ever again.

He was surprised her hands were still so nimble; he could see the knobs of her gnarly knuckles through the gloves she wore to protect herself from her own iron tools. Grit sat on a little makeshift stool with her back to Rinka, her mechanical wing extended and held in place by small metal clamps. She was trying her best not to look nervous, but Carmer could tell by the tension in her shoulders that she was wary about someone else touching her wing— especially someone whose fingers kept changing size and shape by the hour.

Carmer took another sip of his hot chocolate—he had endeavored to have a hot beverage in his hands pretty much at all times since his rescue from the beach—and leaned in over Rinka's shoulder.

"Are you sure you don't want to use a helical gear there?" he asked.

Rinka's gloved hands paused. "You are blocking my light."

"Stop blocking her light," scolded Grit.

Carmer backed away in surrender. "How am I supposed to learn from this if you won't tell me what you're doing?" he grumbled.

"I'll write everything down in my notes for you," Rinka assured him, and turned back to Grit. Carmer could have sworn he'd seen her roll her eyes. So much for the shy changeling he'd met who would barely talk to him. "Later."

Carmer took the hint. The ship *was* starting to feel a little small for his taste.

"Grit?" he asked. He wasn't about to leave his friend at Rinka's mercy if she didn't feel comfortable, but Grit waved him off with a flick of her fingers, careful not to move too much.

"Stop hovering like a mother hen," she said. "I'll come find you when the girl genius is done fixing your mistakes."

Carmer went around to the other side of the table and looked Grit straight in the eye. Her little face looked tired and pinched, but she winked at him all the same.

"As my queen commands," teased Carmer with a small bow.

"I'll boil that hot chocolate right on your tongue."

Carmer smiled and backed out of the ship before Rinka could glower at the two of them again.

He ran into Bell Daisimer at the foot of the hatch.

"Oh," said Carmer. "Um, hi."

"Hi yourself," said Bell with an attempt at his trademark smile, but it didn't quite reach his eyes. They'd barely spoken since Tinkerton and some of the Wonder Show employees had found them on the beach. First there had been some time spent fending off hypothermia, and then Carmer and Nan and Tinkerton had to have a few more strained chats with the Driftside City police department, and now that they each had their share of the reward money in their pockets . . . well, they'd be parting ways soon, wouldn't they?

"Do you want some stew?" Carmer blurted. It was as if his instinct to serve everyone tea in awkward moments and his newfound desire to *never be cold ever again* had turned him into a monster who forced warm food and drink onto every innocent bystander in his path. "I mean, um, the cooks should be serving some. For lunch. Right about now."

Bell nodded. "I never say no to a free lunch."

They exchanged a few updates about Grit and Rinka while they waited in the lunch line, but the talk felt strained, and they soon fell silent. When they sat down at one of the picnic tables set up at the camp, no one else joined them, though they were the subjects of quite a few curious stares. Carmer didn't know how much the crew and performers knew about the events of the past week, but he was willing to bet his presence was enough to start the gossip mill churning.

Carmer dug into his stew, mostly for something to do with his hands, but the other boy merely picked at his, occasionally giving it a listless stir with his spoon and staring off into space. He was staring in the direction of the water—and Pru's castle.

"So," Carmer said finally, "have you decided what you're going to do yet?"

Bell's attention snapped back to Carmer, as if he just realized someone else was sitting across from him. But he smiled when he said, "Actually, I have." He looked almost surprised. "I'm going to work for the Blythes," Bell said. "They're looking for a pilot brave enough to take some of their new planes for a spin."

Carmer shoved a spoonful of stew into his mouth. *Or crazy enough.*

"And"—Bell took a deep breath—"they're going to help me clear my name in the *Jasconius* crash. Robert Blythe isn't too keen on the chance of someone coming out of the woodwork to sue his best pilot, he said."

"What are you going to tell people?"

"Exactly what happened," said Bell. "That I saw an

intruder, but I didn't get a good look at their face. They overpowered me, and I must've hit my head, because the next thing I remember is running over the field."

Bell's eyes were hard, like he was already daring a detective to contradict him instead of talking to a friend who knew the whole truth already. His knees bounced up and down under the table, jostling the whole thing.

"Bell . . ." Carmer started. "Are you . . . okay?"

It was a stupid question. Bell had been terrified. His mind had been manipulated. He'd nearly frozen to death and been captured and held hostage under the ocean in a magical alternate dimension by the same faerie who'd done said manipulating. She'd probably tortured him, just as she had Carmer—maybe worse. And all because Bell had the misfortune to run into Felix Carmer III.

Bell's mouth twitched, a tight line of bitter amusement. "To be honest?" he asked, knees still bouncing. "Not really."

Carmer stared miserably into his stew. He suddenly wasn't hungry anymore.

"I still think I'm there sometimes, at night," Bell confessed. "I still see my guards. I still hear her mermaids singing, in my dreams. You know, they're really not that pretty at all in person."

Carmer made a noncommittal noise. *The suckers might have something to do with that*, he thought. But the lump in his throat kept him from saying so.

"Bell," Carmer finally choked out, "I'm so sorry."

348

"Sorry?" Bell repeated. "For what?"

"If it weren't for me," Carmer said, "if we hadn't gone into the graveyard that day, if I hadn't asked you to come back to Driff City . . . none of this would have happened to you." And suddenly it was all pouring out of him—the story of how he'd met Gideon Sharpe, how Gideon had realized his mistakes and come to Carmer and the faeries with the hope of protection, or at least a fair trial. How Mister Moon had sneered at them and imprisoned Gideon with the Wild Hunt without even a chance to defend himself. How Carmer had just stood there, and then ran, because he didn't know what else to do.

And now the same thing had happened again. Carmer and Grit had promised to protect Bell, to help him face his demons, and the Unseelies had snatched him up barely a day later. Carmer was supposed to be learning about this new, terrifying, magical world he'd entered. He was supposed to be getting better at it. But once again, someone had ended up in the clutches of the Unseelies because of him.

Bell listened patiently while Carmer blabbered, glaring daggers at any curious circus folk who walked too near the table. He handed Carmer a polka dot handkerchief that Carmer strongly suspected belonged to Nan; Carmer took it and blew his nose vigorously.

"Carmer," said Bell, "has it ever occurred to you that my fate was sealed when I overslept for my shift that day? That the minute I saw something I shouldn't have on that ship—long before we ever met, I might add—my life was about to get a whole lot more complicated?"

Carmer's breath came in embarrassing hiccups from crying. He shrugged. Bell pushed the lukewarm bowl of stew at him.

"It sounds to me like that Gideon Sharpe was in the game long before you even knew the game existed," mused Bell, leaning his elbows on the table. "And it also sounds like he was a stinker who did a lot of awful things before he wised up, and he probably had a good kick in the butt coming for a while. Now whether he deserved the kick he got, yeah, that's up for debate. But it's got nothing to do with you."

Carmer remembered what Gideon had said to him when he and Nan had been cornered by the Hunt in the swamp. Gideon had led the Wild Hunt away, probably at great personal risk. *Consider us even.*

"It was for trying to save him," Carmer realized. "He thought he *owed* me for trying to get the faeries to give him another chance. He was paying back the debt."

"You know, for someone so smart," said Bell, reaching over to nudge Carmer's shoulder, "you can be pretty stupid."

"You're not the first to mention it," muttered Carmer.

Bell looked out toward the sea again before fixing his gaze back on Carmer. "I don't blame you, kid. And neither, it seems, does Gideon Sharpe, so you might want to take a stab at not blaming *yourself.*"

It was a bit of a novel concept, but Carmer figured he could give it a go.

"*Consider us even,*" he whispered to himself.

TO THE HIGHEST HEIGHTS

"I CAN'T LOOK," SAID NAN, COVERING HER FACE with her hands. "Tell me when it's over."

"Um, I think the whole point of having witnesses is that they watch," said Carmer, though he looked a little green himself.

"Well, *I'm* going to watch, even if you ninnies won't," said Grit. "Go, Bell, go!" She cheered and flew in figure eights above Carmer's hat, shooting off encouraging sparks in rainbow colors.

"What are you *doing*?" Carmer hissed. The Blythes were on the other end of the beach, it was true, but they were bound to notice sparks mysteriously exploding above Carmer's head. One of their dogs cocked its head.

"Oh, relax," Grit said. "They probably just think you're waving around sparklers. Or, um, aerial signals or something."

"I think they've got all the 'aerial signals' covered," Carmer said. "Let's keep the fireworks to a minimum."

Grit sat back down on the edge of Carmer's hat with a huff, but he was probably right. They didn't want to distract Bell, who was currently strapped into what the Blythes hoped would be the world's first successful manned airplane. He was surrounded by a small crew of Blythe Flights employees; while the event had the potential to be historic, it also had the potential to be disastrous. There would be no cheering crowds of spectators today—just a bunch of antsy engineers, one pilot of debatable sanity, a wire walker, a magician's apprentice, and a faerie princess.

Faerie *queen*, technically, but considering that her territory had barely been hers for a day before a "freak storm" struck and the entire tidal island sank into the sea, she didn't think it counted. Much. And yet . . . she didn't mind the sound of it as much as she used to.

Nan turned and marched up the sand dune, as much for an excuse to turn her back for a while as for a better view. The thrum of the plane's engine and the roar of the propellers were loud enough to carry down the whole beach. Grit would be surprised if they didn't wake up half the city.

If anyone but Carmer had told her that this hunk of wood, canvas, and metal was supposed to fly, she would have laughed in their face. But then again, if anyone had told her, a year ago—when she was a sheltered little fire faerie who thought stepping a single toe out of the Oldtown Arboretum counted as an adventure—that she would soon have a mechanical wing and a human boy for a best friend, create electricity with her bare hands, and willingly be crowned queen of an abandoned rock hundreds of miles from home . . . well, she would have laughed pretty hard at that, too.

The contrast between the chilly tranquility of the beach, the waves gently lapping on the shore, the grasses swaying in the wind, and the long, sleek metal form of the plane—all perfect angles and painted lines—struck her as just about the oddest thing she'd seen on this whole adventure. Anyone who said that airplanes looked like birds had never, Grit was prepared to argue, *ever* gotten a good look at a bird in their life.

Driff City wasn't like Skemantis, where the old and new blended together (relatively) seamlessly. No iron gate could hold back a flying machine like that. They would even, Carmer said, eventually fly too fast for anyone (faerie or human) to think about holding on for the ride. Grit imagined the sky filled with them—noisy, magical not-birds, ferrying people from place to place in ways that no one could have imagined. Ways that were supposed to be impossible.

She had gotten too wrapped up in her own thoughts. One moment, the plane was running down the wooden launch track, and the next, the back wheel had lifted off the ground, and then the front, and then . . . Bell Daisimer was flying.

The cheers from the Blythe Flights crew were instantaneous. Robert picked up Isla and swung her around, like two giants doing a jig, until she batted him away so they could watch the landing. The dogs, sensing the excitement, scampered around the group, yipping at the strange new flying object in the sky.

Grit peeked over the edge of the hat at Carmer's face. His expression was rapt, but guarded, and Grit knew he was concerned for Bell's safety as well. Getting the thing *up* in the air was only half the battle.

She hopped down to Carmer's shoulder and looked at the plane, one hand on her hip.

"It's kind of noisy," she said, wrinkling her nose. They watched the smoke trail it left behind, ribbons of black against the clear sky.

"And smelly," he added.

"But it's happening," Grit said. Whether they were ready or not.

The important part was what they decided to do about it.

Carmer nodded. "It's happening."

And when the plane completed its graceful arc over the water, the sunrise glinting through its wings, Grit thought, just for a moment, that it didn't look so out of place after all.

Acknowledgments

THERE WAS A TIME WHEN THE VERY IDEA THAT I would have a *second* book out in the world—never mind a first—seemed just as impossible as a faerie with one wing. I would like to thank some of the people who helped Carmer, Grit, and me continue on this crazy adventure:

Krestyna Lypen, Sarah Alpert, Eileen Lawrence, Brooke Csuka, Ashley Mason, and the whole Algonquin Young Readers team. *Carmer and Grit* couldn't have a better home.

My partner, David, for continuous support on the good days and the bad, and for nodding enthusiastically when I go off on tangents about the *Hindenburg*.

Brooke Mills, who remembers when this book was about kitsune and spiritualists and the invention of the radio and *actual* magical whales. You've been with me since day one.

Alex Trivilino, walking Harry Potter lexicon, for excellent plot advice—and for boundless patience when, naturally, I ignore said advice.

Harvard John, whose ability to accurately diagnose the deepest, gnarliest problems in my manuscripts is uncanny.

My agent, Victoria Marini, without whom there would be no *Carmer and Grit* at all.

John Logan, for the balloon painting he paid a hundred dollars for in 1983. I wasn't kidding when I said I'd put you in the book.